MANILA BAY

A Sailor's Story

MANILA BAY

A Sailor's Story

Don Walker

MILL CITY PRESS
MINNEAPOLIS

Copyright © 2011 by Don Walker

Mill City Press, Inc.
212 3rd Avenue North, Suite 290
Minneapolis, MN 55401
612.455.2294
www.millcitypublishing.com

All rights reserved. No part of this publication may be reproduced, stored in a retrieval system, or transmitted, in any form or by any means, electronic, mechanical, photocopying, recording, or otherwise, without the prior written permission of the author.

ISBN - 978-1-936780-28-0
LCCN - 2011926616

Book design by Kristeen Wegner

Printed in the United States of America

Remembering my old shipmates and the Filipino bar girls of Cavite City—for the good times.

To Jane S Essa
From an old sailor
lost in his memories

all the best

Don Walker

ACKNOWLEDGMENTS

I am indebted to several people who read portions of this work and made useful suggestions. But none as much as Barbara Haselbeck. She believed in *Manila Bay* from the start and provided continued support and editorial guidance through the many revisions we made to get the story right. Now she knows this old sailor's tale and all its secrets.

TABLE OF CONTENTS

Prologue 2009 / **ix**

CHAPTER ONE: Rosie / **1**

CHAPTER TWO: In the Beginning / **23**

CHAPTER THREE: Joining Up / **33**

CHAPTER FOUR: Shipping Out—The Philippine Islands / **51**

CHAPTER FIVE: Finding a Home / **67**

CHAPTER SIX: The Rape / **77**

CHAPTER SEVEN: Girl Trouble / **99**

CHAPTER EIGHT: A Strange Request / **127**

CHAPTER NINE: Going to Hong Kong / **143**

CHAPTER TEN: Going to Be a Cop / **159**

CHAPTER ELEVEN: Life Is Good / **175**

CHAPTER TWELVE: Big Ben Biegler / **185**

CHAPTER THIRTEEN: Cop Talk / **195**

CHAPTER FOURTEEN: Boats / **205**

CHAPTER FIFTEEN: A Desk Job / **225**

CHAPTER SIXTEEN: Sex 101 / **245**

CHAPTER SEVENTEEN: Crisis Time / **251**

CHAPTER EIGHTEEN: I Lose a Friend / **261**

CHAPTER NINETEEN: The Party / **267**

CHAPTER TWENTY: Lieutenant Delmar Bliss / **281**

CHAPTER TWENTY-ONE: A Bittersweet Time / **301**

CHAPTER TWENTY-TWO: Stateside and Heartache / **319**

CHAPTER TWENTY-THREE: Looking for Love in All the Wrong Places / **329**

CHAPTER TWENTY-FOUR: Back to the Farm / **345**

Epilogue 2009 / 351

PROLOGUE 2009

Jake Becker and I were tight, real close, best friends, I'd say. We met when we served together in the U.S. Navy in the Philippine Islands in the early 1950s. We were weathermen at the Fleet Weather Central at Sangley Point Naval Air Station on Manila Bay. My name is Don Walker. I'm a 77-year-old Korean War veteran.

If I had to describe Jake in those days— well— let's just say the old folks in his home town used words like "clean-cut" and "nice-looking." One of his shipmates summed it up, "not bad looking, nothing out of the ordinary, but Jake had a killer smile that got the ladies every time."

Jake Becker died last year. He had no family, he never married, and his parents were dead. He named me executor of his estate.

Jake had few assets: a government pension that ended upon his death, some stock in a mutual fund, and less than $15,000 in a savings account. But there were personal items: a jewelry box containing a gold, heart-shaped pendant on a chain, registration papers signed by Jake and a Rosa Perez at a Filipino police station, a bundle of love letters tied with a red ribbon, photographs, and a manuscript.

The manuscript is a memoir that Jake had written in 1993. It's about a love affair he had with a Filipino bar girl, a tragic one. I never knew a man could love one woman so much. In the end, I think it killed him.

Here is the story, in Jake's words. He describes sex in more detail than I think necessary, at least for an old sailor like me, but it's his account. Let him tell it his way.

Love really has nothing to do with
wisdom or experience or logic.
It is the prevailing breeze in the land of youth.

— Bruno Lessing, pseudonym of Rudolph Block
(1870–1940), American writer and journalist

CHAPTER 1

Rosie

I squared my navy white hat, handed the marine sentry my liberty card, and stepped out the Sangley Point Naval Air Station main gate and into Cavite City, Republic of the Philippines. It was September 1953, two months after the Korean War had ended with the signing of the armistice at Panmunjon, and Cavite City, on Manila Bay, eight miles across the bay from Manila, was the party town for sailors from Sangley Point and the U.S. Seventh Fleet.

Nineteen years old and fresh out of Aerographer's A School at Lakehurst, New Jersey, I had been assigned to the Fleet Weather Central at Sangley as a weather observer. I was anxious to see Cavite City, but it had rained every day the past two weeks since my arrival and I didn't feel like venturing out. Finally, one afternoon the sun broke through, the sky cleared. Some of the guys from my section were organizing yet another poker game, others were going to the Enlisted Men's Club. I wasn't a card player, and I was tired of watching the usual heavy drinkers belly up to the bar. So I decided to hit the beach alone.

From a book I had learned a few things about Cavite City. For one, it was old. It was a town when the Spanish came to Manila Bay in 1571 and put a fort there. In 1898, the United States replaced the Spanish and built an American naval base near it. I talked to a few of my shipmates. The general consensus: It was a good liberty town. As one fellow put it, "There's not much to see, but it's got the basics: bars, booze, and broads."

It was late afternoon and, although I had a three-day pass, my plan was to wander around the town for a few hours and return to the base. It didn't work out that way. Before the day was over, I would meet someone who would draw me into a world I could never have imagined—far removed from my Minnesota farm boy life and the teachings of my German Lutheran church.

Just outside the base was Radio Drive, a main drag that went about eight blocks to the center of town. Two jeepneys were parked under the shade of a coconut tree along side the road, their Filipino drivers talking, smoking, and waiting for sailors who might want a ride. Jeepneys were the Filipino taxi. Converted from U.S. Army surplus jeeps after World War II, the jeepney was like a minibus with a top and benches along the sides for passengers.

One of the drivers saw me, came over. "I take you downtown, Seven Seas Club, 40 centavos," he said. That was 20 cents American. Not bad if you were the only rider.

"No," I said, "I want to walk."

The driver touched my arm. "Twenty centavos, then. We go now," he said.

Business, I could see, was slow. There were no ships in port, and it was a little too early for the Sangley day sailors. I shook my head and started to walk up the street.

I'd gone about a half block when I heard the soft strains of music. Across the street was a garishly painted, blue wood-frame building. Two yellow circles, each enclosing a black cat with arched back, were on either side of a red doorway. A sign above said "Black Cat Club." I pushed open the door. Inside, a sailor was dancing with a slender Filipino girl. Their bodies were pressed together, moving to the jukebox lyrics of Joni James singing, "Why don't you believe me? It's you I adore ..." Another sailor was sitting at the bar, drinking. Three bar girls were chattering at a table; one saw me and got up. I left. I wasn't ready to start drinking.

I walked up Radio Drive. The early evening sun

was still warm, but a cooling breeze off Manila Bay began to stir the leaves on palm trees that lined the street. It felt good.

About every block, I noticed, was a club or bar catering to American sailors. I poked my head in a few. There was a tired similarity. Each had a jukebox filled with popular stateside songs, a bar, a few tables and chairs, room enough for a handful of dancers, and three or more bar girls.

Here and there I saw little neighborhood open-air stores—one like another. You'd see a lean-to with a corrugated iron roof and Coca Cola or 7-Up signs nailed to its support poles. A counter would run along the front and sides, lined with covered glass jars of candy, cookies, bread rolls, and anything else that needed protection from flies and the humidity. There'd be baskets of fruits and vegetables, and bunches of bananas hanging from a rope across the ceiling. A group of young boys might be grab-assing on a bench out front and a mongrel dog tiptoeing around puddles of water still standing from the rains. And maybe an old woman in a large, peaked palm-leaf hat would be sitting on her haunches nearby with baskets of fresh-caught fish for sale.

I got to the end of Radio Drive where Burcos Street crossed. A two-story building dominated the corner. Huge block letters announced the Pagoda Kitchen on the first floor and the Seven Seas Club on the second. I wasn't hungry yet, but the walk was giving me a thirst.

A few steps down Burcos, I passed a little storefront with the sign Mom's Place on the side. I stepped back and pushed through the swinging doors. It was a bar like all the others, just smaller. In one corner a sailor and a bar girl sat at a table, their arms around each other, cheeks touching, talking softly; in the other corner two bar girls sat chatting.

As I stood, contemplating whether to stay or leave, one of the girls got up and sashayed toward me. She was tiny, with black, curly shoulder-length hair, milk-chocolate skin and an ample bosom that threatened to burst out of a tight-fitting red blouse. She had a practiced swing to her hips, swirling a black skirt around shapely legs. Black high-heeled shoes, scuffed from dancing with clumsy young sailors, completed her ensemble. The total effect was like a diminutive Mae West making an entrance.

"You, sailor boy," the little Mae West said, taking my hand. "You come, sit with us. I get you San Miguel beer." She spoke English like many Filipinos: sentences fragmented and pronunciations a bit jumbled with Tagalog, the native language. Her name was Rosie she said, and she walked me to her table like a drill sergeant taking charge of a raw recruit. I followed along like it was the natural thing to do.

"This is my best friend, Mary," Rosie said, putting her arm around the shoulders of a young Filipina. "She is new girl at Mom's Place." The slender bar girl rose, extending her hand like a shy schoolgirl. She was taller than Rosie and looked a decade younger. She wore a white dress. I thought of the girls in my church confirmation class picture—all clean and pretty. "I get San Miguel beer for you now," said Rosie, "and a drink for Mary—okay?" I nodded, and she waltzed to the bar as if she owned it.

With Rosie gone, Mary began hesitantly asking me a list of questions—my name, my ship, when I came to Sangley—hardly waiting for my response before asking the next question. It was like an interrogation. As we talked, I studied her face. Her skin was poured cream, and her eyes hinted of some Chinese in her bloodline. I asked if she liked working at Mom's Place. She forced a smile. "I am learning to be a hostess," she said, then silence.

Rosie came back with our drinks. I laid a five-peso note ($2.50 in American dollars) and a pack of Chesterfields on the table. Rosie took a cigarette, dragged easily. Mary touched her drink to her lips, set the glass down. From the guys in the office, I knew her "drink" was a nonalcoholic tea. The bar girls got a commission off the drinks they served.

While we talked, the sailor and bar girl who were huddled up when I came in, got up and fed the jukebox. "Harbor Lights," Sammy Kay's 1950 hit about lovers parting, came on. The couple clung to each other. "Sad, very sad," Rosie said, explaining that the sailor, for over a year, was the bar girl's steady boyfriend. "Now he goes back to the States in two days," Rosie shrugged her shoulders in helpless resignation, "and she cries." Then, as one who had seen this woeful drama played out many times, said to Mary, "It better not to fall in love with sailor."

It was evening now and two other bar girls came "on duty" to handle the night trade. A couple of white hats drifted in, regulars it seemed, and waved to Rosie. She got up, gave them the Mae West walk and said something ribald, questioning their masculinity. The sailors shot back they'd just filled up on baluts and Tanduay Rum at the Pagoda and were raring to go. It had the sound of a familiar repartee and all laughed. The sailors threw their arms around the new girls and shouted for drinks.

The jukebox was playing "Rags to Riches" by Tony Bennett and I felt like dancing. I asked Mary. Without enthusiasm, she nodded and we joined another couple on the floor. We danced, her eyes averted, our bodies hardly touching. The song was half over when abruptly she started sobbing and rushed off to the ladies room, leaving me standing on the dance floor. Rosie, talking to the Filipino bar man, noticed and followed Mary. A bit later they came out, Mary wiping her eyes as she walked out the front door. Soon, Rosie returned and sat next to me. I asked what was wrong. Rosie dismissed it, saying it was a sad story, but it was Mary's problem and she'd have to deal with it. She said Mary had taken a jeepney home and would not be back.

I told Rosie to bring another beer and a drink for herself. I watched her joke with the barman as she got our drinks and my change. She was no kid, that was for sure. Fine lines and darkened shadows under her eyes, suggested she'd spent more than a few days and nights in smoke-filled bars. And her coarse familiarity with sailors betrayed the likelihood of extensive experience with the carnal needs of men. But she had a gaiety and sense of fun I liked.

In a lighthearted way, Rosie soon got me talking about myself. She was interested in everything I said. She tried hard to pronounce my Christian name, repeating it to get it right. "Jake," I told her, "call me Jake." And she knew all about Minnesota, she said, from a sailor she once knew. He told her about the ice and snow. She'd never seen snow she said, but couldn't imagine wanting to live in it.

Rosie had a way of studying your face, looking you over, then picking out something on which to comment. She kidded me, called me "Chinese eyes" because of my Clint Eastwood squint. It wasn't an affectation on my part. Two years later at Sand Point Naval Air Station in Seattle, I learned I was nearsighted as well as astigmatic. After I complained my eyes hurt when plotting weather maps, I had an eye exam and was fitted with glasses.

I had another beer and felt a pleasant glow. I asked Rosie to dance. She played the jukebox, selecting a love song with slow tempo. I opened my arms and she melted against me. Rosie moved easily with the music, her body pressed to mine. She nestled her head against my chest, and I caught the fragrance of a flowery perfume in her curly black hair. I felt an erotic stirring in my body. As we danced I became aroused in an embarrassing way. Snug-fitting navy trousers concealed little. Rosie noticed, and when we sat down, she teased me.

She made a raunchy comparison to a bull *carabao,* a water buffalo, then giggled and covered her mouth with one hand—a familiar Filipino habit when poking fun.

Rosie had a stream of chat geared to keep a sailor glued to her table and buying drinks until his money ran out. It involved a good deal of sex talk. She said French sailors were different than American sailors in their approach to love. She explained: A few months before, a French ship came to port. Sailors came to Mom's, ordered drinks, and made plays for the girls. If a French sailor liked a girl, he made his move by first kissing her hand, then her arm, and on up to her shoulder and neck before asking her for a short-time. This was the bar girls' first exposure to French sailors. At first they were mystified, then squealed in delight. In contrast, she said, an American sailor doesn't mess around. If he wants sex with a girl, he reaches for his wallet and asks her, "How much?"

Rosie said she was a teenager during the Japanese occupation of the Philippine Islands in World War II, then asked me if I knew the difference between Japanese soldiers and American sailors. I was getting a kick out of this talk and played along, "No, what?"

"I show you," Rosie said. With one hand she made a circle using her index finger and thumb. With the other hand she pulled a tuft of her skirt through the circle to form the shape of a penis about four inches long. "That Japanese soldier," she said. Then she pulled the dress further out to about seven inches and waggled it. "That American sailor!" She reached over, squeezed my thigh, and got me laughing.

This woman, I thought, was sinking a hook into me, and I was liking it. I wanted to spend the night with her. Although I hadn't eaten since noon, I wasn't hungry. I'd learned that after three or four drinks on an empty stomach, I lost interest in food. But at the rate I was going, I wouldn't last till closing time. I'd noticed a movie theater on Radio Drive, a block or two away, and asked Rosie if she could get away for a couple of hours and go. Except for the two raucous sailors, now well in their cups, and the sorrowful swabbie soon to depart for the States, the place was empty. I'd told Rosie I had liberty for three days and wanted to see the sights.

Rosie smiled, looked me up and down as if to make sure I was worth the effort, and said she'd have to check with Mom, the owner. After a few moments in a private room behind the bar, Rosie breezed back to our table, slipped an arm in mine, and ushered me out the door.

I can't remember anything about the movie, perhaps because I was thinking about how to act. I put my arm around Rosie like I would with a girl on a date back home. I thought about how this night would play out. Would she dump me after the bar closed at Mom's? When the movie ended and we left the theater, I turned to walk Rosie back to Mom's Place. She stopped, "No, we don't go back to Mom's." She wrapped her arm around my waist, "we go my place."

Rosie flagged down a jeepney, and we drove away from downtown. It was dark now and I had no idea where we were going. Within minutes the jeepney pulled up to a group of wooden shacks and *nipa* huts (thatched with nipa palm leaves) scattered amongst palm trees. The air was fresh and smelled of the sea. Rosie said we were only a few blocks from the ocean. We got off the jeepney and Rosie took me by the hand, guiding me around mud puddles in the darkness to a small, one-story shanty on stilts, about three feet off the ground. Through an open window I saw a candle flickering inside. Rosie went to the window and whispered something in Tagalog. In the candlelight a figure appeared. It was Mary, the virginal girl who broke into tears at Mom's. They talked a minute, then Rosie took me up the steps to her door, unlocked it, and we stepped in.

ROSIE

Rosie went to a table and lit a candle. She said the house was separated by a wall into two rooms, each with its own entrance. Mary had one room and Rosie the other. I looked around Rosie's small room. A double bed with a mosquito net strung above took nearly half the space. A stand with washbasin stood in one corner, a pail of water next to it. In the other corner was shelving for clothing and personal objects, and a cord from which hung dresses, blouses and skirts. From a window, open to the sea, came a soft breeze. The candle fluttered, throwing our shadows around the room. From somewhere a dog was barking, muted voices floated in.

Rosie turned to me and asked, "You like Rosie's place?" She put her arms around me, started kissing my ear. "You like Rosie?" Her arms roamed my body, I kissed her mouth. Rosie went to the candle, blew out the flame, and in the faint moonlight began to disrobe. I needed no more encouragement. I pulled off my clothes and laid them on a chair next to the table. Soon we were entwined on the bed.

I was nervous. I fumbled. "You cherry boy," Rosie whispered, "You let Rosie help you." She directed my hands about her body. Her skin was soft and warm. She lifted her breasts to me. "Kiss me, Jake," she breathed, "Kiss me all over." Rosie enticed me into a profusion of voluptuous sensations. Her fingertip caresses and soft words of encouragement were an aphrodisiac to me. Her soft animal sounds of pleasure gave me confidence and spurred me on through the night.

The next morning I was famished. Mary knocked on the door. She seemed to be in better spirits than the night before. I wondered about her "problem" but didn't want to ask. The three of us went to the Pagoda Kitchen for lunch. It turned out to be a dining experience. I told Rosie to order for me, and soon our table was covered with platters of fish, rice, *pansit,* and bananas and papaya. I liked the food, although I wasn't accustomed to eating fish with the heads on and the eyes staring up at me. My favorite was pansit, a baked dish with thick noodles mixed with pieces of pork and vegetables.

All went well—then Rosie ordered three *baluts,* one for each of us. "They're eggs," Rosie said in answer to my question, "and they will make you strong, Jake." She glanced at Mary and giggled. The waitress brought the baluts. They looked like hard-boiled eggs. I ordered a San Miguel to wash mine down. Rosie and Mary waited, watched me crack my egg open. I was surprised, then disgusted. A yellow putrid slime leaked out, followed by a half-formed chick with beak and feathers. The girls watched my reaction and laughed. They said baluts were half-boiled, ready-to-hatch duck eggs. They ate theirs with gusto, daintily picking out the feathers that stuck between their teeth.

Along with baluts, there were two other Filipino dishes I learned to avoid. One was *Aso*, roasted dog. I heard it tasted good, although sweet and too stringy. It was basted in garlic or lime juice, or dipped in a savory sauce. I loved dogs too much to try it. The other was *dinuguan*, finely chopped offal (pork or chicken) roasted in fresh blood and seasoned with whole green pepper corns. It wasn't the blood that made me squeamish—I grew up eating German blood sausage—it was the pig and chicken guts that turned me off.

After lunch we went to Mom's Place. Mary stayed to work. Business was still slow, and Rosie talked Mom into giving her time off until the end of my liberty. Rosie said she'd show me a little of Cavite City. She hailed a jeepney and directed the driver to take us around the bay. The road was lined with giant palm and coconut trees that overlooked the water. The sky was still clear, the sight beautiful.

During the drive we passed several Catholic churches. Each time Rosie made the sign of the cross. Filipinos, I knew, were predominately Roman Catholic and they took their faith seriously. It was their source of strength in times of trouble. Yet, for a bar girl to show this conspicuous adherence to faith struck me as ironic, if not false. I had much to learn.

That evening Rosie packed food and we walked the few blocks from her house to a secluded spot on the bay. The water was inviting and we decided to swim. Rosie was wearing a cotton halter and shorts. I stripped down to my skivvies (drawers). We waded in. Rosie was in high spirits and started splashing me with water. Soon we were in a water fight, laughing like kids. Then, with easy stokes, she struck out for deep water, calling me to follow. I was a good swimmer and soon we were a good ways out. We could see fishing boats, and in the distance, ships on their way to Manila harbor.

We turned back to shore. I was ahead of Rosie and waited for her in chest-deep water. She swam to me, threw her arms around my neck and kissed me. Giggling, she reached down and excited me. She slipped out of her shorts and hoisted her legs around my waist. I discovered making love is possible while half submerged in water.

We toweled off and ate our lunch. We were alone on the beach and sat in the sand, our backs against a log near the water's edge. The sun was setting and we watched it slowly drop below the horizon. Clouds were moving in, and the sky was aflame in shades of gold, red, and purple.

I put my arm around Rosie and watched the breeze off the bay tousle her hair. For a moment I wondered if this was happening to me—or if it was a dream. This was early September 1953. If I hadn't joined the Navy, I'd still be on the farm milking cows and doing chores or drafted into the army.

Night fell; moonlight filtered through thickening cloud cover. We walked back to Rosie's house. That night the rains returned. The next day, except for a brief foray for food, Rosie and I stayed in her little room. Rain poured down, a noisy drumbeat on the corrugated iron roof. We made love. We told each other our life stories.

Rosie said her real name was Rosa Perez, and she was 26 years old. Her parents were poor rice farmers who rented the land and paid the owner a share of the crop. She had a younger brother, Carlos, a miner in the gold mines of Northern Luzon. Rosie had been married once. When the American soldiers liberated the Philippine Islands from the Japanese, she met and fell in love with a young soldier. After the war, the young soldier was discharged from the U.S. Army and stayed in the islands, working as a mechanic, converting surplus Army jeeps into jeepneys. Rosie and the ex-soldier married and tried to make a home.

Then trouble. Rosie's husband cheated on her with a local schoolteacher. An inquisitive boy in the schoolteacher's class secretly followed the couple to a secluded hideaway near a mountain stream. He climbed a coconut tree and watched while they embraced and made love. He couldn't wait to tell his classmates, and soon it was the talk of the village. Rosie was shamed; she lost much face. She confronted her husband. There were hurtful words shouted back and forth, fueled by jealousy and anger. The young ex-soldier became the butt of whispered jokes and snickers behind his back.

As time went on Rosie's husband became despondent. His marriage on the rocks, with few close friends in an alien culture, he walked out of the house one day and out of Rosie's life. He left the islands and returned to the States.

Rosie never said if they were divorced. It didn't matter; her chances of marrying again were zero. A Filipino man would never marry a woman "used" by another man—and certainly not if the man was an American. Rosie stayed with her parents for a while, but they were poor and she felt she must make her own way. Without an education or particular skills, she drifted about, at last taking a job as bar girl in a club in Olongapo, the town outside the huge U.S. Naval base on Subic Bay. For about six years she worked in the bars of Olongapo, mostly in the Greenland Nite Club, and then, just a few months ago, came to Cavite City and Mom's Place.

Rosie talked about her life with little emotion. Whatever feelings she had about the breakup of her marriage seemed long ago lost in the telling. She was quick to turn the talk to questions about me, about my family: What did my parents do? Did I have brothers and sisters? I learned that for Filipinos, family was everything. A Filipino was not seen as an individual, but as part of a family. And along with strong kinship ties came the obligation to help one another. That they could rely upon one another was how they managed to get through the tough times. When I told Rosie of my plans to join my father on the family farm rather than going to college, she nodded in agreement. If you cared about your family, she said, it was the right thing to do.

While I was absorbed in going on about plans for my future, Rosie seemed little interested in her own. I was surprised. Here she was a bar girl, little more than a prostitute, the lowest rung in Filipino society. She had no chance for marriage and children, her own family, yet she seemed content. For her, life was to be lived and loved in the here and now. If she ever thought about the day when her looks were gone, when the young sailors no longer found her attractive, she never talked about it.

Evening was coming on. I had to be back on the job in the morning, at 0800 hours, the day watch. I thought about spending the night with Rosie, but was afraid of oversleeping. I told Rosie I planned to go back to the base. In that case, she said, she'd go to Mom's and help the night girls.

Now that it was time to go, I wondered what to pay Rosie. She hadn't talked money so I hadn't a clue. The boys in the office said the fees varied, depending on whether the ships were in and how busy the girls were. A short-time could cost from four to six pesos, an all-nighter about eight to ten pesos. And then whether the girl liked you entered into the equation. I had left the base with close to 30 pesos. I had picked up the tab for food, drinks, and the movies. I wasn't broke, but close to it.

The rain was letting up, but the humidity was high. I lay in bed in just my skivvies. I got up, pulled on my undershirt, and grabbed my white trousers. Rosie was in a kittenish mood. She was naked, getting ready to put on her working clothes. She snatched my white hat, cocked it back on her head, and danced around the room.

"I think I be sailor man now," Rosie giggled and did a bump and grind like a stripper, her outsized breasts bouncing. "Would Rosie be a good sailor?" she questioned in false seriousness. "Yes," I answered solemnly, "the guys in my outfit would love to have you as a shipmate." Then I wrapped my arms around her and held her, "And to have you to curl up with in their bunk every night." I started laughing. Rosie liked that and kissed my cheek. God, I thought, she sure is a sexy little thing.

When finally I asked her about money, she played the coquette. "Surprise me, Jake," she teased. I emptied my wallet on the bed. There were a few pesos and a handful of centavos—not much. I was afraid she'd be angry, but no, she just put her hand on my cheek. "You see Rosie again. Come by in Mom's Place," she said. She had a funny way of using double prepositions in a sentence.

From Rosie's, the base was about two miles, following a road that ran along the bay. Rosie said a jeepney or two made a regular run about this time to pick up girls going to work in the bars. She'd flag one down for me. No, I said, I felt like walking. I left Rosie's feeling ten feet tall. I was smitten with her. My emotions were awhirl. Was it love or was it lust? I didn't know and I didn't care. I would surely see that woman again.

CHAPTER 2

In the Beginning

I grew up on a farm in southern Minnesota founded by my grandfather, Frederick Becker, who emigrated from Germany in 1887.

Grandpa Fritz came to Minnesota with little education, no money, but with a burning ambition to get ahead. He landed a job with a farmer who spoke German for 15 dollars a month. He was dependable and worked hard. Two years later, he married the farmer's oldest daughter and purchased a tract of land, mostly wooded, "on a handshake." To clear the land, he cut trees and sold fire wood to people in town. He blew out the stumps with dynamite before plowing the land for planting corn.

My grandparents were much like the typical farm family in that area at the turn of the century. They owned about 80 acres, consisting of some plowed land for corn and oats, some pasture for milk cows, and some land for growing hay—feed for the cows during winter. Along with milk cows, they raised hogs and chickens.

Their food was largely home grown. They butchered their own pigs and chickens for meat, produced their own milk, cream, butter, and eggs, and maintained a large vegetable garden and a few apple trees.

Grandpa and Grandma were blessed with two sons: Karl and William (my father). Karl was killed as a soldier in World War I. Dad stayed on the home place. In 1928 Grandma died of cancer of the "female organs."

In 1933 my father met and married a neighboring farm girl, and they moved in with Grandpa. I came along in 1934.

My birth was not an easy one. My mother, thin, pale, and anemic, almost died during the delivery. Two miscarriages later, the doctor advised against getting pregnant again, or it might kill her. Dad took Mom to the hospital and she had a hysterectomy—the removal of her uterus.

At six years of age I began first grade in a one-room country school with one teacher for 13 kids—grades one through eight. I liked school, my favorite subjects being history and geography. I dreamed of sailing the South Seas.

In June 1948 two things happened: I graduated from eighth grade and Grandpa Fritz died of a heart attack while at the dinner table. I remember he was eating green beans and mashed potatoes. He started coughing, gasped "mein Gott" and fell off his chair stone dead.

At my grandfather's funeral, Dad put his arm around my shoulder and said, "Grandpa Fritz loved this land—he cleared it, plowed it, and farmed it. He wanted the farm to stay in the family. I promised him it would. Now it's up to us, Jake, to see that it does."

Three months after my grandfather died, I started high school in Willow Creek, the small town five miles from our farm. I was a shy boy and soon found out for a boy to be anybody he had to play sports. There were three: football, basketball, and baseball. Most of the athletes were town kids, boys who began playing sports when they were little. I had been too busy doing chores around the farm to play games. But I wanted to try out. Football was my best chance, I thought. But Dad didn't like the idea. "It's a waste of time," he said, "and besides how will you get home? Practice is after school after the bus leaves." Yet I was determined. There was a farm kid nearby who played football and drove his parents' car to school. He agreed to take me home after practice.

The first two years, I never got beyond the practice squad. But by junior year I was up to 150 pounds, lean, and well muscled from pitching hay and shoveling corn. I made the starting eleven as a running back on offense and played the secondary on defense. Along with being a jock, I acted in two school plays and found performing under the stage lights liberating.

As I hoped, girls took notice. I was excited by their attention, but lacked the courage to take advantage of it. So I didn't date much, mostly school dances. And that was because boys were almost required to go, so the girls would have someone to dance with. The girls I took on dates were usually from our church, and nothing happened beyond hand-holding.

During my senior year I had to make a major decision that, one might say, could be a matter of life or death. On June 25, 1950, at the end of my sophomore year, the Korean War broke out. Communist North Korean troops and about 150 Soviet-built tanks rolled into South Korea. The United States as part of the United Nations forces stepped in to help South Korea.

In need of soldiers, the U.S. made its first draft call during the summer of 1950. Everyone in Willow Creek was concerned as our young men were called up. Within months, nearly all of the boys in the graduating class of 1950 were drafted or had enlisted. As a sophomore, I wondered if the war would still be going when

IN THE BEGINNING

I graduated.

In the beginning, it looked like the UN forces were winning. Then, in November 1950, hordes of Communist Chinese soldiers, blowing bugles and shouting, swarmed across the Yalu River from Manchuria and attacked the UN army. Savage fighting in bitterly cold weather ensued.

We followed the war in newspapers and on the radio as battles raged across the Korean Peninsula. We worried about our Willow Creek boys. We mourned when Sonny Johnson, 1950 graduating senior and quarterback on our football team, was killed in bloody fighting on Heartbreak Ridge. But we felt proud when Butch Dietrich, the big tackle on the team, got two Bronze Stars: one for gallantry in hand-to-hand combat against the Red Chinese and another for heroism in volunteering to crawl into an enemy mine field and carry out a badly wounded comrade.

In the spring of 1952, as my graduation approached, I was torn by conflicting pressures. Some of my teammates were planning to enlist in the marines or navy after graduation; others were going to take their chances on the draft. I didn't know which way to go.

My parents thought I should wait until I graduated before making any decision. The war was on stalemate now, they cautioned, with peace talks being held in Panmunjom, Korea. The war might be over by then. And even if it wasn't, they offered, the draft quota had gone down in recent months, and chances were better than ever I would not be drafted.

To complicate matters, my minister, Reverend Otto Getz of St. John Lutheran Church in Willow Creek, wanted me to go to college and study for the ministry. A slender man in his early 30s with a high forehead and pale blue eyes, Pastor Getz took a special interest in me. He went to all my football games, cheering me on. He encouraged my participation in church activities. I was active in Luther League and through his influence became president. In time I tried my hand teaching Sunday school, singing in the choir, and ushering. St. John church became my second home.

And Pastor Getz had grave reservations about the war. One evening after choir practice, he and I were sitting in the church office and he started in. "Jake, we should never have gotten involved in Korea. It was a civil war between the North and South. We had no business intervening."

I nodded. I could understand his position. But others in the church thought differently. They asserted, "We have to draw a line in the sand somewhere or the

Communists will take over one country after another."

I wasn't sure which side was right. I just had faith that President Truman and our generals would do what was best for our country.

Then Pastor Getz got going about my future. He wanted me to go to a small Lutheran college in central Iowa, where he had gone, to do my undergraduate work before going on to divinity school. "You would have no problem getting into that college, Jake, with your good grades in high school," his voice soft and caring.

"And," he went on, "I could get you a financial scholarship through the church. You're well thought of here, and it would be quite an honor to have an ordained minister come from this congregation."

I listened with interest. I liked Pastor Getz and knew he wanted to help.

Pastor Getz leaned forward and looked at me intently. "And, Jake, this is important. This war could drag on for years. When it's over, all we will have are good young men dead, wounded, or so damaged emotionally they'll never be the same."

Pastor Getz got up from his desk, pulled a chair next to mine, and cradled my shoulder with his arm. "You're a good, Christian young man, Jake, and you will make a fine minister. And when you're in college and getting good grades, the draft board will leave you alone—you'll get a deferment. You'll escape the lunacy of war and live."

In the months before my graduation, I agonized over what to do. Yes, I could accept Pastor Getz's offer, take the scholarship money from the church, go to that Lutheran college, and study for the ministry. But I just could not see myself as a minister: a robed charismatic figure standing in the pulpit, arms upraised, preaching hell and damnation to the faithful.

Yet, I was intrigued with the idea of college. I had done well in school, and my teachers encouraged me to go. My parents, though, did not have the money to send me, and besides, they wanted me to stay on the farm, eventually marry, and take over when they grew old.

Although, if I were dishonest, I might consider taking the church money, going to college under pretense, taking the deferment until the war was over, then finding a plausible reason to back out. In time, though, people would know it for the ruse it was. I'd be labeled a draft-dodger, a coward in my hometown and even, perhaps, blamed for someone dying in my place. I would never be able to live with the guilt.

In June 1952 I graduated. I talked to several World War II veterans about military service. One had

IN THE BEGINNING

been a sailor and advised, "Take the Navy. You won't be crawling around in the mud with a rifle, slugging it out. You'll get three square meals and a clean bed. And if you do buy the farm, it will be quick—you'll get blown up or go down with the ship."

Finally, I decided. I would join the U.S. Navy and, after serving my country, go back to the farm to help my folks.

CHAPTER 3

Joining Up

In July I drove to a nearby city where there was a U.S. Navy recruiting office. The navy recruiter said the enlistment would be for four years. I signed up. On September 10, 1952, I went to Minneapolis, took the oath, and was sworn in.

The next step was recruit training at the naval training center in San Diego, California—boot camp. I was one of a group of about 28 recruits, mostly from northern Minnesota, who would be going by train. It took us several days to get to San Diego. We were met by a navy bus that took us to the recruit training center. As we passed through the gate, sailors waved and shouted, "You'll be soorreee!"

Our first navy meal was breakfast. We were lined up and given trays. As we passed the steam tables, servers filled our trays with an assortment of food: pork chops, pancakes, fried potatoes, eggs and more—not asking what or how much we wanted. As a boy I was taught to clean my plate, so I ate everything. I went into boot camp weighing 150 pounds and came out three months later at 168.

The first week or so in boot camp we were kept busy getting physical and dental examinations, having our hair shaved off, taking navy classification tests to determine our general intelligence and clerical, arithmetical, and mechanical aptitudes. We were told to send a letter home so our parents knew we were okay.

One of the first things we learned was how to stand at attention and how to salute. To make sure we realized how insignificant we were, the chief petty officer in charge told us to salute "everything that moves or isn't nailed down."

We were issued our uniforms and regulation clothing—all of which had to fit into a canvas sea bag. We had to stencil each article of clothing with our name and service number and fold it in a precise way. We got dog tags with our name and service number and were told to memorize our service number and never forget it; I haven't. I can still rattle it off faster than my telephone number.

One of the toughest thing for me in boot camp was the bag inspection. Each article of clothing had to be spotless, labeled, and folded and rolled in a specific way. On the day of inspection, each recruit had to layout all his clothes in a precise manner for the chief or inspecting officers to review. The slightest deviation meant a loss of points.

Our chief, a salty old boatswain's mate, was a stickler during inspections and would at times use coarse language to set us straight. I remember him grabbing one recruit's rolled-up trousers and banging the soft and limp tube against the metal frame of a bunk. "This is pathetic," he growled in his harsh cigarette voice. "I want this rolled tight—as stiff as a young man's pecker on his wedding night!"

After eight weeks or so, for the first time, we were allowed to leave the base on liberty, and the Navy knew from long experience that young recruits getting their first taste of freedom after weeks of confinement on base would be likely to get into trouble. We were shown filmstrips depicting the ravages of syphilis and gonorrhea and advised not to go across the border into Tijuana, Mexico. Tattooing, we were told, could be dangerous and lead to bloodstream infection or hepatitis and could result in a crude design we'd be stuck with for life. For some, the warnings did not take hold.

We were an excited bunch of "swabbies" getting ready for our first liberty. We spit-shined our black shoes to a high gloss, put on our dress uniforms, and squared our white hats just so. We took the bus into downtown San Diego and joined the sea of other white hats filling the streets.

For some boots the first thing they wanted was a drink. Just about all the guys in my company were underage and the bars were strict about checking IDs. So the joints were out. But where there was a will, there was a way.

There seemed to be a number of seedy liquor stores lining the streets with one or two rheumy-eyed derelicts hanging around out front. As a group of sailors walked by, a vagrant would ask if anyone wanted a bottle. He said if the sailors gave him the money, he'd go in and buy them a bottle of their choice—no charge. All he wanted was a drink out of it. It was a win-win all around, and the liquor stores did a thriving business.

I spent an enjoyable day visiting Balboa Park and the San Diego Zoo and kept out of trouble. That wasn't true for some of the guys. More than a few came back to the base red-faced with drink, proudly showing tattooed forearms covered with eagles and anchors and upper arms with snarling panthers.

Finally, graduation day. Our company, along with a number of others, filed onto the parade ground and marched in review past navy brass to the thrilling

JOINING UP

strains of "Anchors Away." I was proud to be a sailor.

It was December 8, 1952, and boot camp was finally over. I was given leave and spent Christmas with my parents on the farm. My orders were then to report to the Navy's Airman Class P School in Norman, Oklahoma. It would be an eight-week course at a preparatory level for the broad field of naval aviation.

On a cold day on the dusty wind-swept prairie near Norman, about 15 miles south of Oklahoma City, during the first week in January 1953, I reported to the training center. I hoisted the sea bag on my shoulder and went to Barracks 63 and found a bunk.

It felt like I had walked in on a funeral. There was a small group of southern boys almost in tears as they sat around a small radio listening to the records of a country western singer. I asked around and was told Hank Williams had died. (Hank Williams, Sr. died in his sleep in the back seat of his Cadillac on January 1, 1953, at the age of 29.) It didn't mean much to me. I knew little about Hank Williams, having grown up hearing German old-time polkas and Russ Morgan and his big band.

The course work at the school wasn't very exciting—primarily basic mathematics and physics—and the instructors seemed bored teaching it. The first class I had in the morning was physics, and the instructor was a second-class petty officer in his 20s with a red nose and paunch. He was a drinker and would come into class hung over, his hand quivering as he chain smoked cigarettes and drank mug after mug of black coffee.

I did have one memorable experience while at Norman. That once-in-a-lifetime event few men, or women for that matter, ever forget—one's first sexual encounter.

Sailors, perhaps more than most young men, think and talk a good deal about women. Maybe it's because they are confined aboard ships for long periods without seeing women (when I was in the Navy women did not serve aboard ships or on naval stations overseas). Or maybe the Navy just attracts guys with an over abundance of male hormones. Whatever the reason, sailors seem to obsess as much about girls as starving prisoners of war do about food.

It all began one Saturday when a group of sailors from my barracks decided to go to Oklahoma City on liberty. I hadn't been to the city, so I joined them. About five of us took the bus downtown and spent a few hours wandering around looking in store windows. Then one of the guys, a streetwise sailor from a big city out East, asked if anyone was interested in feminine companionship. Of course, if you ask a sailor a question like that, his pride demands a yes—so all of us nodded in the affirmative.

The streetwise fellow said he'd gotten the word from one of the "old salt" instructors at the school. Just follow me, he said, and took us into an older downtown hotel. We trailed after him into the elevator. When the elevator operator asked us what floor, the streetwise guy whispered, "The boys at the base said you're the man to see about some feminine companionship." He winked, "You know what I mean?"

The elevator operator looked us over—we weren't drunk or unruly—then said something like, "go to room 416 and tell the lady that Charlie sent you."

We went to the 4th floor and the streetwise guy knocked and did the talking. The woman who answered was about 30 years old and not bad looking. She had brown hair and was nicely dressed in a skirt and blouse. She looked at us and smiled. "I'd be happy to accommodate you boys, but not all at once," she said. "You all go downstairs to the lobby and decide who goes first. The rest wait your turn."

We went to the lobby and the streetwise sailor pulled out a book of matches and we drew straws. The winner went upstairs and we waited. I would go next.

The guy who drew last was kidded and there were ribald jokes about sloppy seconds. I was nervous and wondered if I could go through with it. Then I decided—yes. I was old enough and in the Navy now. I couldn't back out.

About a half an hour later, the first guy came down. He walked with a cocky swagger. I went up and knocked at the door. The lady, now wearing just a thin slip, motioned me in and told me to strip.

The whole procedure was about as erotic as a doctor's examination. She took me to a washbasin, washed and inspected my equipment, and led me to the bed. On her nightstand I noticed was a half-eaten sandwich and a cup of coffee. The sexual congress was over in a few minutes. I dressed and paid her the required fee—about $10. As I left the room I wondered: Is this all there is?

The jobs in the Navy were called *ratings* and they were grouped according to related knowledge and skills. The Aviation Group had about 13 ratings, including such jobs as air controlman, aviation electrician's mate, aviation machinist's mate, etc. The sailors at Norman's P School would be placed into one of the 13 ratings based on their grades, aptitude, and preference. Then, after graduation they would be sent to an

JOINING UP

A School for intensive training in that particular rating.

I narrowed my preference in ratings to first aerographer's mate, and if not that, then photographer's mate or aviation storekeeper. The A Schools for these ratings were scattered across the country. The school for aerographer's mate was in Lakehurst, New Jersey.

Just before graduation, I was told I would be going to Aerographers (Class A) School. I had done well at Norman, graduating 35th out of a class of 611.

There was a damp chill in the air that second week in March 1953 when I arrived at the U.S. Naval Air Station at Lakehurst, New Jersey, about 10 miles from the Atlantic Ocean. NAS Lakehurst was the headquarters for the Navy's Lighter-Than-Air program. I marveled at the huge hangers on the base for housing the Navy's massive, helium-filled airships. These blimps had been developed during the 1930s and used in World War II for patrolling, hunting submarines, and escorting convoys. I remembered that here at Lakehurst occurred a terrible disaster in 1937 when Germany's giant Zeppelin, the Hindenburg, burst into flames just before landing, killing 35 of 97 persons aboard. And it was where I'd be spending the next 15 weeks studying aerology.

I was one of 56 airman apprentices who mustered for our first roll call at the Aerographers A School. We were welcomed by two petty officers. The first, an aerographer's mate first class (AG1) and our lead instructor happened to have a strange facial tick: He would clench his teeth in a way that made his cheek muscles knot and his neck swell. He got right to the point.

"Boys," the AG1 said, "I'll warn you right now. You'd better knuckle down and study because your grades will decide where you go after you graduate from here. You see, the number one guy in class gets first pick of the duty stations available—and down the line to the last guy who gets what's left." He paused a moment, his face contorting as his tick kicked in. "Two gents from the last class ended up going on an expedition to the Arctic," he chuckled. "Right now they're sitting in a weather shack on an ice flow somewhere, going out every hour to check the weather instruments." He laughed. "And we have weather stations scattered on islands all over the Pacific; some places it's just you and the gooney birds. On the other hand, you could go to the Fleet Weather Central in Japan and spend a tour of duty frolicking with those pretty little Japanese girls. It's up to you." He gave us a stern look, "So if you screw around for the next three and a half months and end up getting sent to some real asshole of the world, don't come crabbing to me."

So it was with this admonition in the back of our minds that we began the intense study of weather and weather forecasting. We learned about air masses, those huge bodies of warm or cold air that constantly move across the earth's surface, and the development of fronts (cold, warm, stationary, and occluded) that form when air masses of contrasting temperatures converge.

We learned that clouds herald the approach of a front, from the high, wispy cirrus clouds that develop as a warm front draws near, often bringing a slow, steady rain or snow, to the dark, ominous cumulonimbus clouds that tower quickly to altitudes as high as 70,000 feet in advance of a swiftly moving cold front, often resulting in high winds, lightning, and sometimes large hail and even tornadoes.

We learned about the formation of high and low air pressure systems and the relationship of a rapidly falling barometer to the approach of a violent tropical cyclone—and the calamity that can occur when that weather indicator is not sufficiently regarded.

We studied the six elements that are used to describe weather: wind, air pressure, air temperature, humidity, clouds, and precipitation—and we studied the instruments to measure them: anemometer, barometer, thermometer, rain gauge, and so on.

We were told how important it was to be accurate in our weather observations and calculations as the lives of our shipmates depended on it. The message got through to me. In a letter to my mother I expressed concern about making mistakes.

There was one step in weather forecasting in which I felt inadequate. Before you could make the forecast, it was necessary to plot and draw a weather map. I had no problem plotting the weather information from the many reporting weather stations. It was drawing in the isobars, those connecting lines between places of like barometric pressure, that left me displeased.

Some of my schoolmates drew beautiful weather maps; their isobars swirled and curved with such symmetry so pleasing to the eye. It was a gift, like having elegant handwriting. My weather maps were accurate, but my drawing was a bit crude, like my handwriting. My isobars were too jerky, more like the lines connecting the numbers on a child's draw-a-picture game. I used an eraser a lot. I got by because my weather maps were correct. I was careful, however, not to post my maps for display.

On weekends, if I did not have duty, I tried to get out and see the sights. New Jersey is noted for its beautiful seashore along the Atlantic Ocean. I went to

Asbury Park, a well-known resort town on the Jersey Shore, and walked along the boardwalk and ate saltwater taffy.

New York City wasn't far away and it drew me like a magnet draws iron: One week my roommate and I saw Eddie Fisher in person at the Paramount Theater. We also saw a new type of movie, 3-dimensional. We had to wear special polarized glasses to see it, but it certainly was a thrill. Everything seemed as if you were actually there. In one scene, two men were fighting, and when one threw a chair at the other, that chair seemed as if it were coming right at me.

If we had the duty and were stuck on base, we would pass the time watching base movies. I remember seeing *Moulin Rouge* with actor Jose Ferrer as the painter Henri de Toulouse-Lautrec—a great performance. And my shipmates and I were all reading the Mickey Spillane books, *I, the Jury* and *My Gun is Quick*, in dog-eared paperbacks.

Finally, June 16, 1953, graduation day. Now we would find out where each of us would spend the next two years of our naval career. We were called into a room. Our instructors had listed on a chalkboard all the available duty stations with job openings (billets) for aerographer's mates. Opposite the duty stations were listed the 56 graduates: starting with the best student on top and down to the guy with the worst grades at the bottom.

The AG1, the instructor with the tick, called out the top man and asked his choice. The top guy, a quiet and serious sort, looked over the list. He had plenty of options. There were weather stations with vacancies all over the world: Alaska, Port-Lyautey in Morocco, Guantánamo Bay in Cuba, the Panama Canal Zone, naval air stations all over the U.S. and Hawaii; as well as on U.S. ships (mostly aircraft carriers and battleships). To our surprise, he took a billet on a stateside naval air station. I think it was NAS Corpus Christi in Texas.

Several of us in the middle of the class standing (I was nineteenth) were holding our breath. Frenchy, one of our instructors, was a colorful character and advised us on the good and bad billets on the list. During World War II he had been a weather observer on an island off the coast of New Guinea. He said the girls there took awhile to get used to, but after a few years he didn't want to leave. He said the best duty on the list was at the Fleet Weather Central in Japan; it had five openings.

Tom Madsen, eighteenth in the class, and I wanted Japan. We watched in dismay as the seventeenth man took the fifth and last slot. The next best,

JOINING UP

we thought, was the Fleet Weather Central in the Philippine Islands where there were two billets. Tom took the first and I the second.

Now that our fate was settled, Tom and I watched to see how the rest of the class would fare. The last man got the weather station at Johnston Island. We shuddered. Johnston Island was a speck in the Pacific Ocean, less than ½ square mile in size, 700 miles southwest of Honolulu—a desolate little naval base of sand and gooney birds. The scuttlebutt was that being assigned to Johnston Island was akin to being sentenced to Devil's Island, the French penal colony—that after two years, if you made it, you came away slightly deranged or an alcoholic. Because a tour of duty there bordered on cruel and unusual punishment, there was talk of reducing the assignment to 18 months. I felt sorry for the guy.

Tom Madsen and I were excited. We were going to the Philippine Islands—the "Pearl of the Orient." Our orders were to report to the naval base on Treasure Island in San Francisco Bay in California. There we would catch a ship to take us to the P.I.

We boarded a train and headed west. During a brief stop in Chicago, Tom and I went into a saloon to use a pay phone to call our folks. While Tom was in the phone booth, two middle-aged gals at the bar saw us and started singing the big band hit, "Bell Bottom Trousers." It included the lyrics, "She loved her sailor boy, and he loved her too." The ladies waved us over and offered to buy drinks. The war was on, and anyone in uniform was considered a bit of a hero. Reluctantly we declined, saying we did not want to miss our train.

We arrived at San Francisco and reported in at the naval station on Treasure Island where we were assigned to the transient barracks. We were told we might have to wait a few weeks before a transport ship would be going to the P.I.

While we waited there wasn't much to do. First thing in the morning we'd muster at the masters-at-arms office for assignment; usually some clean-up job—then be free to go on liberty.

I took every opportunity to take liberty in San Francisco. It was so convenient. The San Francisco–Oakland Bay Bridge went right across Treasure Island. City buses stopped at the gate of the naval station and went downtown. There was so much to see: the hills, the views, the bays and bridges. And it was in San Francisco where I learned about homosexuality—first hand.

Late on a sunny afternoon, I was in a cable car exploring San Francisco for the first time. I was in uniform, those natty form-fitting dress blues. The trousers were the old style with the flap over the crotch secured by 13 buttons, rather than a zipper.

At one stop a portly, middle-aged man in a business suit got on. He sidled up to me and started talking. He seemed friendly. He asked me if I was new in San Francisco, and when I said yes, offered to show me the town. He was an attorney, he said, on his way home. We could stop at his place for a drink or two, then go out for dinner—his treat. I was accustomed to "Minnesota nice" people and in my naiveté said sure, why not?

The man took me to an exclusive residential district. The building we entered was of stone, enclosed by a high, wrought iron fence. The name of the building, the Royal Arms, was embossed on a shield at the entrance.

The man's apartment was large with conservative furnishings. He motioned me to a sofa to sit and said he'd mix drinks. No sooner had I sat down, however, and he was at my side. His demeanor changed; he was excited. He tried to put his arm around me and with the other hand, fumbled with the buttons at my waist. I was taken aback for a moment, unable to respond. I grabbed his hand and pushed it away and got up, saying making love to a man was not my style. I started to leave and he clung to my arm, pleading for me to stay. He took my hand in his, caressing my palm with his fingers. I jerked my hand free and hurried out the door—shaken, my emotions in turmoil.

And this wasn't my last experience with gay men in San Francisco. I didn't have civilian clothes so I was always in uniform. If I stopped in a saloon for a beer and sat at the bar, it wasn't long before some guy would slide up to the stool next to me. He'd offer to buy a drink, and then his hand would go to my thigh. I got sick of it. Young sailors in the city by the bay, it seemed, were like catnip to gay tomcats.

At this time of my life I knew little about homosexuality. If I thought about it at all, it was something perverse. I knew it was definitely forbidden in the Navy, however.

CHAPTER 4

Shipping Out—
The Philippine Islands

Finally the day came. I got my orders and boarded a Navy MSTS (Military Sea Transportation Service) ship. It would take three weeks to get to the Philippine Islands with stops in Hawaii and Guam on the way. We weighed anchor and slowly sailed under the Golden Gate Bridge. The deck was lined with men, their faces all turned eastward as we watched the Golden Gate fade from view.

Our living quarters aboard ship were cramped and not geared for comfort. The bunks were racks of four or five tightly strung canvas hammocks stacked one on top of the other—each about a foot and a half apart. Your face was just inches below the man above you.

Since we were not part of the ship's crew, we had little to do. So we spent the daylight hours playing cards, writing letters, watching flying fish, or reading paperbacks. I can still see myself—above decks one sunny afternoon sitting in the shade, my back against a bulkhead and the ocean breeze cooling my face, reading the absorbing story about a western gunfighter in the book *Shane*.

A few days out from San Francisco we hit rough water. For most of us it caused no problem. But a few got terribly seasick. I remember one unpleasant event. Four guys were playing cards topside. All of a sudden a seasick man from below decks came storming up and rushed to the side of the ship. He threw up over the railing. A strong wind was blowing inboard, however. It sprayed the vomit back and splattered the faces of the card players. There was a howl of anger. For a moment I thought they were going to throw the seasick fellow overboard. Naturally, those of us left unscathed roared with laughter.

We arrived in Honolulu for a brief stopover and were allowed to leave the ship for an afternoon of sightseeing. While still in the Hawaiian Islands we got great news. On July 27, 1953, the Korean War ended with the signing of an armistice at Panmunjom. We didn't have that to worry about anymore.

We left Honolulu, crossed the International Date Line, and steamed into the big U.S. naval base on Guam—a rugged, tropical island about two thirds of the way between Hawaii and Manila. We were not allowed to leave the ship. After a brief stay, unloading cargo and taking on a few passengers, we left for the Philippine Islands.

We were a few days out when I got a hint of the cultural shock I would soon experience. I was topside one evening idly watching the sunset. A small middle-aged Asian man we had taken aboard at Guam came up from below decks. He stood next to me and started talking. He was Filipino, he said, and had been working as a civilian laborer for the U.S. Navy. He had a wife and six children living in the Philippine Islands and it would be his first time back to see them in five years. Proudly, he pulled out his wallet and showed me a picture of his family. I remarked how attractive they were. He showed me another photograph—a young woman, comely. That was his girlfriend in Guam, he said.

I kidded him. "You'd better not let your wife see that one."

"No," he said matter-of-factly. "She would understand. I send money home every month for her and the kids. She knows a man needs a woman."

I looked at him. You'd never get by with that in Willow Creek, I thought.

Several days later we entered the South China Sea. Soon we saw land. It was Luzon, the largest and northern most island in the Philippine Archipelago, a chain of 7083 islands stretching over 1,166 miles.

We sailed into Manila Bay. About 40 miles long, it was here in 1898 that Commodore George Dewey defeated the Spanish naval force during the Spanish-American War and wrested control of the islands from Spain. The Philippine Islands became a U.S. colony. Guarding the inlet to the bay was Corregidor, the small rocky island that was the last bastion of Filipino and American forces fighting the Japanese during World War II.

Someone pointed out Sangley Point, a slender thumb-like strip jutting out into Manila Bay. At the time of the War, it was the site of the Cavite Navy Yard, home of the U.S. Asiatic Fleet and a major ship repair facility. On December 10, 1941, several days after Pearl Harbor, Japanese planes bombed and battered Cavite. Ships were destroyed and sailors killed in the base area. Remains of the sunken ships could still be seen. In some cases a large part of a ship was above water. We were told Filipino fishermen and their families lived on some of these rusted hulks. Now the area was Sangley Point Naval Air Station, my home for the next two years.

It was the height of the rainy season when I

SHIPPING OUT—THE PHILIPPINE ISLANDS

reported in to the Fleet Weather Central. Monsoon winds were driving the rain in sheets, rattling against the corrugated metal roof of the double-sized Quonset hut. Chief Petty Officer Kenneth "Shady" Lane welcomed me aboard. During a brief lull in the rain, a fellow on section watch helped load my gear into a jeep. We drove a few blocks through standing water to a line of Quonset huts at the end of the base.

"This is home," the sailor said, pulling in front of a hut with a banana tree in front. "Two guys rotated back to the States a few days ago so there are a couple of empty bunks."

I grabbed my sea bag and splashed through ankle-deep water to the door. I walked into a darkened room, canvas roll-ups pulled down over the screens. A light bulb illuminated a table with four card players. There was a smell of dampness and mold. A radio tuned to the Armed Force radio station was playing "Swanee River Boogie" by Glen Gray and the Casa Loma Orchestra.

After introductions and handshakes all around, I dumped my sodden sea bag on an empty bed on one of the 20 or so double metal bunks in the hut. I started sorting out dirty clothes and asked about a laundry. One of the card players said not to worry. "You're in the P.I. now" he said. "We have a Filipino hut boy that'll take your dirty clothes to the laundry, shine your shoes, and make your bed. All you have to do is put on clean clothes and take off the dirty ones. He does the rest. We each kick in a little each month to pay him." It turned out that Filipino civilians did just about all the menial tasks on the base.

Later, I joined a few of the boys and ran through the rain to the mess hall for the evening meal. On the way, one of the guys said Manila was just across the bay, about eight miles—easy to see on a clear day. Two weeks later, when it stopped raining I saw the capital city of the Philippine Islands for the first time.

After chow we went to the Enlisted Men's Club for drinks. Jim, an AG2 and one of the Fleet Weather Central section leaders, filled me in. "The best way to save money in the P.I.," Jim laughed, "is to be an alcoholic. You can get drunk every night for less than a buck." In a way, he was right. Drinks were cheap at the EM Club. Beer was 10¢, mixed drinks, 15¢, and you could buy a bottle of Canadian Club whiskey for $1.25. I ordered a Pabst Blue Ribbon beer.

"Jesus," Jim said, "don't drink that horse piss." He called to the bartender, "Make that a San Miguel for the man." He nodded to me, "He just came in from

SHIPPING OUT—THE PHILIPPINE ISLANDS

the States. He don't know any better."

San Miguel Pale Pilson. I had a few that night and felt it. It was good beer, but strong. "Over 6 percent," Jim said. "It's brewed in Manila. Some say that General MacArthur owned part of the San Miguel Brewing Company before the war."

My first watch at Sangley Point Fleet Weather Central was a day watch starting at 0800 hours in the morning. Carroll, my section leader, a serious softspoken AG1, took me into a small conference room. On the wall was a map of the Pacific Ocean. "There are three Navy Fleet Weather Centrals responsible for weather forecasting in this area," he said. "One there," he pointed to Japan, "another in the Hawaiian Islands, and the third here at Sangley. Our responsibility covers this section," he swept his hand in a wide arc around the Philippine Islands that extended north to Formosa, east to Guam, south to the equator, and west across the South China Sea. "We issue weather forecasts and storm warnings to ships at sea and naval stations— around the clock, 24 hours a day."

One of the section crew I'd seen plotting a weather map came in, announced there was fresh coffee. We filled mugs. I lit a cigarette. Carroll went on. "Typhoons, though, are our big concern here," he said.

"A typhoon can be a killer if it hits our ships or a naval base. Our job is to locate and track them and warn the fleet."

It didn't take long for me to learn a good deal about typhoons (called hurricanes in North America). We were in the middle of the typhoon season, June to October, and could expect up to 20 each year in our area of responsibility. They usually started near the equator. Hot, moist air was sucked up from the ocean, creating a whirling cyclone with furious winds and torrential rain. Covering an area from 100 to 600 miles wide and traveling between five and twelve miles per hour, a typhoon tended to move northwest along or across the Philippine Islands, often doing great damage to buildings, bridges, and crops—then sweeping across the South China Sea to hit Vietnam, or swerving further north to strike Formosa or Japan.

During World War II the Navy learned the destructive force of a typhoon through an appalling naval disaster. In December 1944, Admiral William "Bull" Halsey's Third Fleet was near the Philippine Islands. The fleet, in support of General MacArthur's invasion of the islands, was sending carrier planes to attack and bomb Japanese strongholds. On December 18th, a powerful typhoon hammered the fleet, causing grave damage to many ships and planes. Three destroyers were capsized and sunk, taking 790 sailors down to a watery grave.

Survivors of the typhoon reported terrifying experiences. Winds of up to 120 knots screeched and howled through the ships' riggings and guy wires. The spray and spume ripped at the faces of lookouts and signalmen, drawing blood from cheeks and foreheads. One destroyer was completely lost from view as it slid into the trough of a 60-foot wave.

Sailors fighting the storm's fury were swept overboard, never to be seen again. To save his men, the captain of one aircraft carrier instituted a two-man deck order: No seaman was allowed topside unless roped to a shipmate.

One of the few survivors of a lost destroyer gave this heartbreaking account. As the heaving sea hammered the ship, down in the hold he heard some men praying and others singing The Navy Hymn: "Eternal father, strong to save, Whose arm hath bound the restless wave . . . . Oh, hear us when we cry to Thee, For those in peril on the sea. . ," just as the destroyer rolled over and went to the bottom.

The Navy held a Court of Inquiry. The findings included criticism of the fleet's weather forecasting staff in failing to correctly locate and plot the path of the typhoon. As a result, the Third Fleet had run right into the middle of the typhoon. Some said the fleet's aerology officer was hampered by a dearth of weather information on which to locate the typhoon. Others thought he relied too heavily on guidance from the Fleet Weather Central in Hawaii, some 4,000 miles away.

Whatever the true fact, the Navy took action to prevent another such tragedy. After the war, Fleet Weather Centrals were established at naval bases in Japan and the Philippine Islands. More weather reporting stations were set up.

We finished our coffee and Carroll walked me around the office. The FWC was essentially two Quonset huts lying side-by-side with two half-walls forming a corridor down the middle. On one side were our commanding officer's quarters, a conference room, and the "Pibal room." On the other side, at one end, was the duty officer's drawing boards for analyzing weather maps. On the other end was a bank of Teletype machines. In between were tables for plotting weather maps, working up hourly observations, and a cubicle for typing up the weather forecast and warnings.

While Carroll was showing me around, a deafening, high-pitched roar cut through the office. I had never heard anything so piercing. I covered my ears; they hurt. Carroll noticed, pointed out the window to the runway along side our office. "That's one of those new jet fighters revving up," he said. "Probably a Banshee from one of the aircraft carriers. Don't worry about it. We don't get them in that often." It was the first time I'd heard a jet engine up close.

Carroll went on to say we had a squadron of patrol planes, P-2V Neptunes, at Sangley. Along with patrolling they helped us locate and track typhoons. They'd fly right into the typhoon's eye, measuring wind, pressure, and temperature, then report the information to us along with the location and direction of the storm.

It was a job I wouldn't have wanted. Flight crews said when they flew into a typhoon it was like being on a rollercoaster gone mad. Except for the calm in the eye of the storm, winds buffeted the plane so violently that everything loose had to be nailed down to keep from flying around. Down drafts dropped the plane so fast, pencils and rulers would shoot to the ceiling. Definitely not a calling for the faint of heart.

It was dangerous, too. There had been an accident. A patrol plane had crashed and burned, right on Sangley Point, when its JATO (jet-assisted take-off) rocket on one side malfunctioned. Charred bodies of the crew, some of them drawn into a fetal position, their mouths open in a primal scream, were scattered about. One guy in our office said he'd known some of the crew, in fact, had drunk beer with them the night before. It was a sight he couldn't erase from his mind.

The FWC had a total complement of about 60 officers and men; about two-thirds of whom were divided into five sections. Each section worked three eight-hour shifts in a 72-hour period: a day watch (0800 to 1600), an evening watch (1600 to 2400), and a mid-watch (2400 to 0800). Then we had three days off. We could walk out the gate on liberty at eight in the morning after a mid-watch and not come back until the start of our day watch 72 hours later. Fantastic duty.

Each section had about six men to gather, plot, and transmit weather information and forecasts. The flow of work started with one man who took observations. Every hour he would walk up a ladder to the top of our building where the instruments were located. There, he would observe and record the temperature, air pressure, wind direction and velocity, cloud cover, and precipitation.

This information was coded and typed on a teletypewriter as perforations on a tape. At a precise time each hour the tape was taken to an automatic transmitter and the weather report sent out.

As this was happening, another section hand was manning two rows of Teletype receivers, ripping off sheets of coded weather observations coming in from weather stations on land and sea. He dropped the sheets into a box next to a man at a drawing table. This fellow had a weather map covered with tiny circles. Each circle was the location of a reporting station. As the reports came in, he decoded and plotted the information on and around the reporting station's circle.

When plotted, the weather map was taken to the duty officer. He analyzed it and wrote up a forecast. Another section staffer typed it up and drove it a few blocks to the base communications center for transmission to navy land installations and ships at sea.

We monitored upper air conditions using weather balloons. This was a two-man job. John, an old-timer in my section, checked me out. He took me into a back room filled with helium tanks and boxes of pilot-balloons (Pibals). He attached a balloon to a helium tank and blew it up. "Watch this," John said, and went through a familiar routine he pulled on every new guy. He inhaled helium and started talking. His voice sounded weird and strangled, high-pitched and funny. He told a joke and laughed.

We took the balloon out on the landing strip. I held it while John set up a surveyor's telescope called a theodolite. On his signal, I released the balloon and he tracked it though the theodolite. By determining the balloon's direction and angle above the horizon, we could calculate wind speed and direction at various altitudes.

Along with Pibals, we sent up radiosondes: balloons with a radio transmitter attached that recorded the pressure, temperature, and relative humidity as it ascended. This information was transmitted to a ground receiver we operated. We tracked the radiosonde with the theodolite until it was out of sight. The balloon might climb 15 miles or more in the air before it burst dropping the instrument package to earth (usually in the ocean) beneath a tiny parachute.

A tough job was trying to track a weather balloon in gale-force winds. I remember desperately trying to locate a balloon, just released, in the theodolite— then struggling to keep it in sight—almost impossible.

Carroll, my new boss, I soon found out, was a good guy; he treated me right. And my section mates were helpful too and taught me the ropes. Yet my mind too often was distracted. That bar girl at Mom's Place in Cavite city really had a hook into me.

CHAPTER 5

Finding a Home

It was October, one month after I first met Rosie. I was crazy about Rosie; I couldn't get her out of my mind, and I was spending all my liberty time with her. If I wasn't working, I was at her place or with her at Mom's. I started paying her rent and giving her spending money for food and extras. It didn't amount to much; an American dollar went a long way. In exchange Rosie said she wouldn't sleep with anyone but me.

I gave up trying to figure out whether it was lust or love. All I knew is I wanted to be with Rosie all the time, to feel her body next to mine, to make love to her. I never knew it could be like this with a woman. In my wildest dreams, I could never imagine feeling this way.

I blocked out any thoughts about my "sin." The Bible would say I was fornicating with a harlot. I could just imagine what Rev. Getz would think about my behavior; how my mother would feel; and how it would go over with my friends at St. John. My feelings for Rosie, however, overwhelmed rational thinking and cleared my mind of those troublesome concerns.

My shipmates at the Fleet Weather Central kidded me—called me a "shack rat." Most of them were not interested in the Filipino bar girls, rarely went into Cavite City. They were counting the days until they could get back to the States—"God's Country." I didn't care what they thought. I'd found a home.

One thing I wanted Rosie to do, though, was to find another place. Her shack left a lot to be desired. She had no running water, flush toilet, shower, or electricity. Drinking and bath water came from a public spigot a block away; a "piss pot" was kept under the bed for a toilet. And candles provided light. Dirty water and garbage were thrown out the window. The shack had cracks in the floor to let air circulate and permit dust and refuse to drop to the ground. A neighbor's muddy gray hog rooted around the shack, feeding on whatever eatable trash was lying about, with chickens picking through whatever was left over.

I remember the first time I needed a bathroom at Rosie's. It was night and she said I should go outside and do my business alongside the shack. I hesitated, reluctant to go out back and squat in the mud.

"No problem," Rosie said. "The pig; he clean it up . . . He likes."

Having been raised on a farm, I knew something about the eating habits of pigs and chickens. We had a feedlot for cattle and fed whole corn to the steers. Grandpa Fritz allowed pigs and chickens in the lot. Not all the corn was digested by the steers. The pigs followed them and ate their feces. The chickens, in turn, followed behind the pigs and picked through their shit. Grandpa Fritz said in this way we got triple duty from the corn. Yet, for me, there was something deeply unsettling about a dirty razorback hog following behind me and cleaning up my droppings.

Although preoccupied by my romance with Rosie, I found time to keep up a steady correspondence with my parents. In a letter I reported: The weather is warm and it doesn't rain as much as it did before. We had a typhoon that hit close to us but at the last minute swerved into Northern Luzon. In another letter to my mother I thanked her for the stationery she sent me; then said how much I missed her Thanksgiving dinner on the farm. I mentioned how poor the Navy's chow was.

Yes, navy chow was not gourmet, and the cooks were not connoisseurs of delicate taste. That was certainly true of Sangley's mess hall. I remember my first breakfast there. I was standing in line, holding my tray, waiting to get to the steam table for my food. Behind the steam table, the cooks were busy. One cook, grossly obese, was mixing oatmeal in a stainless steel tub with a wooden paddle big enough to propel a canoe. Rivulets of perspiration ran down his cheeks. His undershirt, sweat soaked, stuck to his fleshy back. A damp cigarette with an ash nearly an inch long dangled from his lips.

I watched as the fat cook hunched over the tub and worked the paddle, his drinker's paunch hanging over the rim. His drooping cigarette ash fascinated me. When would it drop into the tub? Just as it seemed to repudiate the law of gravity, he, with a casual, practiced hand, flicked the ash on the floor. When finally the mess cook on the line dropped a scoop of the mush on my tray, I had to wonder: what sort of detritus might be floating around in that mass of goo, hidden to the eye?

And the eggs and milk. The "scrambled" eggs were a churned mixture of powdered eggs and water, splashed on your tray and looking like the snot of some sick animal. The milk was powdered too and, mixed with water, had a chalky taste. Fruit, more often than not, was from a can—peaches or fruit cocktail in heavy syrup.

For dinner, on occasion, the meat was rabbit from Australia. Australia, I heard, was overrun with rabbits; they were a nuisance. The Navy must have gotten the meat cheap. The cuts were lean and looked good but were as tasteless as sawdust. The cooks used no herbs, spices, or garlic for flavor. When we complained, the cooks threw in more salt. Then it tasted like salty wood chips. And when we did get beef, it came chipped and creamed. We called it SOS (shit on a shingle). I started taking more of my meals in Cavite City.

At our October monthly inspection, we got word of a major event in the Philippine Islands—the national election. All hands were lined up in formation outside our office. Our hut boy had our dress whites spotless and our black shoes shining. We listened intently as our commanding officer informed us about the coming Philippine election in November that would select a new president of the Islands. Our skipper cautioned us to behave with decorum when on liberty and not do or say anything that would reflect badly on the United States and the Navy.

As the days went by, we heard the presidential election promised to be tumultuous, passionate, and perhaps violent. During the last one, we were told that at least 40 people were killed in election-related violence. This one pitted the current incumbent, Elpidio Quirino, whose presidency was racked by fraud and corruption, against the popular Ramon Magsaysay, a big, burly figure nearly six feet tall who towered above his fellow Filipinos.

The years leading up to the election had been ones of turbulent political and economic instability. In December 1941, Japanese planes had bombed Pearl Harbor, the U.S. naval base in Hawaii, and attacked Clark Field, the American air base north of Manila. In response, the United States declared war on Japan and entered World War II. Japanese troops invaded the Philippine Islands, defeated American and Filipino soldiers, and occupied the Islands for the next four years.

World War II had ravaged the Philippine Islands. Manila and the other cities were destroyed, and the countryside where the fighting had been heavy was a barren land. Hundreds of thousands of people lost their homes, and many lived on handouts from the U.S. Army.

Even more devastating, during the Japanese occupation the Philippine social order broke down. Robbery and murder were rampant. A Communist-led group, the Hukbong, or Huks, operated out of the jungles and mountains of central Luzon, where many of them had been guerrilla fighters during the war. They sought to convert the Philippines to a communist form of government, dividing the estates of the wealthy landowners into small parcels of land that would be given to poor farmers.

Into this seething caldron was born the Republic of the Philippines on July 4, 1946. Its system of government was similar to the United States: it had a president, congress, and Supreme Court. The U.S. poured in millions of dollars of financial aid. The first president was Manuel Roxas, an intense, chain-smoking friend of General MacArthur. President Roxas died of a heart attack in 1948. He was succeeded by Vice-President Elpidio Quirino, a weak, indecisive figure.

In the presidential election of 1949, President Quirino ran against Jose Laurel, leader of the opposition party. Laurel had served as puppet president under the Japanese. The race was dirty; the election fraudulent. Both sides deployed goons to threaten citizens, stuff ballot boxes, and abduct and often murder rival campaign workers. Names of voters were lifted from tombstones or just invented. Quirino's incumbency enabled him to bribe local bosses. He won by a slim margin.

Under Quirino, corruption in government ruled. Contracts and public jobs were sold to the highest bidder or given to friends in high places. Government service sank into disarray, with civil servants working only to fill their own pockets.

With the country floundering, the Communist-led Huks threatened to overthrow the young democratic government. In 1950, they overran two towns and 15 villages in central Luzon, ambushing army convoys, attacking military outposts, assaulting police stations, and assassinating civilian officials. Large landowners fled as they ravaged estates, and destroyed homes, barns, and animals.

The young republic needed a strong leader, and, by good fortune, one appeared. His name was Ramon Magsaysay. At age 46, he did not smoke, drink, or gamble, though he had an eye for the ladies.

Magsaysay first came to the attention of the Americans when he fought with them as a guerrilla against the Japanese during the war. After the war, he won election to the national legislature and became chair of the Defense Committee. With U.S. financial backing in economic and military aid, he doubled the size of the army, brought in modern weapons, and boosted the morale of the soldiers by purging incompetents and rewarding achievers. With his leadership, the army battered the Huks, and by 1952 they were no longer a threat.

The U.S., through the CIA, began grooming

Magsaysay for the presidency in 1953. Money was provided to further his chance for election. By the end of October the presidential campaign was in full swing.

At Sangley Point, our base had a number of Filipino civilians working as hut boys, laundry women, maintenance men—and they were excited. So was Mom's Place where I had a few beers, danced with Rosie, and listened to the chatter. The bar girls were for Magsaysay; he was their kind of guy.

Magsaysay ran his campaign like an American and it was effective. He smiled, pushed into crowds, shook hands, held babies, and kissed old women—and won by a landslide. The Filipino people were wild about Magsaysay; at his inaugural in January, he was lifted into the air by elated fans who tore his clothes as he tried to reach his car. Thousands poured into Malacañan Palace to see him. And we liked him. He was a friend of America, and we needn't worry that our military bases might he closed.

These were great times. Filipinos liked American sailors. We had money and we spent it. Cavite City was the Navy's party town.

Chapter 6

The Rape

The Philippine Islands, in early December 1953, was to my way of thinking, a paradise. It was the start of the dry season; the sun was shining every day, the sky blue, and the breezes balmy. Flowers splashed color around: brilliant purple-red bougainvillea, showy white gardenias, and sweetly scented orchids with white petals.

Rosie and I went swimming in the bay, and with all the sun, I was as dark as her. Nights, when she wasn't working, we'd take in the movies, and when she was working, dance at Moms. And it was at this time, one night while we lay in bed under the mosquito net, our window open to the moonlight that flowed in through gently swaying palm trees, she told me, her voice grave, that her friend Mary wanted to sleep with me.

Astonished, I rose up on my elbows and looked down at Rosie. Her face was impassive, her eyes told me nothing. What was this all about, I wondered? Had I said something to Mary, or done anything to give her reason? I searched my mind.

In the three months I'd been with Rosie, Mary had become my friend too. More often than not, Mary joined us swimming, went with us to the movies or out to eat. Occasionally, I'd come to the house and Rosie would be out. Mary might be around and we'd talk, joke a bit. She was like Rosie's lovely, yet innocent, younger sister. Rosie looked out for her. I was so romantically involved with Rosie, that Mary was more like a sister to me as well. Strange as it might seem, the thought of making love to Mary never crossed my mind.

"We've got to talk," I said, and got out of bed. "I'll make some tea." Rosie had an iron frame that held candles with a grate over the top. You put a jar of water on the grate to boil and add a tea bag. I must get to the bottom of this, I thought, and I had better be careful. There was something in Rosie's voice that told me a lot would be riding on how I responded to her pronouncement.

Rosie got up and we sat at the table, watching the candles heat the water. "Tell me what happened," I asked, taking her hand, "From the start."

Rosie hesitated, looked up and studied my face. "This afternoon, you at base, when we eat." She sighed, "Mary ask me, 'Rosie, you be mad if Jake sleep with me, make love with me?' I said I must think first."

THE RAPE

I had never made a pass at Mary, I protested, never gave her reason,. Rosie said she believed me, said she questioned Mary and Mary never lied to her. She trusted Mary.

The water in the glass jar was boiling now. I dropped in a teabag, stirred it with a spoon. I knew Mary was having trouble at Mom's. She wasn't making much on commissions, and she was not sleeping with sailors for side money. Rosie helped her out on rent, and I always picked up the tab for her when the three of us went out to eat or to the movies. Was this tied in somehow? "Has Mom said something to Mary?" I asked.

Rosie took a cigarette from my pack on the table, lit it off the burning candle. She took a deep drag, exhaled slowly. "Yes, Mom tell Mary if she don't do short-time with sailors, she must go. Sailors, they say Mary cold, she just wants their money for drinks, then won't do short-time."

I poured the hot tea into two small cups. "But what does this have to do with me?" I asked. "And what's her problem with sailors all about! What is she afraid of?"

Rosie took a sip of tea and looked up, her eyebrows raised as she struggled to explain. "Mary, when she virgin girl, she had bad thing happen," Rosie whispered. I leaned forward to hear. "Men, they drunk, rape Mary, now she afraid."

I remembered how Rosie tried to line me up with Mary at Mom's the first time we met. And how Mary was distant and cried when we danced. Rosie said she had a problem. Was this it? I pressed Rosie for more.

Slowly the story unfolded. Rosie said Mary's Chinese father and Filipino mother had owned a restaurant in Manila. Then came the attack on Pearl Harbor, the fall of Bataan and Corregidor, and the occupation of the Philippine Islands by the Japanese. Mary's father treated the Japanese military officers lavishly, paid bribes to the police, and was able to keep the restaurant open. He thought his family would be able to survive the war.

When the American forces invaded the islands, the fanatical Japanese naval defense force in Manila resolved to fight to the last man. The city was bombarded, buildings leveled, and flames swept through the streets to the slums, igniting the flimsy shacks and panicking thousands. Trapped in the chaos, the Japanese embarked on an orgy of atrocities. They impaled babies on bayonets, raped women, beheaded men and mutilated the corpses. Setting houses ablaze, they shot the fleeing inhabitants and started fires in hospitals af-

THE RAPE

ter strapping patients to their beds. Mary's parents were machine-gunned, the restaurant torched. Mary was nine years old.

Rosie paused, there was emotion in her voice. I knew Rosie had gone through a lot during World War II, but at least her family had been spared. I could just imagine what it must have been like for Mary, a nine-year-old girl, to have lost her parents in the gunfire and flames of those last days in Manila. I urged Rosie to continue, piecing together the story as she spoke, sentences fragmented and interspersed with Tagalog.

With the help of family friends, Mary escaped the horror. An uncle, a storeowner in a small rural barrio, and his family took her in. Mary grew to be a pretty girl, and by age 16 she was engaged to marry a young man of good family.

It was during the barrio's annual fiesta in honor of its patron saint that the sexual assault took place. There was a parade with everyone dressed in colorful costumes. Mary was a princess on one of the floats. A dance was to follow with rich food and drink. Mary planned to meet her fiancé at the dance after the parade.

Watching the parade were three young men, college friends from wealthy families in Manila. They had come to the barrio that afternoon, driving an expensive sedan, honking irritably at the two-wheeled, horse-drawn carts that clogged up the dusty road leading to the village.

"Damn rice farmers," the driver Jose muttered, and took a pull from a bottle of fiery Tanduay rum they'd been drinking. Instead of a fiesta mood, the three fraternity pals seethed with anger. They had bet and lost heavily at the cockfights in Manila the day before and had yet to face the displeasure of their fathers. To make matters worse, after they had parked the shiny sedan, a careening jeepney had passed too close and ripped a gash across the side of the new vehicle, then sped away. Now Jose, known as JoJo, would face the additional wrath of his father who owned and prized the automobile.

As the three young bloods surveyed the floats in the parade, they eyed the pretty Filipinas dressed in their Maria Clara dresses with the long billowy skirts and the blouses with puffy sleeves. As Mary's float passed, Jojo focused on the lovely girl with the Chinese features and leered, "Ah, my friends, how would you like to get between those Chink legs?"

They laughed, hostility rippling through their machismo. The young Filipinos reflected the undercurrent of antipathy held by their fathers toward the Chinese in the Philippine Islands. The Chinese had been in the islands for centuries. They were bright and industrious. Like the Jews in Europe, many became successful merchants and bankers. Some married Filipino women, their children called "Chinese mestizos." And like the Jews, they were both needed and resented.

After the parade, the three sports gorged on roast pig and drank "tuba," the sweetish coconut wine made from the sap of an unopened coconut bud. When the fiesta dance started they swaggered over. Dressed in the latest Manila fashions, they strutted around to impress the country girls.

In the dance hall three Filipino teenagers played guitars and sang love songs. The unattached girls all dressed in their Sunday best clustered at one end of the hall, demurely glancing at the boys who milled around at the other end eyeing them. All heads turned when the three strangers from Manila came in.

Jojo, slim and handsome, noticed the attention and preened himself, running a slender hand across sleek black hair. He surveyed the room, focusing on the group of young girls. Mary, looking anxiously for her fiancé who had yet to arrive, stood out.

"Well, well, look what we have here," said Jojo noticing Mary. "It's the pretty Chinese."

"Jojo," said one of his pals, "Do you think she'd dance with you!"

"No problem," Jojo said, his arrogance inflamed by alcohol. He squared his shoulders and adjusted his *barong Tagalog*, the elegant white shirt he wore made of the fine pina cloth. "It'll be like picking a sweet banana off the tree."

When the music started, Jojo dance-stepped his way across the floor to the group of girls. He singled Mary out. "Come," he ordered. "We dance."

Mary was frozen in place, assailed by conflicting emotions. She was excited by this handsome stranger, so assured, so manly. But she was promised to another. Fearful, she looked desperately for her betrothed. Where is he, she thought, why hasn't he come?

Jojo took Mary's hesitancy as shyness. He took her hand and led her onto the floor. Before she knew it, she was in his arms. He pulled her close, their bodies pressed. When the song ended, Mary, frightened and embarrassed, tried to pull away. "I must go," she said, her voice tremulous.

Jojo held her, his arms around her waist. "You can't go now, little one," he whispered. "We've just started."

"But I must," Mary whimpered. "I'm promised

to another."

Jojo looked around. "Where is he?" There was a smirk on his smooth, aristocratic face. "I don't see him." Then he leaned close, his cheek touching hers and breathed in her ear, "You're just afraid. Don't be."

The guitars began. Jojo swept Mary off, swirled her around. "You dance divine," he said. He introduced himself, got Mary's name.

The barrio girls watched with amazement mixed with envy. Why is Mary dancing with the attractive newcomer, they wondered. She has won the heart of a local man, Manuel, a prominent young man they each coveted. Mary was playing with fire. She could lose what she has.

Finally Mary was able to break away from Jojo's grasp. She hurried to the door. "Wait for me outside," Jojo shouted after her.

Jojo went back to his friends. "We'll get the car," he said. "I think we can have some fun with this country girl."

Mary was standing just outside the hall amidst a throng of villagers milling about in a carnival atmosphere. She was looking for Manuel. He was jealous, she knew, and she had some explaining to do. He lived about six blocks away. His father owned a pharmacy and two rental houses. Should she wait for him, she wondered, or walk to his house?

Just then Jojo and his friends drove up. He got out of the car and walked up to Mary. "This is mine," he said, nodding to the sedan. "How do you like it?"

Mary was astonished, impressed. There were only a handful of automobiles in the barrio owned by wealthy landowners.

"Here," Jojo said, taking her hand, "get in. I'll take you for a ride." Mary hesitated. "Well at least meet my friends," he said, showing a big smile. "There's no harm in that."

The sedan was a four-door. Jojo opened the rear door. One of his friends was in the back seat, the other in the front passenger side. Jojo made introductions. "Get in Mary," Jojo said. "Don't be afraid."

"I'm on my way to see my boyfriend," Mary protested.

"No problem," Jojo said, taking Mary's arm and pushing her into the back seat. "We will take you there." Jojo walked around to the front and got behind the wheel.

A crowd had gathered, dazzled by the sleek automobile, a sight not often seen in the barrio. Mary opened her mouth to protest, but didn't want to make a scene. She gave Jojo the directions to Manuel's house.

Jojo wheeled the sedan through narrow streets swarming with revelers, leaning on the horn as if to blow them away. But when they got to Manuel's street, Jojo kept going, taking the main road out of town. Fear gripped Mary. "Please," she begged, "take me back."

Jojo laughed. "There's no hurry." He nodded to his partner in the front seat, "There is a bottle of rum in the glove compartment; let's have a drink to liven up the party." There was a shout of agreement, and the bottle was passed from hand to hand.

The sedan raced toward Manila, the headlights cutting through the dark night. About ten miles from the city, Jojo jerked the sedan off the road and down a seldom-used wagon trail, hidden from the main highway by a bamboo thicket and high grass. He parked and killed the headlights.

Jojo turned and looked at Mary in the back seat. "It's time we all got better acquainted, don't you think little Chinese girl?" He handed her the half-full bottle of rum. "Take a drink," he said. "You seem very tense."

Mary looked down, slowly shook her head. "I—I don't drink," she stammered.

"Just a little," Jojo insisted, "then we'll take you back to the village." Jojo motioned to his thickset, muscular cohort in the back seat. "Ramon, help the poor girl drink."

Ramon put the bottle to Mary's lips. She shook her head and rum trickled down her chin. "Damn," Jojo exclaimed, "she's wasting it. Ramon, get out of the back seat and let me show you how this is done."

Jojo got in the back seat next to Mary. "Now my pretty one, you will drink," he whispered in her ear. He grabbed Mary by the hair and jerked her head back against the seat cushion. "Open your damn mouth," Jojo ordered and shoved the bottle of rum against her mouth. Mary struggled, her teeth clenched. He slapped her face hard, once, twice, three times, her head snapping back and forth from the blows. Mary broke, sobbing, her chest heaving, gasping for breath. Jojo poured the rum into her open mouth. Mary started choking, swallowing. "See," he said softly, smiling, "it wasn't so hard, was it."

Jojo forced Mary to drink until the rum was gone, then threw the empty bottle out the window. "You'll relax now," he said, "and we can get more friendly." His pals in the front seat chuckled in the darkness.

Jojo put his arms around Mary's shoulders, caressed her hair. She held her body rigid under his grip; tears ran down her cheeks. He kissed Mary hard, bruising her lips. Jojo grabbed her dress, jerking it around Mary's hips, then drove his hand between her legs. She struggled, grabbed his arm. "Please," she begged, "don't hurt me."

"You won't get hurt," Jojo advised, "as long as you don't fight it." Jojo pushed Mary down on the car seat, began pulling off her undergarments. "Just relax and enjoy it."

Mary felt woozy, the rum was a fire in her belly. "I can't let this happen," she thought.

Jojo was determined now. He held Mary down, one arm across her chest and the other prying apart her legs. "Come on, you damn whore," he muttered. Mary fought back, ripping at Jojo's face with her fingernails. Jojo felt blood, "God damn you," he shouted and slammed his fist in Mary's face. Blood gushed from her nose. Pain and fear washed over Mary. She felt sick, her stomach heaved. "Jesus," Jojo let out, "she threw up all over. Let's get her out of the car. I don't want the seat all messed up."

They dragged her out to an open place. Jojo brought a blanket from the trunk. "I don't want to rip up my knees and elbows," he said, and laid it open on the ground. Mary's struggles were weaker now, her brain confused and dulled by alcohol.

They forced her down on the blanket. "Ramon, hold her arms," Jojo ordered. Ramon cradled Mary's head between his knees and knelt on her outstretched arms. He pulled her dress up and over her face. Mary was naked below the waist. Jojo unfastened his belt and unzipped his trousers. He entered her, thrust hard and deep. "There," he grunted with satisfaction. "That will give you something to remember me."

They took their turns raping Mary until the three were satiated. They left her curled up and moaning on a bloody blanket and drove on to Manila.

Rosie stopped and looked at me. There was sadness in her eyes. I was sure she must have heard many hard luck stories from bar girls, but this had to have been one of the most heart-rending. Rosie went on.

It was a teenage boy, a passenger on a bus out of Manila the next morning, who called to the driver to stop. There was a girl on the side of the road, he said, her dress covered with blood. The driver backed up. Mary was sitting, rocking back and forth, dazed.

They took her aboard. When questioned, she just repeated, "I want to go home," over and over. The bus, on a circuit of outlying barrios, went through Mary's village. They stopped and took her to the police station.

Mary's family had been frantic with concern.

Her fiancé, Manuel, late to the dance, was told she had danced with a stranger, then left with him and his friends in an expensive automobile. It was daybreak the next morning, when Mary had not returned home, that her uncle and Manuel went to the police and reported her missing. When the police called to say she was safe, they rushed to her side, only to discover something terrible had happened.

Mary was taken home, a physician called. Once assured she would be alright, Mary's uncle and Manuel wanted to know what had happened. Deeply ashamed, Mary refused to talk. They insisted, demanded, until she broke and told all. Her uncle was enraged and demanded the police take action. Manuel's reaction was different. Silent, his shoulders slumped, he sat looking at the floor, slowly shaking his head. After awhile he got up and left, telling Mary he'd see her the next day. He didn't.

For weeks Mary rarely left the house; she was so ashamed. The whole barrio knew what had happened; the talk was on everyone's lips. She cried, unable to be consoled. For Jojo had taken something from her more precious than life itself—her virginity.

Yet Mary loved Manuel; still dreamed there might be a chance they could marry. She went to him, begged. Instead of sympathy, he turned on her. "How can you ask that of me," he demanded. "You danced with him, you went with them. You asked for it." Manuel turned his back to her, "It's over for us."

The police investigation of the rape proved futile. The local police did get the license plate numbers of Jojo's vehicle. They contacted the Manila police who questioned Jojo and his friends. The three rapists acknowledged they had been in the barrio and had given Mary a ride, but insisted they had nothing to do with the rape. Without witnesses the case was dropped.

Mary, unable to live with her disgrace, left the barrio and went to Manila to look for work. Without useable skills, however, she had no luck. One employer, noticing her youth and good looks, suggested she go to Cavite City and seek employment as a "hostess" at one of the many bars. Despondent and with her last peso, she took a bus 20 miles to Cavite and accepted the first job offer—at Mom's Place. Rosie, recognizing Mary's innocence, befriended and tried to help her. That was a month before I came to Sangley Point.

Rosie leaned back on her chair, breathless from telling the story. "That is why Mary afraid to sleep with sailor," Rosie explained. "She afraid sailor will hurt her like Jojo"

Rosie explained that she and the girls at Mom's had been pushing Mary to do short-times. She'd agree, then back out, terrified when the time came. In a way I could sympathize with Mary. Sailors were not known as tender lovers. Rough and inexperienced, often drunk, sex with sailors, at times, bordered on rape.

I was growing uneasy with the direction of this story. "But why me?" I asked.

Rosie was not smiling. She chose her words carefully. "Mary, she hears us make love. I tell her things about you. She trusts you."

That Mary could hear us make love was a bit embarrassing, but not a surprise. The wall separating Rosie and Mary's rooms was flimsy, strips of bamboo that blocked out little above a whisper.

Then came the big question I knew would come. "You want to sleep with Mary?" Rosie studied my face, waiting for my answer.

I shifted uncomfortably in my chair; took time to light a cigarette. I needed time to think. How I answered Rosie's question would define our relationship from then on. And I cared about her; I didn't want anything changed.

I'd been in the P.I. and around bar girls long enough to know they gathered and clung together like a sorority: a club with a code, a set of unwritten rules of behavior. They formed close friendships and were fiercely loyal. Mary was a friend and Rosie was trying to help her. And Mary was following proper "procedure"; she was asking Rosie's permission to sleep with me. If Rosie said yes, that meant Mary could make a move on me, could flirt and solicit my attention. It also told Mary that Rosie did not value her relationship with me and was looking for a graceful way out of it.

If Rosie said no to Mary, it meant I was Rosie's boyfriend and Mary best keep her hands off. If one bar girl went after another bar girl's steady boyfriend, it was a grave violation of protocol. The most furious arguments and the usual cause of long standing enmities between the girls was when one stole another's boyfriend.

But Rosie was asking me if I wanted to sleep with Mary, sounding me out and wondering how much value I put on our relationship. And there was the threat: Mary was younger, prettier. In the life of a bar girl, Rosie's best years were past. She had a personality though, lively and fun and that helped with the Sangley Point sailors, who, once they knew Rosie, sometimes came in Mom's Place just to kid her and have a few laughs.

For the shipboard sailors, however, youth and

looks were everything. They didn't get into port that often, did not have a chance to know the girls. And when they got liberty, it was just for a few hours, time to cruise the bars in a hurry and pick out the prettiest girl for a short-time. The bar owners knew this. Seagoing sailors had money to spend, and the proverb "To spend like a drunken sailor" was a truism. The bar owners wanted the most attractive girls to draw them in.

So if I told Rosie I did want to make love with Mary, I knew what we had going would be over. Rosie would start sleeping with other sailors, would pass the word among the girls at Mom's that I was no longer her boyfriend.

Of course, I could say I would have sex with Mary only if Rosie wanted me to, to help our friend with her problem, so to speak, but that would be a weasel way out. And it wouldn't be the truth.

The truth was I had no desire for Mary. To me, she was like Rosie's underage sister, innocent and vulnerable. Someone to protect and care for, not to have sex with. In fact, I didn't think I could perform the sex act with Mary even if I wanted to. So I told Rosie no, I can't sleep with Mary.

Rosie giggled, jumped up and wrapped her arms around my shoulders, kissed my cheek. "You like Rosie too much to make love with Mary, yes?"

"Yes," I answered. And that was the truth.

Although my love life with Rosie was on track, there still remained Mary's near phobic reaction to sex. Feeling some responsibility, I took the matter to Tom Madsen, my pal from Aerographer's A School in Lakehurst. Tom, a big, easygoing guy with a gentle disposition, was in another section at FWC. After careful deliberation, Tom announced this was an issue of vital importance. The reputation of the U.S. Navy was at stake, he said with some humor, and took it as a personal challenge.

I took Tom to Mom's and introduced him to Mary. He liked what he saw and started making Mom's his regular stop on liberty. He spent time with Mary, buying drinks, laughing and joking with her, letting the other girls know he wanted Mary as his girlfriend. Mary liked the attention. Rosie, watching the romance evolve, encouraged Mary. A few weeks later, Tom, thinking the time was right, told Mary he wanted to spend the night with her. She accepted.

The next day at the office I saw Tom. Hoping for the best, I asked him how it had gone. He was at the Teletype machine, typing an hourly weather report. Tom slowly turned in his chair, "Not good," he said, and went on to explain the disaster. "We left Mom's and went to Mary's place. We necked awhile, you know, the usual preliminaries, but when it came time to go to bed, she balked. She was tense, nervous. I had a bottle of rum and tried to get her to drink. At first she said no. Eventually, I got her to take a glass. When finally we got into bed, Mary was scared stiff. After we finished, she cried. She didn't like it and neither did I."

Tom got up and I followed him to the pot of coffee on our hot plate. We filled our cups and Tom said, "The girl's got a real hang-up about sex, and I know I'm sure not the one to help her get over it."

About a month later, Mary left Mom's Place and Cavite City and took the bus to Olongapo, the town outside the big U.S. Naval Station at Subic Bay. Rosie helped Mary get on as a bar girl at the Greenland Nite Club there.

I don't know what happened to Mary. Chances are if she stayed on as a bar girl, she took to drink to overcome her fears and ease the shame of her work—not uncommon for some girls. And when her youth was gone, she may have begged for menial work, washing clothes, cleaning rooms, perhaps, for the young bar girls taking her place.

CHAPTER 7

Girl Trouble

Along with blue skies and lush, tropical breezes, December brought news of a different sort, yet equally pleasant. Rosie announced she was moving out of her shack. She'd found new lodging and couldn't wait to show me. She hired a jeepney, we loaded her few belongings, and she directed the driver to a house in a quiet tree-lined residential district about six blocks from the naval base.

The two-story house was surrounded by a five-foot cement and stone wall with shards of sharp jagged glass embedded in the cement on top. There was an iron-spiked entrance gate painted green that could be padlocked at night. Even the downstairs windows were guarded with vertical iron bars. I knew theft was rampant in P.I. city life, and if you had anything of value, security was important.

The house had three apartments downstairs and two on the top floor. I paid the jeepney driver, grabbed a box of Rosie's things, and followed her through the gate and around to the back of the house to the entrance to one of the downstairs apartments. Rosie unlocked the door and I followed her in. We stood in the middle of a large room with a polished solid wood floor, a substantial double bed, table and chairs, and enough space for hanging Rosie's clothes. Just off the bedroom were a lean-to kitchen and a shower and toilet.

Rosie did a pirouette, her hands pointing out all the amenities, "This my place now." Her eyes glistened with joy, "You like?"

Compared with Rosie's shack, this was luxury. "Wonderful Rosie, just perfect," I responded.

While Rosie was showing me around, she described the other occupants of the house. Her landlady, the owner of the house, lived in one of the two apartments upstairs. A girl who'd been a waitress, Marie, lived in the other apartment. Five months pregnant, Marie's steady sailor boyfriend had just left for the States. Rosie explained that the boyfriend left Marie with some money and promised to send money regularly for her and the baby so she would not have to go back to work. The other two one-room apartments downstairs next to Rosie's were rented by bar girls who brought sailors for short-times. The two bar girls, Rosie said, assured her the landlady was fair, and the area was quiet, a good place to live. It all seemed so right for us.

With December comes Christmas. But without snow on the ground and ice on the lakes, it was hard to imagine. The FWC tried, though. We decorated a Christmas tree, played Christmas carols and hymns, and sent out navy Christmas cards. We had a party for all the men with a dinner of chicken and ham, then exchanged gifts. All sane and decent.

Then came New Year's Eve. A group of us went to the EM Club to celebrate. The liquor was flowing, mostly whiskey and champagne. I tried the champagne. It was bubbly like pop and that's how I drank it. It wasn't long before the room started spinning and my legs got wobbly. It was years later before I drank champagne again.

It was about this time that Don Walker came aboard FWC. Several years older than me, Don had previously served in the Army or Air Force and transferred in as an AG Petty Officer—soon to become my Section Leader. A gentle guy, with a soft Kentucky way of talking, Don had a fun sense of humor and soon became my best friend. A lover of poetry, he kidded me and called me "Blackie," after California's legendary stagecoach robber of the 1870s, Black Bart, who scrawled poems and left them at the scenes of his robberies, one of which read:

> *I've labored long and hard for bread*
> *For honor and for riches*
> *But on my corns too long you've tread*
> *You fine haired sons of Bitches*
>   BLACK BART, the Poet

The year 1954 began so well. Work at FWC was challenging, and I had a boss I respected and liked. And off the base I had a girlfriend I cared about. It was blue skies and smooth sailing, I thought. I failed to see the ragged edge of a storm cloud boiling on the horizon.

It all started one afternoon at Rosie's. I was winding up a 72-hour liberty and getting ready to go back to the base. I would have the day watch next morning starting at 0800 hours. I'd spent the last two hours propped up in bed reading a book from the base library while Rosie was cleaning up in the kitchen and doing some sewing. Rosie would be going to work at Mom's when I left for the base, the usual routine—so I thought.

I put a marker in the book, laid it on the table next to the bed and grabbed my white hat. Rosie was standing in the kitchen with her back to me. I put my arm around her waist and kissed her neck, "I'm going now. I'll see you tomorrow after work," I whispered, and turned for the door.

"Wait," Rosie said, clutching my arm. "I not here tomorrow. I go to Olongapo, by in Subic Bay."

"Oh, you going to see Mary, visit some friends?" I asked.

"Yes, I see friends," she answered, her eyes looking away as if to dismiss the subject.

I tried to get more information about the trip, when she'd be back, etc., but Rosie was evasive, never gave me a direct answer. I left for the base with a vague disquietude.

I came back to Rosie's the next day, then every day I had free for the next two weeks. When she didn't show I became concerned. I talked to the girls at Mom's. If they had information, they wouldn't say. The landlady had not heard from Rosie. The rent was paid through the month, but when that time came and went, the landlady said she was renting the apartment to someone else.

I searched my mind as to why Rosie hadn't returned. We hadn't argued, although Rosie, like most Filipinos, avoided confrontations that would hurt another's feelings. She had not expressed any problems. Was there another boyfriend she wanted to see, one she had left behind when she came to Cavite City? Could she be pregnant, I wondered, and wanted to get an abortion—didn't want me to know? If she did, I would understand. Being pregnant and having a child was tough for a bar girl. Marie upstairs was an example. Her boyfriend sent money for a few months after he went back to the States, then stopped. She was expecting her baby any day now and was penniless.

A month passed without word from Rosie. Her apartment was rented to another bar girl. I came to the conclusion she had left because of boredom—with me. She couldn't tell me, didn't want to hurt my feelings.

I started going to the Black Cat, a busy club just outside the base main gate. The Cat had a couple of leather covered booths in the back where a guy could sit and nurse a drink without trouble.

After I'd come in a few times, one of the girls, Linda, became unusually solicitous. She was taller than Rosie and younger, with shapely legs and a flirtatious eye. Whenever I came in Linda would rush to my side, making a fuss as she ushered me to my favorite booth. She'd sit with me, making sexy small talk. And when she got up to get me a beer, she would swing her hips as she walked to the bar, then give me the over-the-shoulder glance to see if I was watching her. I liked the attention. Soon Linda made it clear to the other girls I was her special customer, and they would alert her when I came through the door.

I liked Linda, but I wasn't over Rosie. I kept going to her apartment even though someone else was there, hoping to find her. Then one night circumstance threw Linda and me together and our relationship became intimate.

One of our aircraft carriers came into Manila Bay and anchored near Sangley Point. I learned a friend of mine from boot camp was aboard and would be getting liberty in Cavite City. I contacted him and we got together at the Black Cat one afternoon. Linda joined us and the celebration began. I wasn't accustomed to drinking much, a few beers tops. But by 2200 hours that night we were two happy drunks. My buddy had to get back to the base and catch a liberty boat back to the carrier by midnight. When he got up to leave he had trouble walking. Luckily a carrier shipmate was there and said he'd take care of him. I had two days left on my liberty so was in no hurry to go. I stayed at the Cat until closing and that's when Linda made her move: "Jake," she said, "you too drunk. You come sleep at my place."

"Sure," I said, wrapping my arms around her,

"why not." I was in love with everyone.

Linda lived about a block from the Black Cat. I staggered down the street at her side, gulping night air to clear my head. I followed her up the stairs to a small second-floor room in an unpainted, wood-frame building. Linda struck a match to a kerosene lamp. Her room was Spartan: bed, table, and a rattan wicker chair in one corner. On one wall hung a mirror and a picture of the Virgin Mary.

Still flying high from the alcohol, I looked for a place to land and sprawled in the big wicker chair. Linda sashayed over and snuggled in my lap. "You drink much beer tonight," she giggled, tossing off my white hat and running her hands through my hair. "You get happy when drunk. I like that."

Linda started a line of small talk, all the while nuzzling my neck, working her hands on my chest, finally slipping her hand between my legs. "My, the little sailor, he getting big," she fondled, "sailor big now, very big!"

Linda got up and slipped out of her dress. Wearing only her white panties and high heels, she swung her hips and gave me the walk. "You like my body?" she smiled. "My legs, they nice?" she asked.

"Damn nice," I admitted.

Linda had gorgeous legs, show-girl legs, and she knew it. The rest of her young body was nice too. She slipped out of her panties, cupped her breasts, and posed. "You like? You get hot?"

I was drunk, but not that drunk. I peeled off my clothes and slipped into the bed. Linda blew out the lamp and curled up beside me.

Linda was a master with mouth, tongue, and fingers. I had learned enough from Rosie to know what a woman wanted and responded in kind. We rolled and thrashed in passion. I was strongly aroused, but with the drink came a dulling of the orgiastic hair-trigger of youth. I was reaching for that thunderous eruption—just inches away it seemed—all night. Finally by morning came the blissful release. Satiated and exhausted, we fell asleep wrapped in each other's arms.

About noon Linda shook me awake. I rolled off a tangled bed sheet sodden with sweat and love juices. There was a shower on the ground floor, and Linda took soap and towels for us. In the shower we lathered each other. Linda fondled my manhood, gently soaping it down. "The sailor," she laughed, "he very red, very tired."

I wrapped my arms around her, kissing her breasts. "You're beautiful, Linda," I whispered. We hurried back to Linda's room and made love again.

The building had a kitchen available to the bar girls living there. Linda cooked up a brunch and brought it to her room. We wolfed down plates of fried eggs and hot biscuits with coffee sweetened by condensed milk and sugar. She peeled two tree-ripened mangos. I bit into the orange, succulent flesh. Linda laughed as the juice ran down my chin.

We finished eating and I got ready to go back to the base. I opened my wallet and slid peso notes alongside Linda's plate. She held me, started talking about our night together, our lovemaking. There was an urgency in her voice. She said we were good together. Linda took my hand, giggling, "I feel come many times." Then she held up her hands and counted to nine on her fingers in Tagalog. "You feel good too?" she asked.

I knew what Linda was driving at. Like some of the other bar girls, she wanted a steady boyfriend, a sailor from the base who could bring her gifts from the commissary store: jewelry, cigarettes, etc.; could pay her rent, take her to movies, and buy her a new dress from time to time. In exchange, a bar girl might keep working but only sleep with her boyfriend. If the relationship deepened, the sailor might "shack-up" with the bar girl. This meant bar girl would quit work and the sailor support her—an end to the grind of working every night with drunken sailors who groped and pawed over them. For some girls, especially if they were losing their looks or were not popular, this was a good deal. For other girls, the pretty and popular ones, they might want to stay clear of a steady boyfriend and keep working for the better money in short-times and the excitement of the bar scene.

I stood up and held Linda's face in my hands. "You make me feel very good too," I said. "My little sailor man, he wants to come back to see your Momming."

Linda laughed at my use of the slang expression in Tagalog for a woman's sexual organ. "I wait in Black Cat for you," she said.

I wasn't ready to make a commitment, I thought, but I surely would be back. And it just might be a home.

February 1954, was important for me. It was the month in which the Navy offered the service-wide examination for promotion to the petty officer class—specifically Aerographer's Mate Third Class (AG3). And I wanted that promotion. The test was offered infrequently, perhaps once or twice a year, and would not be easy. So as soon as I got to Sangley Point I started taking the required correspondence courses in Aerology and military proficiency. By January 1954, I had completed the courses. I had the necessary time in the pay grade, and the recommendation of my commanding officer. Passing the test was the final hurdle. I took the test and felt confident. I would know in May whether I passed and got the promotion.

I dearly wanted the eagle and red chevron of a petty officer sewed on the left arm of my navy jumper. Not just for the prestige and the authority to train and supervise men, but also for the extra money. Making AG3 would put about $100 (200) pesos a month in my pocket. I figured that 100 pesos would pay for my life in Cavite City: rent for Linda, food, beer, movies and still leave me with plenty for savings. Everything seemed to be falling into place.

March and April tend to be the hottest months on the island of Luzon, and as the Lenten season began, it was hot—in the 90s. Some of the guys in the office suffered with prickly heat rash. The heat and humidity caused tiny red bumps on a man's belt line and belly and between his legs that itched and burned. Every time they took a shower there would be clouds of talcum powder thrown around as they dusted up. For some reason, perhaps because I didn't sweat much, I was never bothered by the rash. And it was the hot month of March when my love life was once again thrown into turmoil.

My romance with Linda was growing. I was spending all my time with her, had paid her rent for March, even brought her a few trinkets from the base commissary. We were an item. Then one afternoon, after seeing a movie, we were back at Linda's, sitting by an open window to catch a breeze, when there came a knock on the door. Expecting one of the girls from the building, Linda casually walked over and unlatched the door. I was stunned. Standing there in the doorway was Rosie, gaunt and hollow-eyed.

Rosie glanced around the room, saw me, then brushed past Linda and marched in. In a flurry of English and Tagalog, Rosie took the offensive, charging that Linda had stolen her boyfriend. Before I could say a word, Linda lashed back accusing Rosie of leaving Cavite and dumping me. She said I was her boyfriend now.

The argument whipsawed back and forth, the words cutting, becoming personal. At one point Rosie charged that Linda "sucked dick," a form of oral sex eschewed by most bar girls as being perverted. (Rosie's accusation was true. Linda offered me the service, but I declined. Not so much on moral grounds, rather as a matter of taste). Linda ripped back, said Rosie was old and ugly. They moved close to one another, their faces contorted in fury.

I grew alarmed. The whole thing was getting out of hand; there could be serious bodily harm. If it got to hair-pulling and face-scratching, Linda had youth, was bigger and stronger. But Rosie was a survivor. She had a purse, was probably carrying a knife, and I was afraid she had the will to use it.

I stepped between the girls. "Wait," I said, "we don't need to fight." In my naiveté I offered, "We can work it out. We can be together, the three of us." I took Rosie and Linda by the hand. "We can get a nice place," I reasoned. "I'll pay the rent, the food. No problem."

They stared at me—not saying a word. Then Rosie turned, faced me. "No," she said, "You must decide, take one." They looked at me, expectantly, waiting for my reply.

I stepped back for a moment, thinking. This fight wasn't about me, my body, about sex. To them I wasn't some kind of stud, some guy they desperately wanted. No, it was more about professional pride, about status among the other bar girls and about ownership. I was a "rice bowl," an Asian term meaning a source of income, a way of making a living. And a steady sailor boyfriend meant a regular income. If he was easy to be around, even fun, and didn't get mean or abusive when drunk, that was good. And if he was good in bed, that was icing on the cake. Sure, it wasn't unusual for a bar girl to fall in love with a sailor; it happened all the time. Especially when a girl was young, just starting out. When the sailor left for the States, she suffered through a broken heart. But she got over it, got wiser and learned not to let it happen again.

I looked first at Linda, then Rosie. I cared for them. Linda, young and pretty, she'd have no trouble latching on to another guy. But Rosie? She was so thin, her eyes sunken, her dress soiled. She looked sick. What had happened to her the past two months in Olongapo? What had she been through? Looking like she did, she would have trouble getting a job in any of the clubs in Cavite. Rosie's eyes met mine, softened. My heart went out to her. She needed me. Why she left, why she came back, I didn't know, but she was back—that's all that mattered.

I reached for Rosie's hand, then turned to Linda. "I'm sorry," I said, "but its got to be this way." I ushered Rosie out the door.

The first thing Rosie needed, I thought, was food. There was a little restaurant nearby and I took her there. I was still troubled by the fight and the way I walked out on Linda. I tried to think of a way I could have eased the break, but decided it was the only way. To have faltered and been hesitant would have made things worse. Bar girls had no respect for a weak man, especially in matters of love.

As Rosie wolfed down a plate of fish and rice, I asked if she was alright.

"I get sick by in Olongapo. The doctor, he said I could not work until I get well. I have no money so I come back to Cavite."

Like all the girls she had to have weekly medical examinations to insure she did not have a disease, venereal or otherwise, to keep working in the bars. She said she got fever and a cough and the doctor gave her medicine.

"How did you find me?" I asked.

"I come yesterday. I go Mom's Place. The girls say you with a girl by Black Cat." She put her arm around me. "I so happy to see you. I feel better now."

Rosie said she was staying with Marie in the old house until her apartment became available. I paid for Rosie's food and we left, walking slowly down the palm tree-lined street to the house. Bougainvillea grew along the cement and stone wall that in the late afternoon showed splashes of brilliant red. We pushed thought the green iron gate and walked up the stairs to Marie's one-room apartment. At our knock, Marie opened the door.

"Oh, Jake," she said with a soft welcoming smile, "it's so good to see you. Rosie said she would find you . . ." Marie was massively pregnant, and I had to lean over to give her a hug. "Come in," she said, motioning for us to sit in the one chair and on her bed, "and I'll make coffee."

Not yet 20 years old, Marie was not a beauty but had a warm personality that just lit up a room. She reminded me of the character Melanie in the book *Gone With The Wind*. She was not a bar girl. She grew up in an educated family but was orphaned by the war. She had worked in a restaurant as a waitress in Cavite when she met and fell in love with a young sailor. They lived together in this house until he left for the States.

As we sipped coffee, Rosie related to Marie blow-by-blow her run-in with Linda. Rosie had the wan look of a tubercular, and in the excitement of telling, her eyes glistened as if with fever. I watched Rosie and felt a sudden hunger. I wanted to hold her, take care of her, make love to her. On impulse I reached over and stroked her hair, brushed her cheek with my fingers.

With a glance, she—and Marie—understood. Marie excused herself, said she had to go shopping, and left.

I took Rosie in my arms, kissed her. She touched my face, then took a towel and spread it on the bed. We undressed and lay down. I caressed her thin body, felt the outline of her ribs. We made love. "I not leave you again," Rosie whispered. "I stay with you always."

At the end of the month the bar girl in Rosie's old downstairs apartment moved out, and Rosie moved in. I gave her money for the rent, food, and a few amenities. Rosie liked music and we bought a little radio.

Rosie and I talked about the future. I told her she did not have to work in the bars, that I would take care of her. To my surprise she acquiesced with no argument. There was a problem though: the weekly medical exams. Cavite City, like Olongapo, in cooperation with the U.S. Navy, required all prostitutes to have weekly medical examinations. The Navy wanted to control venereal disease, and the towns wanted the sailors' business. Each girl had to have written certification of the exam and the doctor's approval or the girl could not work in a bar or walk the street picking up sailors. The Filipino police could stop a girl with a sailor and ask for her papers. If she did not have them, she could be run out of town.

There was an exception to the medical exam requirement, however. And that was if the girl "shacked-up" with one sailor. It required the girl and the sailor to register at the local police station. They would sign papers and submit a picture of the two of them. Then if a policeman saw the girl and a sailor in a bar or on the street and asked for her medical papers, she would show her registration papers and the picture. If she was with the sailor named in the papers and on the picture, no problem. If she was with another sailor, she had problems.

A few weeks after Rosie had regained her health, a Filipino photographer in Cavite took our picture, a head-and-shoulders close-up of the two of us. We went to the police station to register. The fat police sergeant at the desk directed us to the office of Lt. Miguel Cortez.

Lt. Cortez, a slim handsome man in his early 30s, came around his desk with a smile and offered us chairs. I explained our wishes, then turned to Rosie and nodded. She was carrying a large purse and opened it. I reached in and pulled out a carton of Chesterfields and slid it across the desk to Lt. Cortez.

"For you and your friends," I said, "for your help and kindness." Filipinos loved American cigarettes, but for them the smokes were expensive and hard to come by. And with the low pay the police got, the cigarettes were an expensive gift.

"Ah, you Americans," Lt. Cortez smiled, "always so generous." He opened a desk drawer, slid the carton in, then opened his office door and signaled the desk sergeant, who soon came with cups of coffee on a tray. The desk sergeant was all smiles, too, knowing he'd get a pack or two from the carton.

Lt. Cortez explained the requirements and restrictions of the registration and brought out papers for us to sign. Rosie struggled, frowning as she scrawled her name. I signed and handed him a copy of our photograph for their records. Then Lt. Cortez asked us to stand and held our hands in his. He smiled at us and said, "May your days together in the Philippine Islands be happy ones."

Rosie and I left the police station feeling as if we were married. About a year later, after I joined the Sangley Point Armed Forces Police, Lt. Cortez became my best friend at the police station. Little did we know, though, that before I left for the States, Lt. Cortez would die—a violent and tragic death.

Marie finally had her baby, but along the way she gave us a scare. One afternoon I came home and found Marie in our bed. She lay drenched in sweat, her dress pulled up to her breasts, and her huge belly exposed. She was having trouble breathing. Rosie was heating little glass bulbs and sticking them on Marie's belly.

"Marie sick," Rosie said. "She have baby soon."

Marie's belly was covered with the little bulbs. As they cooled, they drew up the skin like suction cups, and when removed left little red rings on the skin. The Filipinos believed the heated cups drew out the sickness.

Something worked, for in a few days Marie got well. A week after that she went into labor. A midwife was called and Marie had a healthy baby girl. Rosie was as excited as Marie. She passed the news, and the landlady had a party. Some girls from the restaurant where Marie worked came, as well as some of Rosie's girlfriends from Mom's. I took pictures with a little Kodak Pony 135 camera I bought at the base commissary.

It was a few weeks after Marie had her baby that I found out why Rosie had left me and gone to Olongapo.

Late one afternoon, I had just finished a day watch and come to our apartment. Rosie was gone. Marie was sitting on a bench outside our apartment door in the shade of a palm tree nursing her baby. I walked over.

Marie looked up, smiled. "Oh, Jake, Rosie went for rice and pansit for you. She'll be back soon."

I thanked Marie, sat on the bench next to her and touched the baby's leg as she nursed. "She's beautiful, Marie, she looks just like you." Yes, she did, I thought. Although the father was Caucasian, the baby showed no sign of white blood. However, I'd seen the other extreme, too. I knew a bar girl who had a baby with a sailor. The little boy, a toddler, had blond hair and blue eyes—just like his father. The little guy was quite a favorite with the other bar girls.

I knew of only a two bar girls who were mixed-race—Caucasian and Filipino. One was an absolute knock-out with black hair, azure blue eyes, white skin and Nordic features—and with a body, as my shipmates said, that wouldn't quit. She drew sailors like bears to honey. Every guy who saw her wanted to get her into bed. The other was the girlfriend of a FWC shipmate—and a girl I would soon become intimate with after an unusual request.

I sat with Marie and we made small talk. Then I asked her the question that had been running through my mind for weeks. "Marie, why did Rosie leave me and go to Olangapo, and why did she return?"

The baby had quit sucking and was sleeping.

Marie looked up, paused, then said, "Rosie is my good friend. Promise me, Jake, if I tell you, you won't hurt Rosie."

I looked at Marie. What is the big secret, I wondered, why this reluctance to talk. I had asked Rosie several time, and she always deflected the question and changed the subject. Now, even more, I wanted to know. "Of course," I promised, "my word."

Marie looked into my eyes, began talking slowly, carefully. "When Rosie first met you, she thought of you as a boy, fun to be with, but that was all. As time went on she began to think of you as a man, to feel love. She left for Olongapo because she was afraid, afraid when you left for the States, it would break her heart—like so many girls she knew."

Marie went on, "Rosie got malaria in Olongapo, was very sick with fever, couldn't eat. Doctor wouldn't let her work. She had no money. She came back to Cavite City to be with you. She needed you, she wanted you."

Marie touched my shoulder, then in a tender voice, "Please be kind, Jake."

I grew uncomfortable. This whole business about love was a new experience. I'd never had a girlfriend. I was in uncharted waters. Somehow I knew there would be rocks and shoals ahead.

On May 15th, my promotion to Petty Officer Third Class came through. In a letter to Mom dated May 22, 1954, I reported the news. I said I got lucky and passed the test in February with the highest score of those in our office taking it. The next time I had the watch, the duty officer asked me to draw and analyze the weather map. I guess he wanted to see how good I was. When I finished, he looked it over and said it wasn't bad. I think he was being kind.

My letter to Mom was revealing in another way: it showed my conflicted state of mind about being in the Philippine Islands. On the one hand, I was happy at Sangley Point and said "I like the duty out here very much and may stay until my enlistment is up, Sept. 9, 1956." The real reason for my happiness was my relationship with Rosie. But I never felt I could tell Mom or anyone back home about Rosie or any of the girls in the P.I. Later in the letter I expressed guilt about not being home to help out on the farm. I was getting letters from Mom in which she mentioned how much work there was to do and how she wasn't feeling well. I felt guilty about leaving and joining the Navy. And Mom, in a nice way, let me know how tough it was for her. At one point I wrote, "I am anxious to get back on the farm in a way. There is a lot to do and I would like to be helping. I ought to be about ready to start producing." In subsequent letters home I made it clear I would come home to stay after my discharge from the Navy and work on the farm with Dad.

Now that I had the promotion and extra money, I decided to splurge a bit. Base sailors were allowed to wear civilian clothes, or "civvies," when on liberty so I shopped Cavite and bought a pair of sharp-looking light blue sharkskin trousers and a white short-sleeve shirt to go with my black navy shoes.

And I took Rosie to Manila to celebrate. A month of rest and good food had put flesh on her body and given her face a healthy glow. We took the bus to Manila, checked into a decent hotel, and ate at a nice restaurant. The next day we went shopping. We went to an upscale store that catered to women of fashion. I told Rosie to pick out something nice for herself. She pawed through racks of elegant dresses until she found a gaudy blue evening dress that shimmered with sequins. She poured herself into it and, turning and twisting, admired herself in the mirror. She fell in love with the dress. She wanted it.

"Fine," I said. "You'll look great when we go to Mom's Place. All the girls will be jealous of you." I paid the clerk and told Rosie to take off the dress so the clerk could box it.

"No, I wear it now," Rosie said and strutted out the door with me following behind. It was high noon, the sun beating down on a busy downtown Manila street. Rosie was doing her Mae West walk, her head held proudly, right down the center of the sidewalk. She parted the crowd like Moses parting the Red Sea, drawing stares from everyone as they stood aside to give her room. It was her day.

July came and with it the rainy season. The office was on full alert for incipient typhoon activity. And at home, Rosie gave me the news—Marie had a new boyfriend.

I had just gotten off the mid-watch, tired and hungry, and was headed out the main gate for the house. The early morning sky was slate grey and hung heavy with moisture. About halfway home it dumped, and the last two blocks I ran through a downpour. Rosie saw me coming and had the door open for me. I kissed her, pulled off a soaked skivvy shirt and trousers, and popped into the shower. Rosie knew what I liked for breakfast, and soon I could smell eggs frying on the hot plate. I toweled off, put on a pair of clean skivvy shorts, and sat down at the table. Rosie joined me and over plates of eggs, hot biscuits, sliced papaya, and coffee, filled me in on Marie's new paramour.

I knew the sad story about Marie's sailor boyfriend, the father of her baby girl. About two months ago she had gotten a letter from him. He said he wouldn't be writing her anymore and couldn't send her any more money for the baby. He was getting married to his high-school girlfriend in the States—the girl he had been writing to for the whole two years he was in the P.I. He had led a double life. He never told Marie about this girl, and he never told the girl about Marie. The news hit Marie hard; the sailor was her first love. Somehow she thought he would come back to the P.I. and marry her. Rosie, the old pro, helped her get over the heartache and face reality.

As I dipped a biscuit into a runny egg yolk, Rosie, breathless, asked me to guess who Marie's new boyfriend was.

"Some other sailor from the base," I offered. "One of her boyfriend's buddies?"

"No," Rosie giggled, "a rich Filipino from Manila. He old and fat, but he nice to Marie. He pay her rent, give her money for the baby, buy her nice things."

Curious now, I pressed for details. Rosie said Marie met the man through the restaurant owner she had worked for. He was a businessman in Manila, in his fifties, and married with grown children. His wife has been ill with cancer for some time, and they did not sleep together anymore.

We finished eating and sipped our coffee. Rosie continued, adding spice to the story. "He told Marie he want woman with warm heart and hot body to sleep with." Rosie covered her mouth to hide her glee. "He come four times now, he sleep with her, take her out to eat. He like her." Rosie's eyes were wide with excitement, her hands fluttering as if to help her find the right words. "He say someday he take Marie and the baby to Manila, find nice place for them, take care of them."

"Do you think Marie would go to Manila, be his mistress?" I asked. A good deal for some bar girls, especially if they were older and losing their looks.

"Marie say she not love this man, but she would go. She say she must do what best for baby."

Rosie agreed with Marie and so did I. Life in the Philippine Islands was tough, and you had to do what you had to do to survive.

CHAPTER 8

A Strange Request

Around this time I got an unusual request: would I shack-up with another sailor's girl? And it came unexpectedly. I was on the base in our hut getting dressed to go on watch. There was the usual confusion with guys from my section tramping in from the head next door after taking a shower and shave, towels wrapped around their waists and heavy rubber thongs on their feet. Ted Cole, an AG2 and one of our section supervisors who bunked at the far end of the hut, came over.

"Jake," Ted whispered, "I wonder if you have a minute, to talk?" He glanced around at the guys milling around. "In private," he added, and nodded toward the door.

"Sure," I said, wondering what this was all about. I didn't know Ted all that well. He was in another section, and since I seldom hung around the hut, about the only time I saw him was during our monthly inspections or when we relieved his section on watch. I did know that Ted was fun-loving yet respected by the mates in his section. I also knew he was finishing his two-year hitch in the P.I. and would be rotating back to the States in a few weeks. And, most significantly, I knew he was the only guy in the FWC beside me who was living with a bar girl.

I followed Ted out the door. The beach was just behind our hut, and we stood at the water's edge and looked out over the bay. Ted was quiet for awhile, then said, "It's my girl Sally. I'll be going and I'm worried about her. I don't know what she'll do when I'm gone, how she'll live."

Ted didn't look at me, his eyes fixed on something in the distance. He was talking as if to himself. I glanced over, studied Ted in profile. I had to admit, he was a handsome stud, slim with blond hair and dark brown eyes. I'd heard Ted was quite the ladies man in the States, even dated a gorgeous Hollywood starlet. He had her picture hanging in his locker.

Ted continued, as if giving voice to a story he'd run through his mind many times before. "I first met Sally when I came aboard at Sangley, two years ago next month. I was at the Black Cat. She was a bar girl, a young kid really, just starting out, trying to learn the ropes and to fit in. She was sitting with a drunk, some white hat off a carrier in port. He was groping her, and when she grabbed his hand and protested, he started slapping her around. I stepped in and fists flew. I threw a few punches and took a couple in return. Anyway, I ended up going home with her, and we've been together ever since. She's a good girl."

"Yes," I acknowledged, "a pretty little gal. I saw you two at the Cat a few times. Tell you the truth, though, she seemed out of place in a Cavite City bar. She looked like some stateside girl, like a cute cheerleader you'd see in a small-town high school back home."

"Well, you are right on that score," Ted agreed. "She has white blood in her. Her father was a soldier out of old Fort Stotsenburg. He died on the Bataan Death March. I don't know what happened to her mother. She's on her own. I guess I'm her family now."

Ted turned to face me, watched my reaction, then went on. "Funny thing is I really care about Sally. I'm going to miss her a lot. I never thought it would be this way when I moved in with her. I've been with plenty of women before, in the navy and otherwise, but this is different."

I knew the feeling. It was something I was going to have to face in less than a year. I didn't like to think about it. "Yes, I know what you're saying," I replied. "I've been with a woman myself for the past year, and I'm in the same situation."

"I know that Jake, and that's why I'm telling you this. The other guys don't understand."

I did understand. Ted was struggling with feelings called "love." In the navy, though, a sailor was not supposed to fall in love, and certainly not with the women sailors spent time with. If a sailor did, he might want to get married, and that meant complications, problems for the Fleet. When a sailor enlisted in the navy he had to be single. In boot camp, the first thing he was told was "if the Navy wanted you to have a wife, the Navy would issue you one."

So sailors had a macho attitude toward women, especially bar girls. The "old salts" used to say: "Find 'em, feel 'em, fuck 'em, and forget 'em."

Yet there was something about Asian and Pacific Island women. They could get to sailors. History was replete with instances. There were books written: *The Sand Pebbles*, a novel about American gunboat sailors in China during the 1920s and a sailor's love for a bar girl that leads to tragedy; and *Mutiny on the Bounty*, the story of British sailors in Tahiti in 1789 who rebel against their captain so they can stay with their island women;

A STRANGE REQUEST

and then the true experience of James Michener, a U.S. naval officer on the beautiful Pacific island of Bora Bora during World War II. As reported in his book, *The World Is My Home: A Memoir*, Michener was sent to the island to investigate a singular and near unbelievable problem—American sailors, after two years stationed on the naval base on Bora Bora, did not want to go back to the States. Almost to a man, they each were living with native girls, and unless directly ordered, would not leave their Polynesian *wahines* and go home.

As we talked, I assumed Ted just wanted to commiserate, talk out his feelings. Then he came out with it. "Jake," he said, "would you move in with Sally?"

For a moment I was taken aback. If you loved a woman, I thought, you wouldn't be asking another guy to live with her. There was that very human feeling called jealousy. Then I thought, maybe it was love, real love. He cares about her, wants someone to take care of her, someone who won't abuse her. But I wasn't the one to help.

"Ted, I can't. I've got a girl. I'm as hooked on her as you are on Sally."

"Wait," Ted protested, "don't rush to make up your mind. I'm leaving in ten days. After I'm gone, go visit Sally. See her place. Stay with her a few days, sleep with her. Then decide. I told her about you. She wants to meet you."

Well, I thought, it's no use. But he is a shipmate, I should do something.

"I can tell you now—I won't move in with her," I said. "But I will stop in and see that she's alright, that she is getting along."

Ted looked down, thought a minute. "Well, okay. I'd appreciate it." He shook my hand. A week later we threw a riotous going-away party for Ted and saw him off.

I did not forget my promise. The first chance I got I slipped over to see Sally. I was careful not to tell Rosie. There was no way she'd understand.

Sally, like my erstwhile girlfriend Linda, lived in one of the numerous two-story buildings along the streets that radiated out from the main gate of the naval base. It was mid-afternoon when I left the base and headed for Sally's. The rainy season was back, and dark clouds hung ominously in the sky. A cool breeze blew in from the bay as I stepped around puddles of water standing in the street. Ted had told me where Sally lived, and I was familiar with the place—only a block from Linda's.

I pushed open the gate, walked around to the

back of the weatherworn building and knocked on the door of Sally's ground-floor apartment. I heard the latch and the door opened a crack. A childlike Shirley Temple face appeared, dimples and all. Before I could introduce myself, a soft little hand reached out and took mine.

"I know you, you're Jake. I saw you at the Black Cat. Teddy said you would come."

Sally ushered me into a small kitchen with a table, two chairs, a hot plate, and shelving for dishes above the sink. "You sit," Sally said. "I get you something to drink." She hurried about, flustered. "What you like, San Miguel, rum, tea? I have good rum, and pineapple juice." She pointed to a bottle of Tanduay Rum and a bottle of juice next to the dishes.

My plan when I walked in was to make sure Sally was okay, then leave. I didn't want to hang around. If she had a problem, I'd try to help. That's all. But she was so anxious to please, it would be impolite to refuse. "Well, maybe a glass of rum and juice," I said.

"Good. I'll get ice from the store and make a cool drink. I'll be back in a minute." Before I could protest Sally was out the door.

I got up and looked around. The kitchen was cramped but clean and tidy. Curtains separated two rooms off the kitchen. I pushed one aside—a shower and toilet. The other curtain opened to a bedroom. Along with a bed and wooden wardrobe for clothes was a chest of drawers with framed pictures on top.

I walked in and looked closely at the photos. One showed a stocky American staff sergeant with a blond crew cut, not much taller than the Filipino woman standing next to him. He had one arm around the woman, and with the other was holding the hand of a little girl. In the background was a movie theater. I turned the photo over. On the back was scrawled "Manila, 1940." Another photograph was of Ted and Sally in swimsuits at the beach, arms around each other, heads touching, smiling.

I glanced around the bedroom. Everything neat and orderly, clothes put away, the floor polished. Sally's a good housekeeper, I thought.

I went back to the kitchen. A few minutes later Sally returned with the ice. She made a big show of mixing my rum drink, then brewed tea for herself. I watched while she scurried about. She looked a lot like her father, the sergeant. The same round face, small nose, a bit chubby though, baby fat really. Her hair wasn't black, but milk-chocolate, a nod to her father's blondness.

We sat at the table. I leaned back, relaxed. The drink was good. "Sally," I said. "I came by to see how you were doing. I promised Ted I would. So how is everything. What are your plans?"

Sally fiddled with her tea, mixing in sugar and milk. She thought a minute, looked up. Her eyes were attractive—hazel with long eyelashes. "I haven't decided yet." She folded and unfolded her hands. "Teddy left me some money, enough for two months."

Sally spoke well. She must have gone to an American school, I figured. "Would you go back to the Black Cat?" I asked.

"I worked at the Black Cat only a few weeks before I met Teddy. I didn't like it. Sailors, they get drunk, get rough."

Sally finished her tea, put the cup in the sink, turned and looked at me evenly. "I would rather have a steady boyfriend." She smiled, quickly covering her mouth with one hand to hide her embarrassment for being so forward. Before I could respond, Sally hurried over and took my glass. "Here, I will get you another drink."

Well, I thought, the rum was fine. Another drink would not hurt. Sally mixed the drink, then excused herself. She said she wanted to take a shower and that

I should wait. She had a radio and turned it on. The Sangley Point radio station was playing the current hit, "Little Things Mean a Lot," with Kitty Kallen singing the lyrics.

Sally finished her shower. With just a towel around her body, she traipsed through the kitchen, pushed through the curtain and disappeared into the bedroom. I sipped my drink and felt a warm glow. The radio eased into the Spanish love song; "Vaya Con Dios," by Les Paul and Mary Ford. Life surely was good.

A few minutes later the curtain to the bedroom parted and Sally stepped out. I caught my breath. She was dressed in a red silk kimono, the kind Japanese Geisha girls wore. With her soft chocolate hair surrounding that Shirley Temple face, Sally looked like a tiny China doll, soft and virginal.

I whistled under my breath. "You look wonderful, Sally, beautiful dress."

Sally turned, swirling the ankle-length dress, showing dainty feet in black slippers. "The kimono is from Hong Kong, pure silk. Teddy bought it for me when he went there on leave." Sally took my hand. "Come, I show you my bedroom."

Sally led me into the bedroom, now darkened by

a thick drape over the single window. On the chest of drawers was a candle—the photos were gone—throwing off a warm sensuous light. Two incense sticks were burning, filling the room with the sweet fragrance of jasmine. The bed was covered by a flowery bedspread, with two velvet pillows at the head. A stuffed puppy sat in the middle.

Sally put her arm around my waist, motioned to the bed. "Sit. Try the bed. It's soft, nice." She put the puppy on the floor.

With the rum, the romantic music, the jasmine, the little doll in the silk kimono, my simple plan to see how Sally was doing and leave went out the window. I sat on the bed and Sally snuggled against me. "You like my place, my bedroom?" she asked.

Sally lay back on the bed. Slowly she undid the sash around her waist, delicately parting the kimono. Her body was lovely, luscious really, but looked so young. Her breasts and pubis was like that of a girl hardly beyond puberty.

Sally took my hand, covered her breast. She sighed, "Your hand is so big."

I should have stopped there. Looking back I'm embarrassed at how eager I was. I caressed her breasts, her thighs. I leaned down and kissed her throat. Sally's skin was satin, and she wore a perfume of rose petals—something else Ted must have gotten in Hong Kong.

"You're beautiful, Sally," I whispered, touching and kissing her body.

Sally closed her eyes, arched her back. "I'm so hot," she breathed.

I took off my clothes. I grabbed one of the velvet pillows and slipped it under Sally. As I entered her, Sally gasped as it if were her first time, then made sounds of exquisite pleasure, of her multiple orgasms. As we made love, her passion became so intense, I began to think it was all an act for my benefit. When I withdrew, Sally clung to me. "Stay with me tonight," she begged.

Sally was so solicitous, so anxious for me to stay that I became uncomfortable. She must be desperate for a steady boyfriend, I thought. Her performance was so over-the-top, so obviously contrived that I started looking for an honorable way out.

"Look, Sally. I have to get back to the base. I have the duty," I said as I started dressing.

Sally took my arm. "You come back tomorrow. I'll make a nice meal, pancit and chicken. Whatever you want," she pleaded.

"No, I can't, Sally. I'm sorry it went this far. I didn't come here with that idea." I reached into my wallet and took out four pesos, laid them on the kitchen table.

Sally grabbed the money and stuck it in my shirt pocket. "No, you don't pay me for a short-time. You come back. Stay with me."

"I can't. I'm with someone else now."

Sally had put her kimono back on and was holding it closed. "Don't you like me?" There was desperation in her eyes. She opened the kimono. "Don't you think I'm pretty?"

"Sure, I like you. And you are pretty. But I have a steady girlfriend."

"Yes, I know your girlfriend. She is old, and she has slept with many sailors." Sally let that thought sink in. Then she put her hand on her chest. "Me, I'm young. I've slept only with Teddy."

"Yes," I said. "You're young and pretty. You go back to the Black Cat. You'll find a sailor, and if you treat him as nice as you did me—you will have a steady boyfriend, I'm sure."

I took the pesos out of my shirt pocket, laid them back on the table, and put my empty rum glass on top. Sally's shoulders slumped, she looked down. She took the pesos.

After leaving Sally's, I went back to the base and

took a shower. I didn't want to go home and have Rosie smell a woman on me.

The use of the word *home* when I went to Rosie's was apt now. We were like a married couple. Rosie was not working in the bars, in fact, never went into the bars. Neither of us did. I didn't relish the idea of taking Rosie into a bar, having a few drinks, and then running into one of her old boyfriends. Or some drunk who wanted a short-time and thought she was working. I did not need the aggravation.

Rosie still had friends working in the bars though. She went to their rooms when they were not working. And Rosie had them come to our place when I was working. I wasn't interested in these visits. It was mostly girl talk.

But there were other things to do. The Filipino people are gregarious and love to party. There seemed to be a fiesta or holiday of some kind often. And Rosie liked to go. For instance, All Saint's Day is on November 1st and All Soul's Day is on November 2nd. On both days Filipinos visit the cemeteries and the graves of their dead family members. They celebrate all night, setting candles on graves that illuminate pictures of the departed and the faces of the relatives gathered around. They bring food and flowers to a celebration that includes prayers, singing, and remembrances. Stalls are set up selling everything necessary to help people enjoy the day.

Rosie wouldn't miss the excitement. So I'd dress in my civvies and Rosie in a discreet cotton dress—not the blue evening gown with the sequins—and we'd go into town. I took my camera one year, and we went to the cemeteries taking pictures of the people and the graves. We ate at a food stall and later had ice cream cones from a vendor.

Rosie's younger brother Carlos came to visit a few times. He was a slim, shy fellow who worked as a miner in the gold fields of Northern Luzon. He was crazy about American cigarettes, but being poor he couldn't afford them. I always brought him a few packs when he came. His eyes just lit up when he saw them.

Rosie was a good housekeeper. We had a hardwood floor she kept polished in the bedroom. Rosie did it by "skating" on the floor. She put half a coconut husk under one foot and glided it over the bare wooden floor. The coconuts thick outer covering with its oily meat shined it to a high gloss.

Although the house was clean, we had some guests that were not welcome. Critters, like cockroaches—big ones. They were drawn to any food scraps and came out at night. One day Rosie brought home a kitten. A friend's cat had a litter and the friend could not keep them all. When the kitten got older, it went after the cockroaches and killed them. After that we didn't have to worry about mice and rats either. We had geckos too, those small, harmless lizards that scramble along the walls. I didn't mind them. Besides, they ate mosquitoes and flies so we left them alone.

There was one critter that really gave me fright, however. I was taking a shower in the rickety wooden stall just off our kitchen. I always kept a bar of soap above my head on a ledge by the roof. I had the shower going and my eyes closed. I reached up to get the soap. Instead, I grabbed a huge, hairy thing that then fell on my shoulder. It was a spider, bigger than anything I had ever seen. It had a body the size of a quarter, with thick hairy legs. I brushed it off, shouted, and Rosie came running. She brought a broom and killed it. I didn't think it was poisonous, but after that, I looked where I reached.

CHAPTER 9

Going to Hong Kong

November 1954. The rainy and typhoon season was about finished. I had been in the P.I. over a year. In the Navy you got 30 days leave (vacation) per year. You could accumulate up to 60 days. I had over 30 days on the books.

Don Walker and I and three guys from the office decided to take leave and go to Hong Kong, the British crown colony on the southeast coast of China. The old salts said it was an experience not to be missed. The shopping, they said, was great—plenty of bargains—and the food, the sights, and, of course, the women were truly fine.

One fellow who bunked next to me had gone twice to Hong Kong, and spent all his time shopping for clothes. His locker was filled with tailor-made civvies: suits, sport jackets, shirts, underwear made of silk, and especially vests. His vests were beautifully embroidered. He loved to dress elegantly and could not wait to get back to the States to show them off.

One of our chief petty officers heard we were going to Hong Kong and offered to show slides of his trip there. He was a good weather forecaster, but had peculiar preferences. For one, he liked his coffee cold and black. When we had the watch before him we'd set aside whatever coffee we didn't drink in a separate pot. It would sit there for hours, black and cold, and develop an oily film on top. He always thanked us, saying the coffee was just the way he liked it.

One night the five of us met with the Chief in the office conference room. He had a stack of colored slides and projected them on a large screen. We sat in the darkness, expecting to see the usual scenery: harbor sights, buildings, street scenes, that sort of thing. Instead we saw photo after photo of Chinese women getting on or off buses. They all wore the split-skirt, and each time they got on or off they showed a bare leg clear up to mid-thigh. The Chief described in detail how he waited for hours at bus stops, setting the f-stop on his camera fast enough to stop the action. He lingered over especially good shots, his voice raising as he related the time of day, the cloud cover, and the general weather conditions when each photo was taken. He never talked of taking a woman to bed. We concluded he was a pure "leg man." The photo was the thing—

end of story. We had to stifle snickers, but at the end we told him he had great pictures.

We left for Hong Kong, 630 miles north of Manila, on a navy transport ship. We'd be gone one week: two days to get there, three days in Hong Kong, and two days to get back to Sangley.

On the way we ran into rough weather. I got so seasick I could not eat, and when I vomited nothing came but a green bile. For two days I just lay in my bunk. I kept thinking this would be a terrible trip. Yet, once I stepped off the ship onto solid ground, I felt as if I'd never been sick.

Hong Kong is an island (about 11 miles long and 2 to 5 miles wide) on the China coast. It lies in a sheltered harbor just one mile from Kowloon on the mainland. Great Britain gained control of Hong Kong island in 1841 after its capture in the Opium War. In 1860 China ceded Kowloon to the British.

We arrived in the morning and Hong Kong harbor was filled with freighters, sampans, junks, and several warships. We took a motor launch to Kowloon and checked into a hotel near the Star Ferry Pier. We each took a room at five dollars (American) a day. As part of the deal, we were invited to have dinner that evening as guests of the manager.

That afternoon we went shopping for clothes. Our shipmates at Sangley told us of a clothing store in Kowloon that would treat us right. We walked to the store wearing the "uniform of the day," navy dress blues, and were greeted at the door by two Chinese men and a Chinese woman. They were dressed in western-style suits and dress and spoke English well.

The store was different from any clothing store I'd ever seen. I was expecting racks of ready-made suits, shirts, and trousers to inspect. Instead there were counters along two walls with piles of fabrics of various kinds and colors and thick style books. At one end was four or five cushioned chairs and a coffee table.

The Chinese woman smiled, ushered us to the chairs, and asked us what we wanted to drink. "You can have anything," she said, "whiskey, gin, rum, beer." We ordered up and she hurried away to mix our drinks.

The two Chinese clerks queried us about our clothing preferences and brought us thick style books to review. When our drinks came we looked over the books. There were pictures of suits, jackets, and trousers with the latest styles from England and the U.S. The clerks were in no hurry and the Chinese woman brought us several rounds. The booze worked on us and we made our selections excitedly, getting a bit carried away.

I ordered two sport jackets, one navy blue and the other tan, a cashmere sweater, a white silk shirt, and silk underwear. For the sport jackets I selected a fabric called doeskin, satin-soft and expensive with silk lining inside.

The clerks took our measurements and told us to come back the next day for fitting. The third day our custom-made clothes would be ready. After the drinks, we left feeling good, although spending a bit more than we planned.

We went back to the hotel and had dinner with the assistant manager of the hotel. I had never eaten real Chinese food and was delighted with the exotic delicacies and fascinated by a block of butter sculpted in the form of a butterfly .

That night we bar-hopped along Nathan Road. The Chinese girls were dressed in silk cheongsams, with high, tight-fitting collars and split skirts. They sat with us, danced if we wanted, lit our cigarettes, and poured our beers. The girls said they liked the cinema and that several American movies had been made in Hong Kong in recent months. We asked if they had slept with any movie stars. One girl said she slept with D.K., a famous American comedic actor. But, she said, he "make lovey too fast." She giggled, "boom, boom, like rabbit, then over, finished."

I asked, "You like make lovey long time?"

She giggled, "Okay."

Several of us took girls back to the hotel for the night. The next morning Don Walker came to my hotel room and knocked on the door. "Time to rollout," he shouted. "We're going out to see the sights." The bar girl and I were still in bed. Groggy, I threw off the sheets, pulled on my trousers, and opened the door for Don. The girl grabbed her clothes and rushed into the bathroom to dress. When she came out she snuggled in my lap. Don chuckled and said he had to get a photo of us—for my grandkids someday. My camera was on the table and had a flash attachment. He took it and shot off a few photos. The pictures show a slim bar girl with nice legs, wearing a lavender silk cheongsam with split skirt and black high-heel shoes..

Yes, our old chief was right. Hong Kong was a great place for a leg man.

My shipmates and I spent the rest of the day browsing the many curio stores in Kowloon. The Chinese shopkeepers expected us to bargain, so we did. When they said something was ten dollars, we said we'd pay six. We would usually get the item for seven or eight dollars.

I purchased a Chinese chest of teakwood covered with carvings of old Chinese wise men, trees, and birds. I paid 45 dollars American for it and filled the chest with other buys I planned to take back to the States: Irish linen for Mom and Chinese carvings for Dad. I couldn't forget Rosie. I found a jewelry store and bought her a gold heart pendant with rose gemstone inset, chain, matching earrings, perfume and a silk kimono.

We dined at fine restaurants, and not only Chinese. We wanted to experience cuisine foreign to our palates. We ate at Tkachenko's, a Russian place where I sampled borscht, a delicious soup made of beets, cabbage, and tomatoes. And at Springers, an American eatery run by a retired navy chief petty officer (great hamburgers). Wherever we ate the food was wonderful—of course it didn't take much to beat navy chow. And the prices were right. In a letter to my parents I reported that the "fanciest restaurants charged less for a meal than we would pay in Willow Creek."

The morning of the third day we went to the clothing store for our tailor-mades. The Chinese clerk pushed open a curtain at the back of the store to retrieve our goods. Behind the curtain we noticed a long room filled with row on row of young Chinese women working at sewing machines. We tried on our clothes and, with a few small adjustments, everything fit perfectly. We paid in American dollars (about a third of the cost in the States), and there were smiles and handshakes all around.

To show their appreciation and to encourage us to refer our shipmates back in the P.I, the clothing store made available, at no charge, a driver and limousine to take us on a tour of Hong Kong Island. We piled into the limo and the driver took the vehicle ferry from Kowloon to the island. We toured the business district. Then on to the Peak Tram, a funicular railway that took us to the top of Victoria Peak for an incredible view of Hong Kong, the harbor, and Kowloon below.

The Chinese driver took us to the Tiger Balm Gardens, eight acres of hillside pocked and covered with grottoes and pavilions filled with garishly painted statues and models of Chinese gods, mythical animals, and scenes from fables and parables. Built in 1935 by two Chinese brothers with profits from sales of a popular menthol balm, the gardens were great fun to explore.

It was our last night and I decided to see the underside of the British colony. Red two-wheeled rickshaws were lined up near the hotel entrance, their black pajama-clad coolies waiting for business. I walked up to one and said, "Girls, you take me to see girls," and waved several American bills at him. He nodded excitedly and motioned me into the small one-passenger vehicle. We started out, the rickshaw man twisting in and around cars and buses in the congested thoroughfare, his bare calloused feet making a slapping sound on the hard city street, then down a narrow side street.

The rickshaw man stopped at a small bar, raised his hand for me to stay, then talked to a man at the entrance. Soon two or three bar girls came out and stood next to me, awaiting my selection. They were not unattractive, but I was not ready to concede, the night was still young. I waved them off and directed the coolie for "more girls." We went from bar to bar with the same result.

Finally, the rickshaw man pulled up to a decayed store front in a darkened alley and motioned for me to get out. "We go now. You see girl."

The store was closed, and we went around to the back and up a flight of stairs to living quarters above the store. At the coolie's knock, an elderly Chinese woman with gold teeth and dressed in a baggy jacket and trousers opened the door. After a hurried discussion with the rickshaw man, the old woman left for a few minutes and came back. I was led down a hall to a door. The old woman opened the door and waved me in. "There," she said, "is nice girl for you."

I looked, unbelieving, for in the middle of a room barren of furniture was a huge mattress, and on the mattress was a monstrously fat Chinese woman of middle years, naked, except for a small handkerchief over her privates. She gave me an obscene smile, and, with an arm bulging with fat, waved stubby fingers for me to join her. I was mesmerized, for a moment did not respond. To further entice me, she slowly removed the handkerchief from her pubis and spread her legs.

"You likey?" said the old woman.

I shook my head and looked to the rickshaw man, "No good," I said. "We go."

Why in the world, I wondered, had the rickshaw man taken me to this? Maybe after I turned down the host of decent-looking girls he thought my interest ran to the perverted, that I would be satisfied only with the grotesque. Then it dawned. This is where coolies came to find relief, perhaps for just a few grimy H.K. coins. I suppose he would get a generous cut on any deal made.

While the rickshaw man and old Chinese talked, I looked across the hall to an open kitchen where two young girls dressed in black pajamas were working. One, bent over washing dishes, glanced up, and catching my eye, smiled, her eyes pleading "take me!" On a whim, I pointed to the girl and said, "I take that one."

There was an excited babble of Chinese, the old woman shaking her head, gesticulating. In broken English the rickshaw man explained the girl belonged to the man of the house. I said I wanted to talk to him. After another flurry in Chinese, the old woman left. Soon after, a wizened old Chinese man, dressed in a high-necked gown and using a walking stick, joined us. The rickshaw man conversed in Chinese, discussed my wishes, then turned to me and explained—the girl was not available. The old Chinaman, he said, bought the girl when she was 12 years old from a poor refugee family. From the start he used her as a woman, and she has slept with no one else.

Although disbelieving the girl's "purity," I was intrigued. I opened my wallet and withdrew a half dozen American one dollar bills and fanned them, like a deck of cards, in front of the old man. He stroked his wispy beard and stared at the bills, then looked up and shook his head—no.

I decided to bargain. I would add a bill or two to the fan, then wait for his reaction. I got up to three times the going rate for a girl. When he shook his head no, I folded my money and turned to go. He raised his hand, nodded yes. Arrangements were made and she was taken to my hotel room for the night.

When we were alone, I looked over the girl whose services I had purchased. She stood, quietly, still wearing the kitchen pajamas, stained here and there from cooking oil, that covered her like a sack, waiting for me to make the first move. She appeared to be about 17 years old, her face pretty. I tried to put her at ease by asking her name. I quickly discovered she spoke no English. Yet, with enough hand gestures I got something that sounded like May-ling.

I went to May-ling, took her in my arms and felt her tremble. I moved my hands over her body, whispered her name, and felt the feminine softness beneath. I undid the ties and clasps of her pajamas, and as her garments fell to the floor, watched a lovely woman emerge.

When I undressed and went to her, she made signs with her hands she wanted us to bathe. It seemed she had never been to a hotel room and was unfamiliar with showers. I took her hand, led her into the stall, and turned on the shower faucet. She jumped as the cold water hit us, we both laughed. With soap, May-ling lathered my body and I hers. She used a technique that must have pleased the' old Chinaman, and it worked on me. At her touch, in an instant, I became erect. She paused, perhaps startled in the difference in reaction time between a 20-year-old and an 80-plus old man. I put my arms around May-ling and lifted her into bed.

I thought back to when I was with girls in high school. Then I was a fumbling virgin, excited yet fearful, without a clue as to what to do. I recalled my senior prom. I was dragging my feet about asking a girl, not sure I wanted to go, uncomfortable with the whole idea. Finally, Ray Quandt, captain of our football team, collared me in the lunch hall.

"Damn, Jake, you're one of the studs on our team. You can't chicken out."

"I don't know who to ask," I stammered, looking for an excuse, for a way out.

"Ask Marcie, she's hot for you. She nearly wets her panties every time you run the football. She'd go with you at the drop of a hat."

Marcie was one of the cheerleaders for our football team. Cute, sassy, Marcie was considered a hot number who liked to neck. "I don't know, Ray . . ."

"Come on, Jake, we'll double-date. I'll take my Dad's car."

Well, I did take Marcie. And that night after the dance, we parked off a deserted road in a popular lover's lane. Ray was in the front seat with a girl and I was in the back seat with Marcie. I sat stiff, uncertain, unable to take the initiative. After waiting and no action, Marcie took my hand and placed it on her breast. That is where my hand stayed, frozen, until falling stiffly to my side—total embarrassment!

Maybe, I thought, in this way I could make amends to Marcie and those few other girls I dated, who saw me as shy and awkward. Now I could prove myself and make up for the humiliation.

I wanted to make love to this girl, this May-ling, to use everything I had learned from Rosie, everything she and Linda and Sally found sensual—and pleasing. Foreplay is an art, I learned, and it takes time. As I kissed, touched, whispered, May-ling gave herself to passion. She began to moan, thrusting her breasts against my lips. A silken sheen of vaginal lubricant spread over her thighs, her belly. When finally we joined, she enveloped me with her arms and legs, as if to pull me inside of her. Several thrusts and she gasped, I felt her body shudder. I could not hold back and felt a release like water bursting through a dam.

Yet the girl held me tight. We rocked, clasped together, like a boat rising and falling with the waves. Her unquenchable desire drove me, and after a brief diminution, I grew hard again. We moved, driven by some animal need. There came a sequence when her breath would quicken, her body grow taunt, a moan, then to be repeated, perhaps a half dozen times, but still she held me in—until there came a cry like that from some doe-like creature caught in the jaws of a predator on the African plains. May-ling fell back, legs and arms splayed, her head turned to one side, her eyes closed. The French call it the little death. I brushed back the tangle of her black hair and kissed her cheek. I looked at her, this beautiful girl, this woman, and thought of the old man—how sad.

After awhile May-ling aroused. She looked into my eyes, smiled. She traced fingers down my cheek, over my chest. For a time we lay, touching, dreamlike, satiated. A feeling of bliss came over me. Later, as tiredness came, I got up and took towels to cover the wet of our love-making on the bed. Then we slept, she curled in my arms, until daybreak when we showered and made love once again.

It was time for me to go; my ship would leave at midday. I kissed May-ling, tried to tell her how beautiful she was. I took her to the hotel entrance and found the rickshaw man who brought her to me. I gave him money to take her back; back to the old Chinaman. I tried to give her money, she shook her head. She took my hand and slipped a thin paper, folded to the size of a half dollar, into my palm. I opened it and stared—just a blank paper with Chinese characters on top. Confused, I showed it to the rickshaw man and asked what it meant. He turned to May-ling—a babble of Chinese—and, in fractured English, back to me. He smiled, "She like you. She say you pay old man enough. She want you to come again. That is paper from store. Show it to rickshaw man, he take you there."

May-ling got into the rickshaw and it pulled away. I watched until it grew small and disappeared. Four hours later I was on a ship back to Sangley.

CHAPTER 10

Going to Be a Cop

There is an adage, generations old, that goes, "He spent money like a drunken sailor." It supports the image of the American Navy seaman as a drunken lout with uncontrollable urges, roaming harbor dives, throwing money at any woman, no matter how ugly and disreputable, just to bed her and satisfy his lust. There is just enough truth to the saying to keep it from dying.

Well, think of it. You take a boy, 18, 19, 20 years old, by law not yet a man, put him on a ship and send him out on a six-month cruise, without seeing a woman for months on end (women were not allowed to serve on a Navy ship when I was in) and without liquor aboard ship, not even 3.2 beer, with a wallet full of money (if he hadn't lost it gambling), then turn him loose on a 12- or 14-hour liberty at some seaport with a gang of shipmates, all desperately trying to live up to the popular image of a boozing, brawling macho sailor, and you have fireworks.

And the Navy understood. Through the years—especially during wartime when sailors put their lives on the line—the Navy learned to look the other way, to cut the boys a little slack. Even to allow brothels, with the girls checked regularly for venereal disease, to operate near U.S. naval bases in some overseas locations like Subic Bay and Sangley Point in the P.I . But there had to be some limits, some control, for the boys' sake and the Navy's reputation. And that is where the Navy's shore patrol, the Navy's police force came in. I mention this because when I got back from Hong Kong I became a member of that thin line of navy control.

It was posted on the FWC bulletin board: Wanted: a volunteer to spend six months TAD (temporary assignment duty) on the Sangley Point Armed Forces Police detachment (called Armed Forces Police rather than Shore Patrol because it included personnel from the Marine Corps and Coast Guard as well as the Navy). It was commanded by a marine corps captain and was responsible for maintaining order among military personnel in Cavite. Volunteers from each of the divisions on the base filled out the detachment. The volunteer from the Fleet Weather Central was completing his tour and someone had to fill his spot on the complement. I was getting bored with the weather maps and

Teletype machines and thought it would be exciting. I signed up and got the job.

The Sangley AFP was housed in a Quonset hut on the main drag of the base. It had a small office facing the street with a counter, two desks, and file cabinets and quarters for the enlisted men (two-tiered bunks and lockers) in the back. I moved my gear from the FWC hut and took a top bunk with my new shipmates—the police patrol.

On my first day on the job I was issued a white helmet with the block letters AFP on the front, a web belt, and a wooden baton. Mike Connelly, a second class petty officer and veteran of the patrol, said he'd give me a tour of Cavite City, our "area of responsibility." Mike was a burly guy, square-shouldered with tattoos on both arms: on one arm, an eagle with crossed anchors and the words "fight or die" on a scroll beneath, and on the other arm, a snarling panther. He had a bushy mustache with the ends waxed and twisted into long thin strands drawn straight out and then curved up, like the horns on a western longhorn steer.

We took a jeep, with Mike driving, and no sooner had we gotten out the front gate into Cavite City when I was introduced to the "sensitivities" of the patrol. A dog, spindly, its mange-ridden coat showing patches of skin, blundered into the road, intent on a remnant of road kill, right in front of the jeep. The veteran never touched the brakes or swerved. There was a thud, the mongrel rolled under the wheels. The jeep kept going. "Geez," I said, looking back at the mutt lying motionless in the dusty street, "aren't you going to stop?"

"Hell, no," Mike grinned. "When we've seen the town we'll come back this way. I'll show you something."

I held my tongue. Even though I knew half of these dogs belonged to no one and ran wild, living off garbage, what I saw rubbed me the wrong way. I liked dogs. My Dad had a black and white Collie for herding the cows. I had my own dog while growing up. Yet I didn't want to get into a fight on the first day with the guy who might turn out to be my boss.

We wheeled through town with Mike hitting the horn to move out of the way first, an old Filipino woman carrying a basket of fruit, then a passel of kids chasing each other, pointing out a bar here or club there that was a trouble spot.

"When I came to Sangley a year ago," Mike went on, "there was about 50 bars and clubs, now there's 60." He primped his mustache with the fingers of one hand. "Of course this is nothing like the number of joints in Olongapo, the town outside our big base at Subic Bay, or Angeles, the village near Clark Air Force Base. Most of our ships pull into Subic, so there is a lot more guys taking liberty in Olongapo. But we have our share of problems. Any business—bar, club, restaurant, hotel—that's got booze and girls is a potential trouble spot. And then there are the massage parlors." I gave him a curious look. He caught it. "You know, a Swedish massage—a suck and fuck," he laughed, the ends of his mustache quivering.

We pulled up to a two-story building a few blocks from Mom's Place in the center of town. A signpost out front read POLICE. Two brown-clad uniformed Filipino policemen stood near the front door smoking. Mike explained that this was the headquarters of the Philippine Constabulary in Cavite, the city's police force. I knew the place. It was the police station where Rosie and I came to register as a couple. But I didn't say anything. I didn't want to admit that I was a shack rat because I wasn't sure how it would go over with Mike. Mike waved at the two cops and ushered me through the front door and down the hall past a row of offices to a small room. An AFP patrolman, a third class petty officer like me, sat at a single desk next to a metal file cabinet, idly leafing through a stack of papers.

"How's business Mack?" asked Mike, tossing his helmet on the desk.

"Not much happening. No ships in," said Mack, leaning back in his chair, hands behind his head.

"Coffee any good?" Mike strolled over to the coffee carafe and filled two mugs.

"Hot and black," Mack said, turning to me, grinning. Mike handed me a mug, motioned me to a chair against the wall, and slumped in another next to the desk. He introduced me to the third class, then explained the unique relationship between the AFP and the Filipino police. He said the U.S. military had jurisdiction over all American servicemen, on or off the base.

"The Filipinos got nothing to say about us," Mike the veteran expounded. "For instance, if a sailor kills a Flip, the sailor is tried by general court-martial under U.S. military law in a U.S. Navy court, and if found guilty, will serve his time in a U.S. federal prison. Our government won't let a Filipino cop or court touch him. The Philippine government don't argue with us on that point either; they need us too much to say no." He slapped his leg, "And, by God, that's the way it should be."

Mike pulled out a pack of Lucky Strikes, lit up,

and offered the pack around. He took a deep drag and, through a stream of smoke, said, "We get along with the Filipino police though. They gave us this office to use." He smoothed his mustache, "They got their job, we got ours."

We finished our coffee and got up to go. Mack shook my hand, welcomed me aboard, said he'd see me around.

On our way back to the base, we turned down the street where we had hit the dog. Except for a smear of blood, there was no sign of the dog. Mike laughed, "Look ahead," he pointed. There, not far up the street, hobbled an old Filipino man, bent over, dressed in trousers cut-off at the knees and a torn tee shirt, carrying the dog over his shoulder. Mike shrugged his shoulders, "These Flips like dog meat. Hell, I did the old guy a favor by killing the dog. He'd never been able to run it down by himself." He waved his hand in disgust, "Hells bells, they'll eat anything, pig guts, chicken guts, cooked in blood yet, any kind of shit."

We got back to the base and went into the office. Mike checked the in-basket, turned to me. "This job is not bad. We get a few punks come in off the ships, they get a snoot full and want to fight the whole world. Once in awhile, one will throw a punch at one of us patrolmen, then we have to kick ass," he chuckled. There was a twisted smile and a look like he enjoyed that part of the job. This guy's a real hard-ass, I thought. If they are all like this, I'm going to have some trouble adjusting.

The AFP, like police in the States, operated on the buddy system, pairing two patrolmen. My first partner was a "volunteer," not his choice, from the Coast Guard, earnest and taciturn, finishing the last month of his six-month tour and anxious to get back to his job as coxswain of a coastal boat. We were a foot patrol, walking an eight-block beat on Radio Drive from the base's main gate to the police station downtown and back.

On an early evening watch, with a partner not given to talk, it was easy to open one's senses to the surroundings. It was dinner time and the smell of cooking smoke and spices wafted in the air. The click and clatter of mahjong pieces on hard-topped tables mixing with the babble of Chinese and Tagalog floated out from living quarters above street-side stores. Jukebox tunes, "Sh-Boom" by the Crew Cuts and "Mr. Sandman" by the Chordettes, drifted out of bars—their windows and doors propped open to catch the breeze. These current favorites mixed with the shouts of jeepney drivers for fares to take sailors, strolling out the main gate on liberty, to the bars of their choice.

Our job, walking the beat, was to check the bars, stopping in to "show the flag," letting the white hats and bar men know we were on duty. If we smelled trouble—a sailor arguing over his bar bill or squabbling with a bar girl, or sailors from different ships trying to out macho one another—we intervened to stop the dispute before it got out of hand.

We tried to avoid putting a sailor on report. To do so meant writing up the offense, and in serious cases, testifying in a navy court, often done after our watch was over, forcing us to come in off liberty—something we did not relish. And writing up a guy for something like drunk and disorderly could get him a captain's mast—a term from the old sailing days when the setting for this form of naval justice was on the weather deck, at the foot of the ship's mainmast. During a captain's mast, the commanding officer could issue punishment ranging from a loss of privileges for a couple weeks to extra duties for a month or more, on up to demotion in rank and loss of pay and three days in the brig on bread and water. And most patrolmen, except for a few hard asses on power trips, sympathized with a sailor who drank too much and was creating a fuss—we'd all been there, or close to it, and hoped an AFP would cut us a little slack in the same circumstances.

I was "blooded" the first week on the beat. A Filipino boy, seven or eight years old, barefoot and wearing tattered cut-offs, ran up to my partner and me shouting, "trouble at Wagon Wheel, bad trouble!'"

Kids, I was to learn, were the usual way the AFP foot patrol first got word of a problem. These ragamuffins were always hanging around the bars, hustling sailors to polish their shoes or trying to sell them cheap homemade whiskey—the current best seller being Golden Cup Scotch Whiskey going for 36 centavos (18 cents) a pint. We tried to shoo the children away from the sailors and warn the sailors that that firewater could make them go blind. (We knew of a few cases where that had happened, at least temporarily.)

The boy grabbed my jumper sleeve, pointed down the street to the Wagon Wheel Bar about a block away, and tried to pull me toward it. My partner and I broke into a trot, heading for the bar, the boy leading the way. The Wagon Wheel had old-time Western swinging doors, and as we got close, the boy scurried under them and disappeared inside.

I pushed through the doors, my partner behind, and caught a flying beer bottle on my left cheekbone, just under the eye, the bottle glancing off and crashing against the wall behind me, beer and shards of glass exploding about. I staggered back, then took in the scene. A young marine private, tall and raw-boned with close-cropped red hair, stood next to an overturned table, drunk and wild-eyed, throwing beer bottles and shouting, "You dirty sons of bitches, you cheated me. You took all my money." There was a broken mirror behind the bar, and splattered beer and broken glass against one wall. The bar girls huddled in a corner, the bar man crouched behind the bar.

My partner pushed past me and directed. "Get on the phone by the bar, the bar man will give it to you. Call for backup and the paddy wagon." I called our man at the police station and had a paddy wagon on the way.

I turned to join my partner, now talking quietly, trying to placate the marine who had backed against the bar, a broken beer bottle in one hand. "Stay away from me you bastards," he threatened.

My partner moved toward the marine. "Take it easy, pal," he said, "don't do anything foolish." He kept talking, moving slowly until he got an arm's length from the young private, faked with his left hand, as if to grab the marine's right hand holding the jagged bottle, then crashed down on the crazed drunk's wrist with his baton. The marine let out a yell and dropped the bottle. We piled on top of him, struggling, until finally wrestling him to the floor and getting his hands cuffed behind his back.

Soon the paddy wagon arrived. Mike Connelly, the burly guy with the tattoos and mustache, barged through the doors, his partner trailing behind. We explained the situation. Mike noticed the swollen knot on my cheekbone, the trickle of blood.

"This fucking Gyrene do this to you?" he growled. I nodded. "Get him up on his feet," Mike ordered.

We pulled the young marine to his feet. He came up kicking. "You swabbie faggots, cock-suckers," he shouted, his face contorted in rage.

Mike stiffened, his eyes glaring. "You need some manners, asshole," he snarled. He grabbed his baton in the middle and drove it up, like a spear, into the marine's stomach. The marine sagged, pain swept his face—then doubled over and threw up, vomit splashing the floor, spotting Mike's spit-shined shoes. Mike looked down in disgust. "Jesus H Christ," he raged. "Let's get this puke-ass bastard into the wagon."

Mike and his partner got under the young marine's arms, jerked him to his feet and dragged him out the door to the paddy wagon parked along the street. Then each with a hand on the marine's collar and belt, hoisted him, like a log between them, head first in to the back of the wagon, the marine's face skidding on the hard floor.

Mike bolted the wagon door, turned to my partner and me and ordered, "I want papers on this bastard. Assaulting a patrolman, damage to property, drunk and disorderly, the works." He walked around to the front of the wagon, drew out a rag from the glove compartment and wiped the vomit from his shoes. "And talk to the bar man and the girls, get an idea of damages." He threw the soiled rag into the street. "Look into this guy's story he got cheated, not that we'll ever find out. The Flips won't admit it, and he was alone without buddies to back up his charge. He walked over and examined my cheek, saying "We'll send over a jeep to take you to sick bay, have it bandaged."

My partner and I watched Mike gun the wagon from the curb, go about 30 feet and slam on brakes, the tires squealing on the street. We could hear the marine, his hands cuffed behind his back, banging around inside the wagon. My partner turned to me, a wry smile on his face. "He likes to do that—hit the brakes. A prisoner with his hands cuffed behind his back bounces off the wagon's metal sides like a pinball, sometimes doing as much damage as beating him with a club."

"How does he get by with that," I asked, knowing there were rules against the AFP abusing prisoners. "And that business in the bar, slamming that baton in the marine's gut. That surely isn't allowed by regulations."

"Hell," my partner said, "who's going to say anything? The Filipinos in the bar won't complain. They'll think the marine got what he had coming. That's how their police handle troublemakers, punch 'em around." He looked at me evenly. "And we're his partners. Any charges against him, we back him—right." He said that as a statement of fact, not a question, then added, "If the marine gives the guys any lip on the way to the base, they might stop in the boondocks somewhere, where no one will see, and use the club. Not on the face, that leaves marks, in the kidneys. A club can do a lot of damage, and it hurts like hell."

We went back into the bar and interviewed the bar man and the girls. As expected they denied cheating the marine. He came into the bar all alone, they said, and just wanted to drink. He wasn't interested in the girls, seemed angry about something, got drunk, started yelling he'd been overcharged and began throwing bottles. We estimated the damages to the bar and took notes for our written report.

A jeep came awhile later and took me to the base sick bay. A corpsman checked the cheek, said nothing was broken and patched the slight cut. I went back to the AFP hut and, with my partner, typed up the charges on the marine and gave it to Mike for review. We learned Mike had taken the marine to sick bay for cuts and bruises from resisting arrest. In checking his ID and liberty pass, we found the marine was attached to an aircraft carrier in port, part of the carrier's security detachment. He was held until the masters-at-arms (MAA) from the carrier came for him. The MAA boys said the marine was a troublemaker, a loner and probably screwed up mentally. At any rate, he wouldn't be hitting the beach for awhile, most likely cooling his heels in the brig on diminished rations.

CHAPTER 11

Life Is Good

As soon as I got back from Hong Kong and got liberty, I hurried to Rosie's with an armful of gifts. I caught her coming out of the shower clutching a bath towel that covered her little body from shoulders to ankles, her damp hair curled around her neck. I put the gift-wrapped packages on the table and opened my arms. She rushed over, bath towel tumbling to the floor behind her, wrapped herself around me and planted a wet kiss on my cheek.

"I miss you. I so lonely when you are gone," she said. She noticed the packages and clasped her hands together. "You bring something for Rosie?"

"Yes," I said, "but you have to close your eyes first." Rosie, like most of the bar girls liked surprises, little games, to keep the suspense going. She jumped up and down, child-like, clasped her hands over her eyes, fingers open enough to see.

"No," I said, "you can't watch." Rosie closed her fingers to prove she couldn't see. I had the pendant and chain in my pocket, opened it and slipped it around her neck. "Now, open your eyes and go to the mirror."

Rosie hurried to the mirror and cried out in delight. She studied the pendant, turned her body this way and that, to see how it looked on her.

"Turn around," I said. "I want to see you wearing it."

Rosie turned to me, posed, one hand on her hip, the other outstretched. She was naked except for the tiny gold heart that nestled between magnificent pendulous breasts.

"You like?" she asked, a mischievous smile on her face.

There came a feeling, so powerful, of lust and love, for a moment I was speechless. A desire, painful in its urgency, overwhelmed me. I swept Rosie into my arms and carried her to the bed, fumbling in haste, finally stripping off my clothes.

"I like," I whispered, "very much."

Rosie struggled in my arms, playfully, as if to ward off a crazed brute intent on rape. "Help," she giggled, "somebody call police, shore patrol."

I pinned Rosie's arms down, buried my face in her bosom. I smelled the clean scent of soap, of woman. I licked her breasts, mouthed first one brown nipple, now growing turgid, then the other, sucking and play biting.

Rosie's struggles weakened, she closed her eyes, her back arched. "Oh, oh," she breathed, "oh, oh."

I let go of Rosie's arms, held her, caressed her belly, her thighs. With fingers, I gently entered her, fondling, finding the place, feeling it swell, undulate.

Rosie moved with my hand, groaned, her breath coming fast. She opened her legs wide, rocked faster, warm vaginal fluid gushed in my hand. "Oh, please," she moaned, "do it, do it."

I slid a pillow under Rosie's hips and mounted her, entering, not fully, searching for that spot with my cock. Holding steady above her, I gave Rosie room to move, to control the pace. She moaned, whimpered, moving fast, ever faster, her sounds telling me she was getting close. I waited, struggled to hold off, wanting this delicious ache to go on, to never end. Then she gasped, pulled me deep into her. We came together, breathless, trembling.

We lay entwined, slippery with sweat and the secretions of lust and love. I held Rosie close, my cheek against hers, my face nestled in her curly damp hair.

"Oh, God," I whispered, breathing in her ear, "Oh, God all mighty."

I lay back, satiated, mind and body at peace. And then a thought, odd for now, came to mind. Sunday school at St. John, how we tried to describe heaven. The green pastures, the fragrant flowers, cool waters, warmth, peace, love. But, of course, no mention of physical love, sex. I wondered: Could there be anything more blissful than this? Happiness, paradise, love, here, now, at this moment, at this time, in this place, this small room, the distance sounds of voices, Tagalog, children at play, 10,000 miles from home, with this woman, this woman I found, who found me. The wonder of it all.

Rosie stirred, raised up on an elbow and looked into my eyes. "Do you love me, Jake?" She kissed my lips. "Do you want me for all time?"

I hugged Rosie and held her close. "Sure Rosie, sure, you know I do." I kissed her. "There's no one like you." I stroked her back. But I didn't say the words.

I took Rosie's hand and said with a smile, "Let's clean up. You've got more presents to open."

I could tell from Rosie's eyes, the way she waited, she wanted more from my lips. She looked down at the tangled wet sheets. "Yes we messy," she said, pulling the sheets off the bed, "very messy." Usually Rosie put towels down before we made love. This time we got too carried away to take the precaution.

We showered and dressed. Rosie went to the table. There were three wrapped packages: two small and a larger one. Her eyes brightened, her mood changed and excitement grew. She opened each package slowly, shaking it first to guess its contents. She opened the box with the matching earrings, held them to her ears, looked in the mirror, and liked how they looked with the pendant. She was full of questions: "Where did you get this? Big store, many pretty girls, Chinese girls in store?" Then the question, always lurking in the mind of a bar girl about her boyfriend: "You get short-time with any girls?" Somehow I danced around that one without an outright lie.

Rosie opened the box with the perfume, sniffed it, liked it, put a dab under each ear and made me smell. I took a whiff, yelled out, "Oh, my God," as if intoxicated by the voluptuous fragrance; then, acting as though overcome by desire, tried to pull her down on the bed while at the same time ripping open my fly.

Rosie laughed, "You crazy sailor." She pulled away and pointed a finger at me in playful reprimand.

"You behave now," she ordered.

When Rosie opened the big box the show really began. It was wrapped with colorful paper and tied with a red ribbon.

Rosie stared at the gift box, turned it this way and that, savoring the moment. She carefully untied the ribbon—of course the ribbon would be saved—and unfolded the paper; all to be saved. When finally she opened the box and took out the red silk kimono—just like Sally's, the one Sally got from Ted—there was a gasp of surprise. She rushed to the mirror, held the garment against her body to see how it looked, and rubbed the smooth fabric against her cheek. She stripped to her panties and wrapped herself in the kimono, turned this way and that in front of the mirror. She was wearing all the gifts I had given her.

I was sitting in a chair watching Rosie. She noticed and came to me with the Mae West walk. I opened my arms. "You look like a movie star now, Rosie."

Rosie snuggled in my lap. "You best boyfriend," she said, wrapping her arms around my neck. "I think I love you now." She gave me a kiss like she saw the girls do in the movies: full on the lips with her eyes closed. "I show all my friends what you brought me from Hong Kong."

I knew the drill. Rosie would invite her friends, bar girls mostly, to come to the house. It would be theater, with Rosie the producer and star. The gifts would be rewrapped and on the table as her friends came in. There would be coffee and sweets. After gossip and small talk, Rosie, very nonchalant, would mention that her boyfriend had just returned from Hong Kong with presents for her. However, she had been too busy to open them. Now, she would say, would be a good time. She would pass the boxes around, wondering aloud as to their contents, giving ample time to each girl to fondle and speculate. Rosie would open each gift with painstaking slowness, adding to the suspense, then savor the "oohs" and "aahs" from the group.

Rosie would open the gifts in a certain order to maximize the dramatic effect. First the perfume, passing it around for each girl to smell, then daintily applying it to her neck and earlobes, then the chain and pendant, followed by the earrings, wearing each after the girls had a chance to look and fondle. Finally, the crème de la crème: Rosie would slip into the red silk kimono and do the movie star walk in front of the admiring bar girls as a grand finale. All this to prove how much her steady boyfriend cared about her.

Later, when I walked back to the base, I thought about Rosie's question: Do you love me, Jake? I wasn't pleased with my answer. Somehow I couldn't say the words "I love you." These were powerful, mysterious words, words I had never said to anyone, words I never heard said in my family. At home growing up, I never heard Dad tell Mom he loved her, never saw them kiss. Maybe it was a German thing—never show your feelings, unless it was anger, then it was okay to rant and rave. Yes, the only time I ever saw a man tell a woman he loved her was in the movies—and that was make believe.

And how did I really feel about Rosie? When I got involved with her, it was to be fun and sex. I assumed Rosie felt the same way. After all, she was a prostitute, that was her job. She told Mary not to fall in love with a sailor, he will go away and break your heart. What did Rosie want from me?

And what was love anyway. The Chinese girl—was that love? I felt wonderful after making love to her. But wasn't that male ego, a macho thing, feeling big because I made an inexperienced girl come. But would I want to spend every day with a girl I couldn't talk to?

LIFE IS GOOD

With Rosie I wanted to be with her every day. I liked her laugh, her gossip, swimming with her, the movies. I felt good when I was with Rosie—like a man. I had never felt this way before. I missed her if I was away from her for a day. Is that love? Maybe.

Then the question: If it is love, where will it all lead?

CHAPTER 12

Big Ben Biegler

Christmas was coming, my second in the P.I. The Fleet Weather Central had its own Christmas cards, and I sent out a bunch to relatives and friends. The card was designed by Our leading chief and had a local spin: a picture of a Filipino two-wheeled cart drawn by a carabao with two native men in straw hats, one driving the carabao and the other holding a stick from which hung the Star of Bethlehem. In the background was a nipa hut and a coconut tree. Inside the card, listed by name and rate was the entire FWC complement of officers and men.

Christmas Day did not seem like Christmas—it was sunny and 80° F. I went back to FWC for the office party, a repeat of last year: Christmas tree, carols and hymns, and a dinner of chicken and ham. Later, Rosie and I went swimming on the beach.

On New Year's Eve I joined Don Walker and a few FWC shipmates at the EM Club. I laid off the whiskey and champagne this time and nursed a couple of San Migs. It was a good time to catch up on the office scuttlebutt.

We were sitting at the bar, feeling loose, letting the alcohol work its magic. Don turned to me and raised his bottle. "Here's one for Ben Biegler—and his wife." Everyone laughed. I didn't get the joke.

"What the heck has happened now?" I asked.

I knew the background. Ben Biegler was a stocky AG3, round-faced with a beginning beer belly, from someplace in the South. He married his high-school sweetheart—she said she missed her period and he believed her, finding out later it was a false alarm—before finishing AG school at Lakehurst. When he shipped out to the Philippine Islands, his wife wanted to follow. Impossible, he told her, the Navy did not provide base housing for enlisted men, and the off-base housing was primitive. Besides, he said, on a $100 a month he could not support her.

Ben, we came to discover, had an enormous sexual appetite, and it wasn't long after coming to the P.I. he set a goal of banging at least one bar girl from each of the 50 bars in Cavite City, plus a few assorted joints in Manila. And his sexuality was on display often and got to be a joke. Ben had a bottom bunk near the back door of our hut that led to the shower hut. Every guy coming in after a shower had to pass by Ben's bunk. On the days he slept late after an evening or mid-watch, Ben's outstretched form, naked except for his skivvy shorts, was on exhibit. Invariably, as he snored, dead to the world, he'd have a massive erection, his skivvy shorts like a tent with his cock the tent pole. It was a running joke, with guys wisecracking as they came in from a shower: "When's Ben going to take the tent down." and "When the hells that hammer handle going to get tired."

Ben didn't seem to miss his wife. She, however, her head filled with visions of a tropical paradise, did not give up wanting to come to the P.I. Every mail call it seemed we'd see Ben sitting on his bunk, letter in hand, a cigarette dangling from his mouth, reading the latest from his wife. He'd finish reading, grumble a few choice swear words, ball up the letter and fling it into the waste basket in the corner of the hut.

Ben tried to dissuade his wife. His letters back to her were filled with the harsh demands of the weather central: the typhoons, the long hours, the unreasonable demands of officers. When he wrote of the P.I. it was in the most inhospitable terms: the heat, humidity, dirt, the crude housing, the native thievery—no place for a decent white woman. He'd try to get a transfer back to the States, he promised, knowing he would not make the effort; also knowing it was next to impossible except for exceptional humanitarian reasons. The fact was he loved the P.I., the women, the sex, the booze, the freedom from any restraint: religious or social. He looked foreword to completing his two-year tour—without his wife.

Ben's world was wonderful until one day when he was sitting on his bunk reading yet another letter from his wife, he leaped up. "Jesus Christ, Jack," he shouted to his bunk mate up on top who was idly leafing through a girlie magazine, "she's coming. God dammit, she's coming."

Jack and four poker players at a nearby table were jolted at the outburst and waited for the details. Ben stormed around the room. "She had to do it, just had to do it," he growled, his florid face growing even more crimson. "After I warned her. She just would not listen."

Jack, Ben's pal on some of Ben's forays through Cavite City's dens of iniquity after he'd gotten worked up over a tit shot in a girlie mag, tried to calm Ben down. "Maybe she'll change her mind. She's been telling you she's coming for months now."

Ben paced back and forth. "No," he rejoined, his head shaking, "she is coming. She left San Francisco on a ship a week ago. This letter is 10 days old. She had some money saved from her clerk job in the discount store, and her folks gave her the rest—so she could join her husband," he added derisively. "Two weeks from today I'm to meet her at the dock in Manila."

Jack tried to put a good spin on it. "Ah, man, it might not be so bad. Your wife's a good looking woman." Jack had seen her picture hanging in Ben's locker: blond, blue eyes, nice figure.

"Yeah, good lookin' all right, but cold as ice." Ben stopped pacing the floor, turned to Jack and the poker players like a prosecuting attorney addressing the jury. "She's a Baptist, goes to church all the time. Don't drink or smoke," he stated evenly, hammering his points home. "Thinks sex should be done in the dark under the covers, maybe once every two or three weeks." Ben paused for dramatic effect. "Then its, "are you through yet" or "it hurts too much."

Jack tried an optimistic approach. "Maybe your wife will loosen up in the P.I., you know, the tropical breezes, the flowers. It could happen."

A poker player chimed in, "Sure, it stands to reason."

Ben could not be convinced. He went on, spewing out his marital grievances—as if he were lancing a boil to get all the pus out. "Nah. She's been looking at this deal through rose-colored glasses. She read about the beautiful sunsets and thinks she and I will be sitting on some veranda drinking lemonade and watching the sun go down through palm trees. Of course, she expects church every Sunday and one or two nights during the week, and girlfriends she can have coffee with," he added with a wry smile.

Well, Ben Biegler did meet his wife at the pier in Manila. He found a cheap, two-room apartment in Cavite City near the base and moved in with his wife. Every time we passed his empty bunk we wondered how it was all going to turn out. It was about this time I transferred to the Armed Forces Police.

The EM Club was noisy. It was getting close to midnight and the boys were starting to whoop it up. I raised my voice and asked again. "So what did happen to Ben Biegler and his wife?"

Don Walker snubbed out his cigarette in the cut-off metal shell casing that served as an ashtray. "Things went to hell in a hurry," he said. "His wife had no friends to talk to. The only women her age living around them were bar girls. As a white woman she couldn't get a job in Cavite City, and the only travel in the P.I. she got was when Biegler took her to the bars in Manila as a change from the bars in Cavite."

"It was a shame," said Tom, a thoughtful AG3 with two years of college before joining the Navy. "She seemed like a nice woman. Not at all like Biegler said. I think all his talk was to make it seem he was the aggrieved party. I met her at the base chapel the first Sunday she was here. Ben wasn't with her. She recognized the specialty mark on my uniform and knew I was in the FWC. We talked every Sunday at church. She seemed sad and lonely." Tom sipped his coke. "How she got tangled up with a slob like Biegler I'll never know."

Tom represented a majority of sailors in the Fleet Weather Central who had no interest in emulating Ben Biegler's lifestyle. They had no truck with Cavite's bar girls, rarely if ever went into the bars, drank little, if at all, and spent their free time on loftier pursuits: reading (Tom was halfway through Edward Gibbon's *The Decline and Fall of the Roman Empire,* and his messmate was well into the third volume of Winston Churchill's four-volume *History of the English Speaking Peoples*), taking sight-seeing trips (Corregidor, Baguio, Lake Taal), or playing a hand or two of cards. Although steady and dependable workers, they could not wait to get out of the navy. Their dream was to go to college—as a group FWC had the highest navy general intelligence test scores of any division at Sangley—on the G.I. Bill of Rights, obtain a good job, get married and have a home and family. And they wanted a woman like Biegler's wife: attractive, decent, someone who would be a good wife and mother.

"So what happened," I asked. "Is she still in the P.I.?"

"Well, no," said Tom. "She got pretty depressed. Seeing all the sailors with bar girls, and Ben, drunk and stepping out all the time, she just couldn't take it. She went to the base chaplain for counseling. She wrote letters to her parents about the situation."

Another FWC shipmate, a slender guy with a crew cut, jumped in, "But that's not the worst of it. Biegler got a dose of the clap in Manila and gave it to his wife. He and his wife went to a Filipino doctor and got penicillin shots. That way Biegler kept it hushed up, the Navy didn't know about it. That finished it for his wife though. She called her folks, and they wired money for her trip home. She left a month ago."

"I bet Biegler was happy about that," I added.

"Yes," the crew cut said. "He was all smiles. He moved back into our hut and his old bunk. Biegler was back to drinking and whoring like always."

Don Walker waved to the bartender, called for

another round of drinks. "It all caught up to Biegler though. His in-laws, his wife's folks, wrote to their congressman. That's when the shit hit the fan. The congressman raised hell with the Navy. Said it sounded like the Navy was fostering prostitution and corrupting the morals of our young fighting men. Our skipper called Biegler in, asked him what the hell was going on. Biegler tried to weasel out of it, but it did no good. Skipper had Biegler's orders cut for the States and told him to shape up or he might be booted out of the Navy. Biegler was on a ship back to the States in a week's time."

The crew cut toyed with his beer, looked up, and asked, "The thing I wonder about is why Biegler's wife got involved with him in the first place?"

Tom paused a moment, then said, "I guess some women see a guy like Biegler and think they can change him. They never do."

The bar was jumping now, the cigarette smoke so thick my eyes were watering. It was ten minutes to midnight and the boys were starting the count down. When the clock struck twelve, we raised our glasses and sang "Auld Lang Syne." It was my last New Year's Eve in the P.I.

CHAPTER 13

Cop Talk

When I got back from Hong Kong, Rosie and I resumed our relationship, even more passionate now after I had showered her with gifts. But when I transferred to the Armed Forces Police, a black cloud of suspicion moved in and hovered above our little nest. Rosie didn't trust me, and she had her reasons.

For one thing, walking a beat as a patrolman put me in and out of Cavite bars all the time, not like the FWC when I seldom went bar hopping and then never without Rosie. And the AFP guys, like civilian policemen in the States, held a fascination for women. Bar girls went after the sailors with the white helmets and batons of authority. It was the power the AFP commanded. They could close a bar down by putting it off limits to servicemen. The AFP could cause all kinds of trouble to a bar owner or bar girl with a word or whisper to their friends in the Cavite police. When the AFP came into a bar, it was as if a wet sheet had been drawn over the festivities: sailors hunched over their beers and lowered their voices, trying to look inconspicuous. It was the fear. The effect was apparent. Bar girls who hardly gave me a second look before, now, when I walked through the door in my AFP uniform, approached smiling and slyly, but not so subtly, offered themselves to me.

The Black Cat Club was on my beat, and I was in and out of the club several times a shift. Linda, my old girlfriend, was still working there. She was popular, and when I came in she made a point of fawning over some guy, then giving me the walk every time she went to the bar to get beer. She wanted to remind me of what I was missing. Sally was at another bar and was doing okay. Some young sailor, a recent arrival at Sangley, was ga-ga over her, blowing every penny he had on her.

Rosie knew all this and had her antenna out. She had her friends, bar girls, reporting on my activities. I knew that and was careful. I made sure she knew where I would be and when I would be home. Everything went well until one night.

I had finished a day watch, showered, and was getting ready to go to Rosie's. A call came in—a brawl at the Black Cat. All hands were to turn to and help quell the riot. I changed into my AFP garb, joined other patrolmen, and rushed to the Black Cat.

The scene when we arrived was utter chaos. Fights were going on all over the place: Chairs were flying, bottles crashing, sailors shouting, and bar girls screaming. We piled in to break it up. When it was all over, we had one AFP patrolman with a broken nose, and there was blood splattered on the floor with broken furniture scattered about. We found out it all started with two sailors fighting over a bar girl. Then their buddies jumped in, and the whole thing got out of hand.

We had plenty to do. By the time we finished taking injured combatants to sick bay, assessing damages, and writing reports, the night was half over. I showered and, instead of going to Rosie's, decided to sleep on the base.

When I got to Rosie's the next day she blew up. "You stay with Linda last night," she shouted, her eyes blazing. "My girlfriend, she told me, you were at Black Cat. You were talking to Linda, you go home with her."

"Wait a minute," I protested. "There was a fight there. I talked to most of the girls—to find out how the trouble started."

Rosie wasn't hearing me. She kept up the tirade. "You like Linda. You sleep with her. She suck your dick, I know. You like that!" Just saying those words inflamed her more. She reached into a stack of books I had on loan from the base library and grabbed my current favorite, *The Scalpel of Scotland Yard: The Life of Sir Bernard Spilsbury*, and threw it at me. "You butterfly," she screamed, using the most disparaging word a bar girl could use to describe her boyfriend. A guy who could not be trusted to be true to one girl—like the butterfly that flies from one flower to another.

Other than dodging books, I did little to defend myself. I let Rosie's rage play out. I knew the truth would come out. Two days later Rosie heard from a friend that Linda went home that night with another sailor. Things went back to normal.

A few weeks after the brawl at the Black Cat, I sat in on a bull session with half a dozen other AFP patrolmen. It was a quiet afternoon, guys hanging around the coffee maker in the AFP office, telling sea stories about cases and problems. Mike was there, the tough guy who had worked over the young marine, and a third-class boatswain's mate they called "Boats," a salty fellow with over eight years in the Navy and plenty of experience in the masters-at-arms and shore patrol aboard ships and on bases.

The confab was rambling and at one point a rookie patrolman asked: "How do you get along with these Filipinos?"

Mike, the old pro, leaned back in his chair and said, "It's not hard. They are easygoing by nature, and friendly, always ready for a laugh, but," he paused, toyed with his mustache, "don't ever make them lose face, if you can help it."

"I'll second that," said Boats, stirring two teaspoonfuls of sugar in his coffee. "You heard about that killing a couple of years ago, the Sangley sailor?" There was a nodding of agreement. "A perfect example of what not to do," added Mike. "I heard about it from the patrolman who was in on the investigation."

I was intrigued and asked for details.

Mike settled back, took a swig of coffee, relishing the chance to tell the tale. "The white-hat was a big guy, a heavy drinker in the Cavite bars. He was a mean drunk, though, always giving the bar girls and counter men a hard time. He had a way of picking out a physical flaw: bow legs, bad teeth, fat butt, bad skin, something like that, then ride the Filipino girl or counter guy, making fun of them in front of everyone. He'd give them a nickname, like 'fat ass' or 'pimple face' and call them by that name every time he came into the bar. He was hated and feared. The girls didn't want to wait on him, and no counter man, small as they were, had the size and courage to throw him out."

There was a high-pitched whine of a Banshee on the runway. Mike paused, then went on, "One day this big sailor went too far. He was in a nice restaurant and had a load on. The cliental was Filipino with a number of well-dressed young couples. For some reason, the sailor made a derogatory remark to an attractive young Filipina. The Filipino husband stepped in, words were spoken. The sailor grabbed the husband by the shirt front, slapped his face, and threw him to the floor. "You pussy Filipino cunt he called him, then kicked him in the ass every time he tried to get up."

Mike got up and filled his coffee mug before going on. "When no one intervened, the sailor waved his hand in disgust at the crowd now on its feet and called the Filipino men gutless cowards in Tagalog, then swaggered out the door and was gone. Now the husband was not hurt physically, but was deeply humiliated in front of his wife, his friends, and the others who knew him in the restaurant. To the machismo Filipino man, it was a terrible loss of face."

"The Filipinos call this shame, or *hiya* in Tagalog," interjected Boats who had a working knowledge of the native language.

"Well," continued Mike, "it's this whole notion

of face, or saving face, that's so damn important to their self-esteem. Anyway, the Filipino restaurant owner complained to our office, saying he did not want the sailor in his place again. Our records show we talked to him, told him to stay clear of the establishment, and let it go at that.

Mike shifted in his chair, fired up a Lucky Strike, and continued. "A few weeks later, our boy was in a Cavite bar, drunk. He stumbled out at closing time, hailed a jeepney to take him back to the base, and got in. It was dark and our guy was the only passenger. Before the driver could pull away, a lone figure jumped in and plunged a knife nine times into the sailor's heart."

I stared at Mike, captivated. Like us, he was dressed in white trousers and skivvy shirt, the tropical uniform of the day. As he drew deeply on his cigarette, the snarling panther tattoo on his flexing muscular arm seemed to claw its way up his bicep. "You know," he said, "the patrolman I talked to said he saw the body and that all nine stab wounds were grouped so closely you could have covered the cluster with your white hat."

"As you might have expected," added Boats, "the jeepney driver couldn't identify the killer, too dark he said, and the AFP got no help from the bar people.

The Filipino police said they'd check all leads, but the case went nowhere."

"And that's not the only example of this loss of face business," said Mike. "Since I've been here there have been two others that were linked pretty close. You remember the sailor that was tied to the tree, Boats?"

Boats picked it up. "Sure, some white hat off a ship in port. A bunch of young Filipinos caught him alone walking down a dark street. They threw a sack over his head, hauled him out to the boonies and tied him to a tree. They stripped him naked, pulled knives and started cutting him, not deep, superficial—taunting and tormenting him as they did so. Kept it up for hours. Had the sailor, who couldn't have been more than 17 years old, bawling and begging for mercy. The kid lived, but looked like shit when they got done with him."

"There was one other," said Mike. "A sailor was standing on a street corner. A jeepney pulled up and a Filipino reached out and slashed the sailor with a knife. Damn near took his ear off. And we never solved any of these cases."

"Hey, and let's not forget that case in Manila awhile back," said Boats grinning. "you know, the one where the bar girl cut off the sailor's pecker."

Boats had all our attention now.

"He was a sailor off a destroyer in port in Manila," said Boats, "and he picked her up in a bar and went to her place for the night. Something happened to make her mad, we're not sure what, and when he fell asleep she got a knife and cut it off. He had had enough to drink, and before he could get help, he bled to death."

"Well, I don't know if that was a loss of face, but she sure as hell was pissed off," added Mike, laughing.

We all looked at each other and shuddered. None of us had heard of such a thing.

Mike snuffed out his cigarette in the ashtray. "The point to all this is when you're out on the beach, treat the Filipinos with respect," he paused, chuckled, "and that includes the women." He stood up and brushed off a speck of cigarette ash from his trousers. "Just treat them as equals and you won't have a problem."

CHAPTER 14

Boats

It was a week after this discussion when I got a new partner—Boats. My old partner, the Coast Guard coxswain, completed his six-month tour of duty and went back to his unit. I had just walked into the AFP office and Boats handed me the assignment sheet. "Welcome aboard partner," he said, shaking my hand.

Boats drove a paddy wagon, like Mike, so I wouldn't be walking a beat. In his late twenties, Boats was an unusual looking guy. From the neck up he was handsome, with aquiline features that in profile resembled John Barrymore the actor. But from unremarkable shoulders down, he spread out like a pear with overflowing love handles and a fat butt grown soft from too much time behind a desk or in the front seat of a navy vehicle.

On our first afternoon out, with Boats behind the wheel, we toured a strip of bars I was not familiar with. "See that joint," pointed Boats out the window, "that's where 'the Arab' hangs out."

By reputation, we in the AFP all knew the man nicknamed the Arab. The Arab was an aviation machinist's mate second class (AD2) attached to the base patrol squadron. At 6 feet 7 inches, with steel grey eyes, a dark complexion, broad shoulders and slim hips, he was an imposing guy. Added to that was the mystery that surrounded him. Word was he had killed a man with his fists in a bar fight in San Diego, but got off on self defense because the guy came at him with a knife and cut him first.

The Arab was a quiet guy, a loner, who drank by himself in the same bar in Cavite. He never got drunk and tried to avoid trouble, but trouble had a way of finding him. The Sangley sailors knew him and stayed at a distance, but every so often some shipboard swabbie hitting the beach for the first time and looking for a fight would spot the Arab and challenge him.

"It's a funny thing," said Boats. "We've never put the Arab on report. He skates on thin ice, but has a way of never falling through. See, he never causes trouble in the bar. He's respectful to the bar girls, tips generously, and if braced by some asshole white hat, will take the fight outside and beat the shit out of him. End of story. The Filipino bar owner never complains, and the sailor he beat the hell out of is too shamed to say anything. I've got to hand it to the Arab though, he's some kind of stud. But handle him with kid gloves, it would take a truck load of us to put him down—if it came to that."

While Boats and I cruised the bars, we were in constant contact by two-way radio with AFP headquarters on the base as well as our office at the Cavite police station. If there was trouble anywhere and we were needed, we'd get the call. We pulled into a squalid street of hole-in-the-wall bars, seedy one-room apartments, and rickety food stalls. Boats stopped in front of a dingy club with the word *Montana* above the door. "Let's see if Monkey John is in," said Boats.

The late afternoon sun was bright, and when we walked through the door I had to strain to see into the gloom. The place was dead. The jukebox wasn't playing and the tables were empty. At the far end of the bar, in a smoky haze illuminated by a single lamp, sat a lone sailor, a bar girl next to him, talking softly. The counter man sat on a stool behind the bar idly riffling a deck of playing cards.

At the sound of our footsteps, a small figure leaped from the floor, perched on the sailor's shoulder, and started screeching at us—it was a monkey. Boats stopped a few feet from the sailor, safely out of reach of the monkey. "How do, John," said Boats to the sailor, a tall gaunt man, with gray-streaked hair and a cadaverous face. "Why is it even Cap don't like the shore patrol." Boats nodded at the little brown monkey whose eyes stared at us angrily.

"Don't pay ol' Cap no mind, Boats," said Monkey John, squinting through a trail of smoke from the cigarette that dangled from his mouth. "We just got in, and he ain't had his first drink of the day yet."

John turned to the fat bar girl next to him. "Blanca, can't you see. When a man needs a drink, he needs a drink." Blanca eased her heavy legs off the chair and waddled off. "You see," said John as he swigged from a bottle of San Miguel, "the Captain don't like beer, he's a rum man."

Blanca came back with a little baby bottle and laid it on the bar next to John. At the sight of the bottle, the monkey quieted, then began trembling. John held up the bottle. "This is water with a little sugar in it," he said. "Now for the good part."

The counter man, as if by long habit, reached behind him and grabbed a bottle of "top shelf" Tanduay rum and handed it to John. "Cap likes nothin' but the best," said John as he poured a dash of the fiery drink into the baby bottle.

The monkey crawled into John's lap, waiting as John tightened the bottle cap, then grabbed the bottle and plunged the nipple into its mouth, sucking furiously. "By God," said John smiling, "Cap's sure got a terrible thirst." He cradled the tiny monkey in his tattooed arms, like a baby, watching as the soft furry body gentled, laid its head against John's bony chest, and suckled as if from a breast. "Thing is though, I've got to ration out the booze or Cap would drink himself stiff in no time. When I've had about four beers, Cap gets another bottle. We go on that way until we've both had enough."

We watched until the monkey finished his bottle. John took a red collar with a cord attached that was lying on the floor near his chair, hooked the little collar around the monkey's neck, eased him to the floor next to a dish with an assortment of raisins, peanuts, and banana slices, and a ragged tennis ball. "There," said John, "he's got some grub and his toy to keep him happy."

Then John tied the cord to his chair. "I don't like Cap wandering around loose. The Sangley boys will be coming in soon. I'm always afraid some drunk will fool with him, rough him up. Old Cap, he don't have time for some asshole—might take a bite out of him."

We watched as the monkey played with the tennis ball, batting it back and forth with its hands. When Boats reached out as if to take the ball, the monkey snatched it and held it against its chest protectively. "He'll let Blanca or I take the ball," said John, grinning, "but nobody else."

"Well," said Boats chuckling, "in this world a man has got to fight to keep what's his."

Boats changed the subject, asked John some questions about the paddy wagon, said it was running a little rough, asked his advice which John answered with knowledge. Then Boats thanked him, wished him well, and we left.

"Monkey John's a lifer," said Boats as we drove away, "with 18 years in. He's a mechanic at the base motor pool, can fix anything—when he's sober." Boats nosed the wagon around two parked jeepneys. "John's shacked up with Blanca. She's not much to look at, but she takes good care of John and the monkey. By closing tonight they'll both be drunk. Blanca will take them home, feed 'em, and make sure John gets up in the morning and back to the base to make muster."

In the days that followed, I was to learn a good deal from Boats about navy law and handling men. He was smart, and he was cool when the shit hit the fan. Two examples.

One night we got a call on a bar fight. But when we got there, the joint was quiet, sailors were sitting down drinking, nothing out of the ordinary. Then one of the bar girls pointed. Over in one corner was a sailor stretched out flat on his face, bloody, and not moving. We rushed to his side and turned him over. His face was a mess: one eye was swollen, cuts on his cheek, and his nose bleeding. We shook him awake—found he was more drunk than hurt—and lifted him into a chair.

Boats got the sailor to pinch his nose to stop the bleeding, then asked, "Who did this to you, pal?"

"Don't know," mumbled the sailor through a swollen lip. "I was at the bar drinkin', minding my own business. Someone caught me from behind with a sucker punch. That's all I remember."

Boats stood up. "Who did this," he shouted, looking over the crowd. Everyone, it seemed, was looking down at the floor or off to the side. He picked out a sailor here and another there, asked the same question and got the same answer: "Didn't see anything."

I wondered what Boats would do next. It didn't take long to find out. He ordered every sailor in the bar to stand up and hold out his hands while he checked them. One sailor, surprisingly slight of build and without a mark on him, had the knuckles on his right hand skinned to the bone. At first he denied being the assailant, but Boats got a bar girl to identify him and he gave it up. It seems there was bad blood between the two sailors, and the smaller one had been whipped before in a fight. He figured he'd get his nemesis when he was drunk and not looking.

Boats told me later he figured the sailor that got beat up knew who did it, but did not want to rat him out. "He'll take care of the matter in his own good time," said Boats. "We'll probably see the littler guy that won this round knocked on his ass and kicked around good in round number three."

Less than a week later we got another call on a bar fight. When we stormed through the door of the joint, in the middle of the floor was a circle of white hats with two fighters in the center. One sailor held the other around the neck with one arm while punching his face with the other. Boats waded in, shouted, "shore patrol" and tried to separate the two scrappers. At that moment, the guy getting his face battered threw a haymaker and caught Boats flush on the jaw. Boat's helmet flew in the air, his knees buckled, and he fell backward. Then I jumped in, ordered, "break it up, dammit, shore patrol," and got between the fighters. That ended it.

By this time, Boat's head had cleared and, except

for a nasty bruise on his cheek, he was okay. We hustled the two fighters into the paddy wagon, took them to our office at the police station, and wrote them up.

Since they were Sangley sailors, we took them back to the base. Boats told them they were in "deep shit, especially you, dickhead," he said, jabbing the sailor who hit him in the chest.

The next day I was in the base AFP office pouring a cup of coffee, waiting for Boats to get his gear on so we could go on duty, when in comes the sailor who had punched Boats on the jaw. His face had little band-aids covering the cuts, and there were two or three knots on his head. He recognized me and came over, looking like a whipped puppy.

"Is your partner in, the third class boatswain's mate?" he asked, nervously twisting his white hat in his hands.

"Sure," I said, "I'll get him."

I went through the door to our living quarters in the back of the hut. Boats was hitching on his web belt. "Dickhead, from the fight yesterday is here to see you," I said.

I followed Boats out to the desk. Boats was brusque. "So what do you want with me?" he asked the sailor.

"I just want to apologize for last night," said the sailor. "I didn't mean to hit you. It was an accident." Boats didn't say anything, waited. The sailor shifted from one foot to the other. "I was wondering, did you write me up?" he asked, his eyes downcast, meek.

"Hell, yes, I wrote you up," said Boats. "You clipped me good." Boats turned his head so the sailor could see the bruise on his jaw. Boats went to the file cabinet, leafed through a folder. "I've got my handwritten notes and will type it up today," said Boats. "Your commanding officer will get the report today or tomorrow."

The sailor, an electrician's mate third class in the base patrol squadron, kept twisting his white hat. "God, Boats, when my skipper gets that report I go to captain's mast. I'll get busted for sure, and I just made third two months ago. Is there anything I can do?" he pleaded.

"Listen, pal," said Boats, "nobody hits a patrolman and walks away. You know that."

"But I didn't know you were shore patrol. I was drunk, and the guy hitting me had my head down. I couldn't see. I was just punching to save my life. As soon as I knew you were shore patrol I stopped punching."

Boats turned to me. "What do you think, Jake?"

"Well, what he says sounds right. As soon as he

saw who we were he stopped, gave us no trouble," I said.

Boats thought a minute. "You're going on report, there's no way out of that. But I'll write it so you didn't seem to know you were hitting a shore patrolman, and that you stopped and followed our orders after that." Boats took the sheet of notes and slipped it into the in-basket. "If you are a good worker with a clean record, your skipper might not bust you, might give you extra duties and restrict you to the base, something like that."

The sailor did not seem happy, but thanked Boats, said he would appreciate anything Boats could do and left. Boats turned to me. "You know, we get guys coming in here all the time, trying to sweet-talk their way out of a jam. Now this guy, if I tore up the report and let him off, it would get all over the base how he blew smoke up my ass and got away with it. We can't let that happen." I looked at Boats. What he said made sense to me.

In the two weeks working with Boats I had grown to like and respect him. Then something happened to shake my judgment.

It was dark, about 9:30 one night. Boats and I were working the evening watch out of our office in the Cavite police station, casually leafing through some paperwork when Boats checked his wristwatch and said, "Jake, there's an errand on the base that needs doing. It won't take long."

"Sure," I said, following him out the door and into the paddy wagon. Boats wheeled the wagon through the base *main* gate, casually waving at the marine guard as he drove through—a comrade-in-arms. The marine guards were responsible for checking the identification of drivers of trucks and jeeps and the contents of the vehicles, but never checked the paddy wagon. They trusted us, we were in the same business. It would be like cops checking cops.

We pulled up to the loading dock behind the mess hall. A sailor, sitting on the dock with his back against the wall, was smoking, his cigarette flaring in the darkness. He got up and peered into the cab. "Hi, Boats," he said, his voice low, "you're right on time. He looked over at me, turned to Boats and whispered, "Who's your partner, new guy?"

"Yeah, he's okay though. What you got for me this time?"

"Good stuff, a few boxes. Wait here, I'll bring it out."

The sailor, who I recognized as one of the cooks, started carrying out boxes and piling them on the dock.

BOATS

Boats opened the back of the wagon and began loading them in. I looked back, asked Boats if he needed help. He said no, that it would take him just a minute, and told me to wait in the cab. In the darkness I couldn't tell what was in the boxes. I was curious, but figured Boats would tell me in due time.

When Boats finished loading, he turned to the cook and said, "I'll see you in the morning like always and settle up."

"Sure, in the morning," the cook whispered, hurrying into the mess hall and closing the door.

Boats drove quietly with the lights off until he got on the main street. He gave the marine guards a friendly salute as we drove out the gate. What's the deal, I thought. When Boats did not say anything, I asked, "What's in the boxes?"

"I've got a little deal going. I'll tell you about it later. I've got to unload this stuff now, before we go off watch."

We drove into Cavite and turned up a darkened alley. Boats cut the headlights and parked behind a small club, then got out and went through the back door into the club. Soon he came out with a middle-aged Filipino who unloaded the boxes. "I'll see you tomorrow," Boats said to the Filipino, and we went back to the office.

A little while later our relief came and took us back to the base. As we were stripping off our AFP gear in the hut, Boats turned to me, "Let's stop over to the EM Club before it closes and have a beer, we can talk."

It was two days before payday, and the club was quiet. A few sailors were at the bar and almost all the tables were empty. Boats went to the bar, ordered and paid for two bottles of San Mig, and headed for a table in a vacant corner. He set the beer down, pulled up a chair and slid a pack of Luckies toward me, motioning me to take one. We lit up and drank slowly, the cold beer tasting good.

Boats leaned over, talked softly, "You know, Jake, the Navy's been real good to me. This is my third hitch. It's true I haven't moved up in rate very fast, but I don't care. I've learned that if you're smart, there's ways of making a hell of a lot more than a petty officer third's pay." Boats watched my face, gauging my reaction, then said, "But it means more than peddling a few cartons of smokes."

When Boats mentioned cigarettes, I knew what was coming—a black market deal. American cigarettes were in big demand in the P.I. Sailors could buy a carton of cigarettes for 90 cents at the base commissary and get two or three times that much by selling to the Filipinos.

Navy regulations prohibited purchasing items at the commissary and selling them for profit off the base, but it was hard to control. Cigarettes were like currency. You could sell them, or trade the cigs for sex, booze, food, whatever. In order to curb the problem, the Navy at Sangley restricted the sale to each sailor of no more than one carton per week. Although sailors found a way around that—buying up the cigarettes from nonsmokers—the regulation made the problem manageable.

Boats hunched his shoulders and went on, "There's a lot of groceries that go through the mess hall. It isn't hard for a guy on the inside to skim some off without anyone knowing. The only problem is getting it off the base—past the marine guards." Boats smiled, "You follow?"

I did follow, and for a moment my heart stopped. It all came clear: the boxes Boats loaded at the mess hall, driving without headlights, the Filipino at the club, this was more than simple black market, this was theft of government property.

Boats hurried on as if to smother any questions I might have. "We don't move any perishable goods, canned stuff mostly: tins of beef, spam, cans of peaches, fruit cocktail, that sort of thing. And we're not greedy, we take a little here, a little there. I make pickups every two or three weeks, small amounts. And it's not a problem moving the stuff off the base, the marine guards never check the paddy wagon."

Alarmed, I reached over and grabbed Boats's arm. "Jesus, Boats, that's stealing from the government. You get caught, that's a navy prison and a dishonorable discharge."

"Ah, don't worry," Boats said, "the chance of getting caught is damn slim. It's near foolproof. The cook that hauled out the boxes also keeps the books. When I sell the stuff to the Filipino, I pay off the cook. The Filipino takes it to Manila and sells it to fancy restaurants that cater to rich Americans and Filipinos. It's a sweet deal." Boats paused, took a deep drag on his cigarette, gazed at me evenly and said, "There's something in it for you too—if you play ball."

I did not think twice. "No way," I said, my voice rising, "as soon as I finish my four years, I'm out of the navy. I'm going back to my hometown and work with my Dad on the family farm. I can't afford to take any chances."

"Hey, take it easy. Don't be in such a rush to

make up your mind. I'll tell you something. Me, the cook, and the Filipino have had this operation for over a year now. From my piece of the action, I live high on the hog here in the P.I. I go to Manila, eat at nice restaurants, drink good liquor. I got a girl I see. It's a nice setup." Boats paused, leaned over, and touched my arm. "And listen to this. I make enough on this sideline so I'm able to send my whole navy paycheck back to the States to an account in a bank. Some of it is invested in stocks. I got a nice pile built up already. My last two partners were in with me and got a nice taste—you can too."

"No Boats, it's no go for me. I want no part of it."

"Listen, this isn't my first go at this sort of thing. When I was stationed in Yokosuka in Japan, I worked out the same deal. I'm no amateur."

"Boats, it's not just the danger, the chances of getting caught, it's the stealing. I've never stolen anything before; I don't think I could live with myself if I did."

"Wait, think about it for a minute. It's not like we're robbing a bank. Being the navy's police force is a dirty job, and we get paid peanuts. This is just a little payback. Hell, the cooks at the mess hall waste ten times what we lift, and the navy don't care. I sleep good at night."

For a few moments we sat in silence. Then Boats snubbed out his cigarette in the ashtray and looked up at the clock on the wall. "It's about time for last call. I'll get us another round before closing."

"No, it's my round," I insisted and went to the bar and came back with the beer.

We sat drinking, not talking, then Boats said, smiling, "You know Jake, in a way, you're in already."

"What do you mean," I asked, "I don't follow?"

"Well, you were in the wagon with me tonight when we got the goods at the mess hall, and you were with me when we made the delivery to the Filipino, just like my last two partners. The cook and the Filipino know I always give my partners a cut on the take, so if we get caught . . . " Boats let that thought hang.

What the hell have I got myself into, I thought. What do I do now?

When we finished our beer and got up to go, Boats said, "Keep this conversation under you hat and think about it. We can talk again tomorrow, and I can give you an idea about what your cut would come to on each trip."

That night I couldn't sleep. I lay thinking about

how easy it was to get drawn into something, to get tangled in a crime before you knew it. I thought even if I told Boats no, and later he gets caught, he could say he paid me, I was in on it. I would be implicated. And being shacked up with a bar girl wouldn't help me any. Prosecuting naval officers would have no sympathy for me and a little jealousy too. They would think I was living it up and needed the money for my degenerate lifestyle.

The next morning I made up my mind. Boats and I did not have the duty. He was standing next to his bunk putting on his civvies. From what he said last night he would be going into Cavite to see the Filipino to get his money, then pay the cook his cut. I strolled over to Boats. "Before you go," I said, "let's take a walk outside. I've got something to say."

"Sure," he said, shrugging his shoulders, "no problem."

We went out the back door of the hut and down a gravel path that led to the landing strip. When we were out of earshot of anyone, I turned to Boats. "I've decided on your offer. I want no part of it. When you use the paddy wagon for deliveries, leave me at the office or somewhere. I don't want to be in the wagon when you're dealing."

Boats looked at me. "You're sure about this?"

"Yes," I said. "I won't squeal on you, I'll keep my mouth shut. But If you guys get pinched by the Navy ONI (Office of Naval Intelligence), and I'm put under oath on the witness stand in a court-martial trial, I make no promises."

Boats stopped walking, looked at me for a moment, then said, "Fair enough. We'll let it go at that."

We walked back to the hut and Boats went into town. I sat on my bunk thinking. I wasn't out of the woods yet. Now I had to pray they wouldn't get caught.

About a week after I told Boats I wanted no part of his "sweet deal" selling stolen goods from the base mess hall, Boats took a two-week leave and went to Baguio, a resort area in the mountains of Northern Luzon, less than a day's drive from Manila. Baguio served as the summer capitol of the Republic of the Philippines and was a favorite R&R spot for Sangley sailors. Since I turned Boats down, our relationship cooled but continued to be professional, and the subject was no longer discussed.

CHAPTER 15

A Desk Job

With Boats gone, I was assigned a temporary desk job at the base AFP office. I was working the desk one morning when a seaman apprentice, appearing all of 15 years old, came in. He had a hangdog look on his face and glanced around nervously. "Is this the shore patrol office?" he asked. "I was robbed yesterday and our chief boatswain's mate told me to come here, that you might be able to help."

Handling the desk at the AFP office involved answering the telephone and dealing with street traffic. Along with maintaining discipline, the mission of the AFP was to assist military personnel and protect them from being ripped off by unscrupulous civilian establishments. "You came to the right place," I said. "Maybe we can help. So, what happened?"

"I'm off a destroyer that came into port two days ago. Yesterday I got liberty and went into Cavite. It was my first time in the P.I. I was alone and went in this bar.

I could imagine what was coming. This kid was cherry through and through.

The sailor went on. "I had a beer and this bar girl asked if I wanted to go to her place for a short-time. She was pretty and I'd never done it with a girl before ... " he stammered, "so I agreed."

"Then what happened?" I asked.

"We went to her place. She asked for ten pesos. I paid her and we took our clothes off and we did it. When we got done I left and went barhopping. I ran into some of my shipmates at another bar and when I went to buy a beer, my wallet was empty. I'd been cleaned out. I was robbed, but I don't know how."

I felt sorry for the guy. He looked so young, like a high school sophomore. I went ahead and asked the standard questions—names, places, times—for the record. He turned out to be a hell of a witness, he remembered everything. Yet, I couldn't figure out how he'd been robbed. His wallet was never out of his possession. It was time for experience. Mike Connelly was completing assignment sheets. I called him over.

Mike was the second class, the one with the handlebar mustache. Since I joined the AFP, he had been promoted to acting second-in-command, right under our commander, the marine captain. I never really got over the cold-hearted way he had driven over the dog on my first day on the job, or the brutal way he put down the drunken young marine in the bar. He was tough, alright, but he was smart, and for the guys under him, he was fair. If you did your job and did it right, he was on your side. If you were lazy and incompetent, look out. I must have been doing something right because we were on a first name basis now.

Mike sauntered over, a bored look on his face. I ticked off the details. He looked at the sailor and started asking questions rapid-fire. "How long were you in the girl's room?"

"It was a short-time," the sailor said, "no more than 15 minutes."

"Did anyone come in or leave the room while you were there?"

"No."

"Were you sober?"

"I was cold sober. I only had one beer."

"How much money did you lose?"

"Forty pesos. I had 50 pesos in my wallet when I went into the girl's room. I gave her 10 pesos. After I left and went to another bar, I went to pay for a beer and my wallet was empty."

Mike paused and looked at the sailor intently.

"Now think carefully; When you took off your clothes in the girl's room, where did you put your wallet?"

The sailor thought, curiosity wrinkling his brow. "The girl told me to put my clothes on a chair next to the wall. I put my wallet under my trousers and jumper. And my wallet was just where I left it when I put my clothes back on. Why?"

A long waist-high counter with a door that latched from the inside separated the waiting room from the office area. Mike leaned over the counter, with one hand fondled his mustache. "Well, you probably got ripped off by a trick used a lot in Manila. It's the trap door hustle. The girl's apartment had a chair next to the wall. She told you to put your clothes on it. While you and the girl were getting it on, a kid in the next room opens a hidden trap door in the wall next to the chair, reaches in and lifts your wallet, cleans out the money and puts the wallet back under your gear. Everything is in order when you leave and you never miss the loss until later. Usually the sailor in these con games is drunk and has no idea what happened."

"Will I get my money back?" the sailor asked.

"Not much chance, it's too hard to prove. What we will do is talk to the bar owner, and maybe the girl. Tell the bar owner if it happens again, we'll put the joint off limits to sailors. That'll really shake him up. If the sailors can't come in, he goes out of business. More likely the girl is new, from Manila. He'll give her hell, maybe fire her outright. We've cleaned up Cavite pretty much now on this swindle."

The sailor looked down and shuffled his feet. "Losing those 40 pesos cleaned me out. I won't have a dime until next payday, and that's a week away."

"Well," said Mike, "you learned something. You're not the first to be taken, and you won't be the last. Charge off the 40 pesos to experience."

"Yeah, thanks anyway. When you guys lean on that bar owner and bar girl, maybe that will teach them a lesson too."

I watched the young sailor walk out the door and turned to Mike.

"Why is it that the best lessons learned are the ones you learn the hard way?" Mike laughed, "Ain't that the truth."

By the second week on the desk I was feeling more comfortable. Mike was in the office all the time now, practically running the place. Our skipper, the marine captain, would come in the morning and go over any complaints, any charges we filed, and sign off on the paper work. He'd leave a telephone number where he could be reached, then take off, coming back late afternoon for a look-see before heading out for the day. Mike liked it that way.

It was Friday morning of my last day on the desk. Boats had just gotten back from Baguio, and I would be joining him on the paddy wagon. I had just finished on the phone with a yeoman from base communications who wanted more information on a report we had written on one of their men for disorderly conduct in Cavite City, when I heard Mike growl loud enough for me to hear. "What the fuck, a report on a homo. Christ All Mighty, that's all I need this morning."

Mike had been reviewing the hand-written reports by patrolmen from the night before. Curiosity got the best of me and I wandered over. Mike noticed and shoved the papers in my face. "Look at this shit. Mack wrote up some poor bastard on a violation of Article 125 of the UCMJ. That's major, big-time."

Mack was the patrolman that Mike had introduced me to in our office in the Cavite police station on my first day. As I scanned the report, I could recognize his small precise handwriting. It seemed Mack and his partner had walked in on a sailor getting a blow job by a Filipino binny-boy in a hotel room. I whistled, "Poor bastard is right."

This was a homosexuality case alright, but I couldn't remember the significance of Article 125 of the Uniform Code of Military Justice, the Armed Forces basic disciplinary law. I searched my mind, recalling the orientation I had gotten on the UCMJ when I was in boot camp and when I started in the AFP. I knew the UCMJ became effective in May of 1951 and governed all branches of the armed forces: Army, Navy, Air Force, Marine Corp, and the Coast Guard. Before UCMJ was "Rocks and Shoals" the Rules Governing U.S. Navy and Marine Corps Personnel. Prior to that time, the Navy operated under laws derived directly from the British Articles of War, which had been in force since before the Revolutionary War. Punishments included execution, flogging, and hard labor with ball and chain. Over the years there were patchwork changes. In 1850, for instance, the Navy outlawed flogging.

I handed the papers back to Mike. "I know homosexuality is a no-no in the Navy, that you can get kicked out, but in a case like this, how would it be charged? What's an Article 125?"

Mike flipped the report on his desk and leaned back in his chair. "You know on homos, there's guys getting kicked out all the time, especially now after the Korean War is over. During a war, the Navy needs every swinging dick on the line. After the war they clean house. All it takes is for somebody to say you're a fag, that he saw you kissing or fondling some guy. The Navy hauls you in, confronts you, and gets you to confess that your a homo, then boots you out on an undesirable discharge."

"So how is this different?" I asked.

Mike picked up the report and slapped it with the back of his hand. "Mack wrote this guy up on a violation of Article 125 of the UCMJ, the provision outlawing sodomy. That's oral or anal sex with another man. That's usually hard to prove, but in this case Mack and his partner observed it, were witnesses."

Mike paused, took a swallow of coffee and went on. "Listen, you get caught sucking off some guy's dick, or getting cornholed up the ass—you've had it. That's an undesirable discharge for sure, but it could go higher, as high as a court-martial with a bad conduct discharge and five years in a Navy prison. As far as the Navy is concerned, you're better off killing some guy in a fight than getting nailed on a sodomy charge."

"Jesus," I said, "that's harsh, real harsh."

"And that's not all," Mike continued, "you go out with less than an honorable discharge and you could lose your benefits. I'm talking pension, G.I. Bill for college, and all the other stuff. And on top of all that, how do you explain all this to your parents, your family, buddies back home. It's major shit, alright."

"Why is the Navy so tough on sodomy?" I asked. "It's like committing murder. Sure, a man who gets his kicks sucking off another guy, or getting fucked up the ass is a weirdo alright, but who's he hurting other than himself?"

Mike paused, thought a minute, then said, "When you think about it though, it isn't any tougher than in the States. Every state in the union has laws that make sodomy or unnatural sexual acts a felony punishable in most states by prison sentences of five or ten or even twenty years. I heard about that in a training session on the UCMJ." Mike smoothed out his mustache and went on, "I don't know how much the states enforce those laws though, but it is the law, by God, and if they want to hang some poor son-of-a-bitch, they can. And so can the Navy.

"But in this case," I argued, "if this guy went to a court martial trial on sodomy, wouldn't there be mitigating circumstances?"

"You're right. I can see a few right off." Mike grinned. "Let's see how smart you are. What are the mitigating circumstances you see?"

"What about the binny-boy doing the oral sex on the sailor, sucking him off. Maybe the sailor thought he was a woman."

Binny-boy was the Filipino term for homosexual. Binny-boys dressed as women. With the small features and lack of facial hair of young Filipino men, when they wore their hair long, dressed in evening gowns and high heels, it was almost impossible to tell they were men in drag. And the binny-boys were accepted in the Philippines. Beauty contests were held and there were binny-boy parades. I'd seen a parade and, until Rosie told me, I swore they were pretty women. I was fooled.

"I'll grant you that one too," said Mike, "what else?"

"Sounds like the sailor was drunk," I added. "Mack's report said he and his partner found the sailor naked lying flat on his back in the bed with the binny-boy kneeling between the sailor's spread-out legs doing a number on him. When confronted, the sailor smelled heavily of booze, slurred his words, and had trouble explaining himself—'seemed to be in a fog.'"

"I agree on that one as well," said Mike.

Mike and I kicked around the pros and cons of the case for awhile. Mack had left for the commissary store and would be back in the afternoon. Mike needed to see Mack regarding clarification of several items in Mack's report.

It was close to noon, chow time, when a petty officer second class slouched through the door, the insignia on his shoulder indicating he was an aviation electronics technician. He didn't look good. His eyes were red and swollen, and he had that pasty white color like he hadn't seen sun in months. As I got up from my desk, he leaned over the counter and confidential-like said, "I'm looking for a red-headed shore patrolman, a petty officer third. I got into some trouble last night, and he said he was going to write me up. I've got to talk to him before he does."

"That must be Mack," I said. "He's not here right now, but you can talk to his supervisor. He went to the head and will be back in a minute." I pointed to the coffee pot in the corner. "Help yourself to a cup of coffee."

I watched as the sailor shuffled over and noticed his hand tremble as he poured a cup. His breath when he talked to me had that sweet-sour smell of booze that comes from the lungs, and hangs on even after you haven't had a drink for hours.

Mike came back and I nodded to the sailor. "He wants to see Mack about a problem last night. I thought you might want to talk to him." I was showing the guy respect. He was a petty officer second, and the three hash marks on his left sleeve indicated he had at least 12 years service in the Navy.

Mike told the sailor to bring his coffee and ushered him to a chair next to his desk. I busied myself with paper work, but my desk was next to Mike's, and I couldn't help but hear the conversation.

"The smoking lamp is lit," Mike said, tapping his cigarette pack and offering a smoke to the sailor, "so what's the problem you got with Mack?"

The electronics tech lit up, took a deep drag and through a cloud of smoke said, "This whole thing is crazy. I was with a Filipino woman in a hotel room last night and this red-headed shore patrolman and his partner busted in, pulled my ID and liberty card, called me a fag, and said he was writing me up on a charge of sodomy. I was damn drunk, I admit, but there's got to be some mistake. I'm hoping I've been dreaming and that I'll wake up and find its all been just a horrible nightmare."

Mike fingered his mustache. "Well, it might be a nightmare alright, but there's no mistake. I've got Mack's report. Now let's hear your side of the story. Start from the beginning."

The sailor took a deep breath, sighed. "I'm off the aircraft carrier Wasp. We just got into Manila Bay yesterday morning. I hit the beach on the first liberty boat yesterday noon with a bunch of my shipmates. We'd never been to the Philippines before so we went a little crazy in Cavite City, barhopping and boozing it up. Well, after a while the guys decided to get laid. Our liberty was up at midnight so they didn't have much time. I'm married so I wasn't planning on joining them. I got drunk, though, and remember leaving the bar alone and walking by this hotel. I see this good-looking Filipino woman and she comes up to me, real friendly-like. The next thing I know we go into the hotel and I pay for a room. I must have blacked out in the room, because I don't remember a thing until the shore patrol came in."

Mike gave the sailor a hard look, then asked, "Do you know you were in bed with a Filipino man?"

The sailor flinched, his face grew scarlet. "No, by God, she was a woman. She was dressed in an evening gown, high heels, the works. I'd swear to that on a Bible."

"Well, you got fooled. You were with a binny-boy, a young Filipino man dressed as a woman. Mack's report says you were flat on your back getting a blow job."

"I can't say about that. I just don't remember. But I swear I'm no homo," the sailor said, slamming his fist on the desk, "I'm not a goddamn faggot!"

Mike reached over, patted the sailor's arm. "Easy pal, no sense getting all riled up."

The sailor's shoulders slumped. "Look, I'm a married man." He reached for his wallet, pulled out a picture and slid it on the desk to Mike. "This is my wife and two kids, our house in Norfolk, Virginia. I've got 13 years in the Navy, just about all in the Atlantic, the Sixth Fleet. Two months ago I got my orders transferring me to the Wasp. This is my first time in the Pacific."

Mike leaned back, letting the sailor get it off his chest, watching his eyes.

"Listen," the sailor continued, "the wife and I got plans. I passed my first class test and should get promoted soon. I've got seven more years to go for a pension, probably make chief petty officer by then. I'll only be 39 years old when I get out, then I can take the G.I. Bill and go to electronics school, or maybe even college and get a degree in electrical engineering. I'm in aviation electronics now, and I'm good at it. This whole field is exploding. There'll be plenty of good jobs on the outside in private industry when I get out." He looked over at Mike, his eyes pleading. "If I get written up on this charge, I'm finished—in the Navy, my marriage—my life is finished."

Mike nodded, said nothing, his face impassive. Mike was a damn good interrogator. He always said, "Listen first. When you have a suspect talking—listen, then watch: his face, his eyes, his body language. Learn, then ask questions."

The sailor rushed in, desperately trying to prove his case. "I joined the Navy right out of high school, 1942—the war was on. After the war I married my high school girlfriend. Since then, with the kids, things have gone real good for us. I've got a 4.0 record in the Navy. Now this!" He reached out, palms upturned. "You've got to help me—please!"

Mike rubbed his mustache, thought a minute. "I hear what you say," he said. Mike reached into the in-basket and pulled out Mack's report. "I've got to talk to the man who wrote you up. I can't promise you anything."

Mike stood up and ushered the sailor to the door. The sailor turned, reached out his hand to Mike. "I'm no homosexual. I swear to God on that." Mike took his hand without comment.

Later in the afternoon Mack came into the office. Mike called him over and handed him his report. "Your man came in and argued his case. He said he was with a woman—that he wasn't a homo."

Mack took the report and waved it in the air. "Well, he's dead wrong on one thing," he said. "The guy was not with a woman. The binny-boy who was going down on him was bare-assed naked, and I could see his cock and balls swinging while he was doing it." His voice raised an octave, "He's lying—just trying to weasel out of it."

Mack, I knew, had no time for homosexuals. Every time the subject came up he went into a tirade. I was with him one time when we drove past a certain Quonset hut that housed yeomen, the navy's male secretaries. With the wave of a limp wrist, he muttered with distain, "fucking queers!"

"Dammit Mike, I wish I'd been here when he came in," said Mack. "We could have broken him down. It's easy. I talked with a petty officer once who worked as an investigator with navy intelligence. He had handled a lot of queer cases. He said homos were the easiest to get a confession out of. You use the good-cop bad-cop approach, push a little and they break right away. He said when a male queer admits he's a homosexual, his voice sometimes turns higher and he becomes like a woman; he breaks down and cries. On top of that, they give up all the other queers they've been involved with."

Mack was excited, really pumped up. "You know Mike, we could have taken him to that little room in the base brig, the one with no windows. It would have gone as smooth as shit through a tin horn. We could have rounded up the names of a whole bunch of queers and given the list to the captain. You know how the captain hates fags—he thinks they are security risks—and the Navy is really pushing to nail queers and run the fuckers out of the service. We'd have been heroes." Mack's eyes just glistened with the thought of it.

Mike leaned back in his chair, comfortable-like, his hands behind his head and said, "Yeah, I appreciate all that. Yet after reading your report I still have some questions. For one—how were you tipped off?"

"It was Laurel, the Filipino beat cop in that area. He knows we don't want binny-boys working around the bars and hotels for sailors. He told me he saw a binny-boy taking a drunken sailor into the Paradise Hotel. I grabbed Jim, my partner, and we went over and got the night clerk to take us to the room. He opened the door and we walked in and saw what was going on. I pulled the sailor's liberty card and ID and got what info

I could out of him. Then I kicked the binny-boy in the ass and ran him out of the hotel. I told the night clerk if I ever caught the hotel letting a binny-boy bring in another sailor, we'd put the place off limits. I chewed his ass out good."

Mack's face was flushed with self-satisfaction. He pulled out a pack of Luckies and with a practiced hand, flared his Zippo lighter, keeping the burning cigarette in his mouth as he inhaled deeply. Then, as the cigarette drooped from the corner of his mouth, the smoke curling around his face, growled, "That night clerk will never fuck with me again." Mack was the tough cop. He'd read all of Mickey Spillane books about Mike Hammer, the tough private eye. A man not to fuck with.

Mike eased out of his chair and took the report from Mack's hand. "You did fine Mack, with the night clerk and all, but this sodomy charge—it won't fly."

"How so?" said Mack. "We got two witnesses—an open and shut case."

"This guy's no homosexual," Mike countered. "He's married. He showed me a picture of his wife and kids."

"You're not going to let him walk, are you?" Mack objected.

"Look, getting sucked off don't mean you're queer," argued Mike. I know half a dozen guys right on this base who prefer binny-boys to women. Not because they'd rather have a man than a woman, but because they don't have to worry about getting the clap and because it's cheaper."

I knew what Mike was saying. It was common knowledge where the binny-boys hung out. A sailor could go in the alley behind at least two bars and a hotel in Cavite and get a blow job—no muss, no fuss. If the binny-boy did a good job, the sailor might tip the kid a peso or two, and if the sailor was broke, he could get it for nothing. The binny-boys liked it that much.

"And another thing," Mike continued, "if the captain gets a hold of this, he'll have the navy intelligence boys sniffing around." He looked at Mack evenly. "You don't know what they might stumble on to."

Mack's shoulders slumped, he looked down at the floor, nodded. It was then I realized Mike knew about Boat's little deal—and Mack did to. Probably Mack had his own scam going.

Mike took Mack's report, tore it into little pieces, and dropped it into the waste basket. "We'll just forget about this thing, shall we. And Mack, talk to Jim. Make it clear the case is closed. It never happened."

CHAPTER 16

Sex 101

I t's funny when thinking back all those years ago, the things that pop into one's mind, bits and pieces of memory that somehow stick in the brain. The important historical events of the time are often gone, wiped clean, and then something nonsensical remains, clear as a diamond.

It was morning and I had just crawled out of the rack. I wrapped a towel around my waist and trudged over to the head to do the sailor's basics: a shit, shower, and shave. There were three other AFP guys in there, showering, laughing, and grab-assing, when a patrolman, an odd duck, a transfer from base communications, slunk in. When he slipped off his towel and tiptoed into the shower there was a moment of stunned silence, for the guy's penis was encased in white hospital bandages.

Then the jokes came. "Holy shit, man, you stick your pecker in the wrong hole?" "You been fucking with one of those binny-boys and he got pissed off and bit the hell out of you?"

"Nah," he said, looking at the floor embarrassed-like. "I got circumcised yesterday, a Filipino doctor. They wouldn't do it in sickbay."

The four of us in the shower looked at each other, not knowing what to say. As I said, the guy was a bit odd, quiet, stayed to himself, read books all the time, religious books. Then one guy asked the question we all were thinking, "Why get circumcised now?"

"I . . . I just thought it was the thing to do," he stammered, turning on his shower, cutting off further comment.

After he'd finished showering and left, the guys speculated: "Did he do it for health reasons?" "Maybe he wants to be a Jew," laughed one. Then another: "They say sex is better when your circumcised." And finally, "I'm damn glad I had it done when I was a baby," joked another, "I wouldn't want to face the knife now."

I didn't say anything then, but later I got thinking about it. I had never been circumcised even though it was customary when I was born. Mom said she didn't want to see me cut. A question ran through my mind. "Did it make any difference when making love if the man was circumcised—for the woman or the man?" I didn't know, and Rosie and the other bar girls never said anything about it.

One thing I did know was that bar girls were keen observers of men's genitalia, and from years of experience could discuss the subject with professional expertise. Rosie, for one, was a walking encyclopedia about men's sexual apparatus and lovemaking, and shared her knowledge with me like a college professor to an eager young freshman taking Sex 101. She categorized a man's penis as big, regular size, and small. But, she said, a man is very sensitive about his size. "I tell sailor his dick is big or regular size if he asks me, but if small, I say regular size. I never tell sailor his dick is small, that hurt him very much."

And, Rosie said, there were many shapes. "Some long, some short, some skinny, some fat—and some bend when it get hard." Rosie was describing her ex-husband, the young American soldier. She said his penis curved to the right when erect and hurt her when they made love.

But the size and shape of a man's penis was not so important when making love—"unless too small." What was important was how the man used his hands and fingers, his mouth and lips—"and the words he say when he make love." Rosie said when making love some bar girls fake passion, moaning and groaning, to make the sailor feel good, or to hurry his orgasm if they are not interested. She never faked it, but "when making love is over and he asks, I say it was good."

Making love was a wonderful thing to Rosie, and the organs of love were given names. She called mine "Junior," and hers "Moming," the Tagalog word for a woman's sexual organ. She would talk to Junior: "Is Junior tired today?" Then she would fondle my cock. "Now Junior, he stand straight and tall, like sailor man at attention." And Rosie would say: "Moming is hot," or "Moming just warm." She never said Moming was cold.

With all the knowledge bar girls had about sex and lovemaking, you would think sailors would be curious, would want to learn from the girls if for no other reason then to be able to please their girlfriends and wives back home. But no, sailors reflected the thinking of men in the 1950s, before the sexual revolution of the 60s, that the goal of a man was to seduce the woman, get her to submit. If she did so, the man thought, it meant she loved him and would enjoy the sex because of it.

Prior to meeting Rosie, I knew nothing about sex and lovemaking. I remember how shocked I was when a shipmate of mine at the Navy's Aerography school at Lakehurst, NJ, told me of a night of incredible sex he had with his girlfriend in the office of his father's furniture store. He was from a big city on the East Coast and saw himself as quite a lover. It was hard for me to believe because he was so ugly: a little guy that looked like a frog with bulging eyes and a mouth that stretched from one ear to the other. Anyway, he said, they laid on his father's huge leather couch and he took off her clothes and then his own. He opened a bottle of wine and dribbled the wine over his girlfriend's body, from her mouth to her ankles. Then he licked it off. By the time they had sex, she was wild with desire and so was he. It was pure ecstasy, he said, a surefire sexual technique. At the time I thought he was a bit deranged. How wrong I was.

When a sailor went with a bar girl he went to please himself with little thought of the girl's pleasure. If he cared and asked, she would say it was fine, whether or not it was. She wanted the sailor to come back—for the money at least—unless he was abusive, or mean, or liked unnatural sex.

CHAPTER 17

Crisis Time

One night something happened that was funny, yet frightening, if that is possible, because I thought the United States was going to war with Communist China—World War III—and that we at Sangley Point in the Philippine Islands might be among the first Americans to fall.

It all had to do with the mountainous island of Formosa, or Taiwan as it's now called. Laying about 100 miles off the South China coast and a few hundred miles north of Luzon in the Philippine Islands, Formosa was a colony of Japan until the end of World War II. In 1949, when the Communists took control of China, those Chinese who opposed communism fled to Formosa.

Fearing a Communist takeover of Formosa, the United States signed a pact to protect the island. In 1954, the Communists started shelling Quemoy, a tiny cluster of islands between Formosa and the coast of China. The U.S. thought this might be a prelude to an attack on Formosa. The U.S. Navy's Seventh Fleet was assigned to patrol the Formosan Straits and protect the island. On January 22, 1955, President Eisenhower, in order to strengthen the fleet, directed three aircraft carriers from Pearl Harbor to join the group.

It was feared that any incident could set off another world war. There was talk of setting up machine gun nests around Sangley Point to fight off the Chinese if they tried to attack or invade us. We sailors would have to man the guns. We wouldn't have a chance with the few men on this base. It was not a pleasant thought.

By February 1955, the crisis in the Formosa Straits had heated up. The aircraft carriers joining the Seventh Fleet steamed into Subic Bay, the main U.S. Base in the Philippine Islands, and into Manila Bay near Sangley Point. Two carriers, the *Wasp* and the *Midway*, anchored in Manila Bay.

The liberty boats brought hundreds of men from the *Wasp* and *Midway* into Cavite City. These sailors had never been to the Philippine Islands and were tearing the town apart. We in the Armed Forces Police had our hands full. On one night, the men from the two carriers got into a brawl at one of the Cavite bars. There must have been twenty men involved. We brought in every available patrolman to quell the fight. One of our patrolman broke his shoulder in the melee. The bar was demolished: mirrors were smashed, furniture splintered, shards of broken beer and whiskey bottles covered the floor, and blood pools and splatter were all about.

Boats and I were working the paddy wagon. The carriers' sailors had to be back to the liberty boats by midnight. We were hauling drunks from the bars to the boat landing on Sangley. The area was littered with drunken sailors, passed out, throwing up, their uniforms torn and bloody. It's was if the boys wanted to live it up before going to war. The bar girls and bar owners never had it so good. The sailors were throwing money around and couldn't get enough of the Filipino girls and the booze.

Then on another night, the absurd yet fearsome thing happened. It was about 3 a.m. and I was dead asleep in the AFP hut when, through the heavy fog of sleep, I heard a persistent ringing of our office telephone. It had been a busy night for our patrolmen. Boats and I had the patrol wagon going, hauling the last few drunken white hats in Cavite City back to the base so they could catch the midnight liberty boats back to their ships. Finally, after clearing the streets, we had closed the AFP office and went to bed.

Then came the telephone call. Since no one was getting up, I stumbled to the phone and heard an excited yet commanding voice on the other end. "This is the OOD (Officer of the Day), Lt. J __. We Just got an emergency notice, the carriers are pulling out now. Ships' officers and chief petty officers are to report to their ships immediately." The base watch officer took my name and rate, then ordered, "Take another patrolman and check each hotel in Cavite City for ships' officers and chiefs. Get the hotel desk clerk to give you their room numbers, bang on their doors, and tell them to report to their ships on the double."

"Aye, aye, sir. Right away, sir." I responded, adrenalin flooding through my body, my brain on full alert.

We had gotten all the white hats back to their ships, but officers and chiefs had overnight liberty. And they wouldn't be caught dead in a bar with enlisted men. If they wanted a woman, they went to one of the hotels in Cavite and ordered one up to their room. Thus the watch officer's directive to check the hotels.

My mind was racing. I struggled to control panic. Are we in a shooting war, I wondered? My next thought was whom to get as my partner to check the hotels. Boats was off on liberty. There were about fifteen men flaked out in bed, dead to the world. It would be hell to get anyone on their feet to go with me. They'd all say they were sick or would have some other excuse. My heart was banging away. It was my problem.

There was, however, one man in the AFP hut I could depend on—Tom, the only Black guy in our outfit. A slim, easy going guy with a soft southern drawl, Tom was a good patrolman, although he kept to himself. In a way he was like me. He didn't hang around with the guys, instead spent all his time in Cavite shacked up with a bar girl.

I grabbed a flashlight, hurried to Tom's bunk and shook him. "Tom," I said, "get up." He moaned, mumbled something. I put the light on his face. "We got orders. Get on your gear."

Tom sat up, wiped his eyes, recognized me. "Yes, suh," he said, and rolled out. Tom responded to me as his superior even though we were the same rate, and he had seniority in years of service.

We strapped on our gear, jumped into a jeep with me at the wheel, and drove out the gate. There were only a handful of hotels in Cavite City, all small, two-story, wood-frame affairs with anywhere from five to twelve rooms.

We pulled up to the first one, ramshackle, with

half a dozen rooms. A single light bulb surrounded by a wire mesh guard burned dimly over the hotel's name. I tried the door—locked—then hammered away, shouting, "Police, open up." No answer. "Open up, shore patrol."

The hotel door opened a crack. An elderly Filipino woman with tangled gray hair peered out and shined a flashlight in our face. "What you want?" she asked.

"Any American sailors in your hotel?" I asked. "We must talk to them."

"No Americans tonight. No American sailors here," she answered and closed the door.

The next hotel, the Starlite, was "higher" class, with twelve rooms. We roused the night clerk and explained our mission. "One American officer here," said the young Filipino, wiping away sleep. He swung around the hotel register. I read the name: Lt. John K _____.

Tom and I followed the clerk to the room. We knocked and identified ourselves. The Lieutenant, a short stocky man with a beginning paunch and dressed in skivvy shirt and shorts, opened the door. "What the hell you want at this hour?" he asked in a whiskey breath.

"Orders, Sir," I said, straightening my shoulders. "All officers are to report to their ships immediately." I glanced over his shoulder and saw a Filipino girl huddled in the bed, a sheet held to cover her breasts. I explained we had to check a few other hotels and then would come back to take him to the base.

"Christ almighty," he muttered, the seriousness of the situation flooding over him. "I'll have my gear packed and ready when you come."

Tom and I hit two more hotels and got one more officer. I radioed the base OOD and reported. He said he'd have a motor launch ready to take them back to their ships.

At the last hotel in Cavite, we found a Lt. (jg) registered. We followed the hotel clerk to the room and knocked, no answer, continued knocking, no response. "What do we do now?" asked Tom. "There's an officer in there and we got to tell him."

I turned to the clerk. "Unlock the door," I ordered, following him into the darkened room. I switched on the light, and stared. In the single bed, under a mosquito net, two figures were locked in sexual congress. Although obscured by the netting, I could see the man was white, his ass pounding up and down like a trip-hammer, his face buried in the thick black hair of a native girl rocking under him whose slim brown legs were wrapped around his thick waist. For a few moments the three of us stood, transfixed, mouths agape, as we watched the two fuck, grunting and groaning, the girl's eyes closed, he striving mightily for the big "O"—both seeming oblivious to our presence.

Finally, Tom made the first move, snapping to attention, eyes fixed at a point well above the writhing bodies, arms locked to his sides. "Permission to speak, sir," he said, clear and respectful.

Abruptly the trip-hammer stopped. Although still engaged, the officer turned his head and looked at us. "What the fuck are you assholes doing in my room. Get the fuck out—now!" Apparently, through the netting, he didn't recognize we were the shore patrol.

I approached close to the bed. The girl disengaged and turned her back to me, hiding her face in the pillow. "Sorry sir," I said. "We're shore patrol on special orders. The carriers are leaving port. All officers are to report back to their ships immediately. We can take you back to the base. Our OOD says there will be a motor launch waiting to take you to your ship."

"Ah shit," he said, sitting up, his voice angry. "I've been at sea for two months and haven't had a piece of ass in six, now you guys break in. Get out and let me finish what I got started."

"Begging your pardon, sir. We got direct orders from the base OOD, we're to bring you back right away. We'll wait at the desk for you. There are two other officers waiting for us."

The officer ripped back the netting, stepped out and stood, naked, his shoulders back and chin out in a position of command, his glistening penis drooping, "By God," he exploded, "you'll wait—God dammit! Now carry on."

Before I could respond, Tom stepped up next to me, clicked his heels, and rendered a salute right out of *The Bluejackets Manual,* right forearm inclined at a perfect 45 degree angle, the tip of his forefinger touching slightly to the right of his right eye, and, in a voice clear and resounding, shouted, "Aye, aye, suh," did an about face, and marched out the door—with me and the clerk following.

Instead of waiting at the desk, Tom and I decided to pick up the two officers waiting at the other hotels and come back for the Lt. (jg). We had a feeling he'd be ready. "From the looks of his pecker when we left," laughed Tom, "I don't think he had much left."

Sure enough, when we walked in the Lt. (jg) was sitting slumped over, eyes downcast, his overnight bag at his side. He followed us to the jeep and, except for a word with the other officers, never spoke.

We got the officers back to base in time to catch their carriers before they left port. The OOD gave Tom and me a "well done." It was too early for morning chow so we went back to the hut and hit the sack. We never found out why the excitement, why the carriers had to leave port in such a hurry. Thankfully, the incident, whatever it was, never led to a shooting war with the Chinese.

CHAPTER 18

I Lose a Friend

A week later I finished my temporary additional duty with the Armed Forces Police and returned to the Fleet Weather Central. I had built up 30 days of liberty so I decided to see more of the P.I. It was getting hot, and February was a good time to go to Baguio, the summer capital of the Philippines, high in the mountains of northern Luzon. Little did I know that I would spend the coldest night of my life in Baguio.

Don Walker and I and three shipmates from the FWC packed our cameras and civvies, piled in a navy automobile, and headed out the gate on a week's tour. First we went south, less than 30 miles from Cavite City, to the Taal Volcano. On the way we passed rice fields and stopped to snap photos of carabao, then up 2,500 feet above sea level to the Tagaytay Ridge on the rim of a giant caldera or volcanic crater. With the cool breeze on our faces, we looked down on an incredible sight: a huge lake, Lake Taal, and within the lake was the Taal Volcano, an active volcano. It was a volcano within a volcano.

The next stop was the town of Pagsanjan 50 miles farther south. Pagsanjan is known for its many waterfalls that flow into the Magdapio River, the largest of which is the Magdapio Falls that cascade from about 100 feet. (Years later the Hollywood director Francis Ford Coppola would use this area for his epic film *Apocalypse Now*). Along the way, we saw villagers bathing and laundering in the river and got some great shots.

Next Richard Long, our shipmate and designated driver, turned the Ford around and headed straight north past Manila and about 200 miles to Baguio. Richard was the most moral and decent man at the FWC. He didn't drink, smoke, or touch women. Yet he was friendly, a good worker, and best of all, ready and willing to sit and make a foursome in a game of cards.

Soon we approached the foothills of the rugged Cordillera mountain range in northern Luzon and began the drive up the narrow, winding, zig-zag road, nervously watching the long drops on the curves. The mountains were terraced, like the rice farms in Japan, by the Ifugao tribesmen. It was an incredible sight to see the rice terraces as they rose step-by-step toward the mountain top.

I LOSE A FRIEND

When we arrived at Baguio, 5,000 feet above sea level, the air was crisp and invigorating and filled with the fragrance of pine trees. It reminded me of northern Minnesota and the Boundary Waters Canoe Area. We checked into barracks at Camp John Hay, a recreational facility for American servicemen, about two miles from town. There was a huge stone fireplace, and each bunk was furnished with a thin blanket. It was a warm, sunny day, and we scoffed at the idea of getting wood for the fireplace.

That night it got below 50 degrees F. It was so cold I started shivering, shaking. In my sleep, I reached out for Rosie—like a child grasping for his teddy bear. I needed Rosie, not just for her warmth, but for her very presence. Slowly, I began to realize how important Rosie was to me. She had become a part of me, as essential as my arms and legs. She was my food and drink, my love. What would I do without her when I left for the States. I didn't want to think about it . . . The next night, Don Walker and I got a fire going in the fireplace.

The weather was a bit unusual: clear and sunny in the mornings and cloudy in the afternoons. Mornings we took cameras and went sightseeing; afternoons we spent golfing or swimming in the 500-foot-long pool.

We went to Baguio and wandered through the public market, a series of alleys with stalls, selling fish, meat, rice, and crafts of all kinds: wood carvings, baskets, silver jewelry, and tribal ornaments. Sometimes we'd see members of the Igorot tribe, small dark aborigines—the men dressed in loincloths, the women in colorful dresses. Their practice of cannibalism had been outlawed some years before. I bought ashtrays of dark mahogany with figures of native women and carabao.

Soon after my return from Baguio I lost a good friend who was shot to death in a gunfight. I had finished a mid-watch at FWC and walked into the house when Rosie rushed up to me. "Jake, your friend the policeman, he killed last night."

Stunned, I waved down a jeepney to the Cavite City police station and got the news. There was a plot to kill a senator in Manila. The Manila police uncovered the plot and went after the conspirators. They escaped and fled to Cavite City where the Cavite City police cornered them in a cemetery, only a mile from our base. In the ensuing gunfight, Lieutenant Cortez, a friend of mine when I was with the Armed Forces Police, was shot and killed, along with one of the conspirators.

Lt. Miguel Cortez was movie-star handsome, gregarious and friendly, an officer with whom the AFP coordinated cases involving sailors and Filipinos: rapes, fights, thefts, and murders. But it was more than that; our offices in the police station were close, and he'd often stroll over just to talk politics, tell stories, and kid us about our love lives. When Rosie and I registered at the police station, he was the man I dealt with. Although registering was simply formalizing a relationship between a sailor and a prostitute, the lieutenant gave the proceedings a certain reverence, like getting a marriage license.

 The wake for Lt. Cortez was held in the back of the police station on March 10, 1955. I know the date because in a letter to Mom I described the gunfight and the day of the wake. The room was crowded: an honor guard of uniformed Cavite City police, family, and friends. Rosie and I joined a long line of people that entered through an open door and snaked past the bier.

 There was a cardboard box half full of pesos next to the casket. I turned to Rosie, a question on my face. "It for the family," she said. I reached for my wallet, opened it and fanned the bills. "Four or five pesos," she whispered. I drew out six, cupped them in my hand, and slipped them into the box as we passed.

 The casket was of wood, the inside padded in a white satin cloth. The lieutenant looked as if asleep, younger than his 30 years, his well-formed face unmarked except for a bullet hole in his chin—from a .38- or .45-caliber slug, I guessed. From the entrance wound, it looked like the bullet coursed upward, probably blowing out the back of his skull. In the Philippines, not much was done to cover the ravages of death, natural or otherwise.

I talked to my police friends after the wake. They said the conspirators, the slayers of Lt. Cortez, were gangsters, common hoods. I wondered. There was so much corruption and fraud throughout the government, the courts, and the political parties. It was said that in the Philippine Islands, the first responsibility of a political leader upon gaining office was to put his compadres in positions of power, to secure government jobs for them, to swing government contracts their way. It was the accepted practice.

An election was like a war, winner take the spoils. When I came to the P.I. I was told that in the previous election 40 members of the competing parties were murdered. Vengeance and retaliation were common, and perhaps the motivation behind the plot to kill the senator. Whatever it was, it got my friend killed.

CHAPTER 19

The Party

It was March—the middle of the dry season. Just about every day was sunny and hot. We were winding up the day watch in the office when Don Walker, my section leader and best friend, strolled over to where I was sitting at the plotting table and suggested, "Jake, let's stop over to the club for a beer before chow."

"Sure," I said. "I could use a cold one."

The EM Club was quiet, a little too early for the rest of the base sailors. But it was cool and dark, and the overhead fans were moving the air. We found a spot at the far end of the bar and ordered up. We were silent a moment, enjoying the first swallows from icy San Migs. Then Don turned to me, "Jake, you'll be leaving in a few months—going back to the States. You still plan to go back to the farm when you get out of the Navy?

"That's the plan," I said.

Don broke open a pack of Old Golds and slid the cigarettes over to me. "Christ, old buddy, milking cows and shoveling shit. Think about it."

I lit up. "I'm not crazy about the idea, but I made promises."

"Promises, hell. Look how you're living now. Shacked up with Rosie. Spending all your free time in Cavite City. How are you going to go back to that small-town farm life after this?"

I shrugged my shoulders. I didn't have an answer.

Then Don started in on an idea he'd had for months—one he'd been trying to sell me. "You and I, Jake, we could take our G.I. Bill money when we get out of the Navy and apply to the University of Mexico in Mexico City. We could live it up for a few years while we pick up a degree. It'd be Cavite City all over again for you, except higher class. You'd find a woman just like Rosie, I tell you."

I had to admit Don's plan sounded better and better each time he told it, but I couldn't let on to him. I was locked in, and I knew it. "Don, I wish I could. But I gave my word—and I can't go back on it."

Don took a drag on his cigarette, thought a minute. Then he tapped his beer bottle on mine and raised it. "Well, hell, we've had some good times, though. That Hong Kong trip—that was a corker." Don rattled

THE PARTY

off our high jinks in Baguio, Manila, and a few places in between. "But last year's Fourth of July—that was something. Remember, old Gene Tolliver? You and I—we could have gotten in a hell of a lot of trouble, but we skated clear."

Yes, the blow-out Fourth-of-July party, just nine months ago. How could I forget? I thought back and recalled how easy it was to get sucked into something real bad before you knew it.

It all started when the section leaders got together and decided we had to celebrate the Fourth in a big way. They agreed a party was in order with three main ingredients: booze, girls, and food. Since I was in Cavite City a lot and knew some of the Filipino bar owners, they asked Don to get me to make a deal. Don was hesitant to put me on the spot, but I said I would do it. He was my pal.

I contacted a few bars and settled on the Seven Seas Club. The owner said for a price he would supply all the food, liquor, and girls we wanted. After some hard-nosed bargaining—and laughs over drinks at the owner's club—we agreed on a price: 300 pesos ($150 American)—a good chunk of change.

Don and I broke down the cost. The total complement of the Fleet Weather Central was 54 enlisted men, (including four chief petty officers) and eight officers, including the officer-in-charge. Because of the Navy's strict caste system that separated officers from enlisted men, officers would not come to a party such as this, even if invited. Officers were gentlemen, people to be respected. None of us enlisted men at FWC had ever been invited to an officer's home.

Chief petty officers were on the highest rung in the enlisted ranks. Their uniforms were like the officers'—no white hats for them. We invited the chiefs, but not one agreed to come. I think they suspected the depths of depravity the party might sink to and didn't want to be part of it.

Of the 50 white hats, 30 signed up. Five dollars a head would cover the cost.

The site of the festivity was a small secluded strip of sandy beach on Manila Bay, hidden from the road by a thick grove of palm trees about two miles from the base. The day before the Fourth, three guys from our section borrowed a panel truck and some supplies from the motor pool and drove out to the locale. They set up a volleyball net for those athletic types, and a clothesline between two palm trees for those wanting to swim and in need of something on which to hang their clothes.

THE PARTY

The afternoon of the Fourth, Don and I and 28 other sailors were waiting as the Filipino club owner and a half dozen of his bar girls pulled up with three jeepneys full of food, drink, and eating utensils. The girls carried out the victuals and laid them out buffet style on tables.

We looked over the tables loaded with food, much of which was the traditional Filipino menu: fish of every stripe, rice, pancit, and tropical fruits: mango, banana, papaya, and pineapple. But there were other dishes, some luscious to the eyes, such as juicy suckling pig, and others strange and exotic, which most of us shied away from.

Along with food, there was plenty to drink. Cases of bottled San Miguel beer were stacked at the end of one table, and at another table were lined up quart bottles of Tanduay run, half-gallon jugs of Tuba, a coconut wine, and empty catsup bottles and fruit jars filled with a horrible tasting drink, probably brewed in the back alley of some barrio in the boondocks, hand-labeled with the words "Golden Cup Scotch Whiskey," the ingredients God only knew. One of the girls warned me not to drink too much of it because "you go blind."

I turned to Don. "What do you think?"

Don looked over the tables of food and liquor,

studied each of the six bar girls, and pronounced, "It's everything the guys wanted. You did good, Jake, damn good." He threw an arm around my shoulder and ushered me to a table lined with bottles of beer and offered, "How about a San Mig?"

I cracked open a bottle and watched the guys laughing and joking. They were lining up at the tables, filling their plates, and grabbing drinks. It had the look of a hell of a swell time. I felt good.

After a few hours of eating and drinking, joking and grab-assing with the bar girls, some of the guys organized into volleyball teams and got a tournament going. By dusk, though, with all that booze flowing, the contests fell apart with players stumbling and falling in the sand, laughing and arguing over points, and finally ending when one disgruntled loser flung the only volleyball out into the bay, and a drunk at one of the tables shouted he'd get it, jerked off his clothes and bare-assed it into the water. The next thing you knew a bunch of the guys stripped and ran, shouting, cock and balls swinging, into the water. One guy grabbed a girl and, as she screamed, dragged her into the water with him.

When nightfall came, some of the guys brought out Roman candles and shot balls of fire out over the water. Firecrackers were popping off, and girls were

THE PARTY

shrieking. Someone broke into song, and we roared out "Anchors Aweigh" and "The Star-Spangled Banner." Later, excited and flushed with booze, here and there a sailor would take a girl into the palm grove for a short-time, although paying extra for that service.

About 0300 in the morning, the party broke up. Don and I had hired a couple of jeepney drivers to shuttle all the guys back to the base. Everyone was accounted for except Gene Tolliver, a section leader.

I turned to Don "We've got to find Tolliver. His section has the day watch, less than five hours from now."

Don nodded, and we headed over to the tables where the bar owner was directing his bar girls to clean up and pack into the jeepneys what remained of the food and drink. We talked him into letting us use his girls to help us in the search. Don had a flashlight, and there was a full moon so there was enough light for the girls to see. We fanned out and walked through a grove of trees.

Suddenly we heard a woman's cry. We rushed toward the sound and found a bar girl standing and pointing down, "He drunk, very drunk."

Don's flashlight took in the scene. Gene Tolliver was snoring, his back against a coconut tree, a half empty fruit jar of Golden Cup Scotch Whiskey in his hand. Don looked down. A medley of concern and disgust whipped across his face. He leaned over and shook Gene's shoulder. "You okay, Gene?"

Gene aroused, then mumbled something about it being a damn fine party and wished it could go on forever.

Gene Tolliver was a spree drinker. He'd go for weeks without a drink, then stay drunk for four or five days, spending all his money and humiliating himself by begging a few dollars from the new guys to keep the binge going. Yet, he was a good-natured supervisor, and the veterans in his section would always cover for him until he sobered up.

Don helped Gene to his feet. "Can you make it partner?"

Gene blinked his eyes and shook his head as if to clear his mind. "I'll be okay, I'll make it." Gene was drunk but coherent. He could drink a lot and still function.

Don looked into Gene's eyes to make sure he was comprehending. "In a few hours you and your guys got the watch. You've got to stand tall."

Gene said he was good to go. We got under his arms and walked him to a jeepney. As we piled into

THE PARTY

the jeepney, Don turned to me, "No sense you coming back to the base with us. You got two days left on your liberty. We can drop you off at Rosie's on the way."

"Are you sure?" I asked, concerned.

Don glanced at Gene, now fully conscious. "We'll do okay, Jake. You've done enough. There's four hours left 'til watch time for Gene and his guys. We'll get back to the base. Gene's been though this before." Don nodded to Gene. "He'll get cleaned up and be in the office. A mug or two of strong coffee and a cigarette and he'll do fine."

The jeepney driver left me off at Rosie's and the rest went on their way. I wasn't comfortable though. I noticed Gene kept the half-full jar of whiskey with him in the jeepney. Something told me there'd be hell to pay before the day was done.

Rosie opened the door at my knock. She was half asleep, waiting up for me. "You have good time?" she asked, checking me over to make sure I was okay. Rosie had been to sailors' parties before and knew how drunk they got—and how quickly a fight could start.

"It went good," I said, kissing her. "No problems." I washed up and we slipped into bed. Rosie curled up in my arms as she liked to do. Before I drifted off, I lay thinking. I felt guilty. Rosie wanted to go to the party, but I said no. I was afraid some shipmate from the office would get drunk and hit on her. Then I'd have to step in—fists might fly. I didn't want that. I tried to explain to Rosie, but I wasn't sure she believed me. She knew there would be bar girls there, and she hadn't forgotten Linda.

When I got back from liberty, I got the rest of the story about Gene Tolliver. Gene made it to the office all right, but he snuck in that jar of whiskey and hid it in the instrument shelter topside. He avoided the duty officer by pretending he was taking weather observations on the observation deck. He kept nipping the booze to keep his spree going.

Then, as luck would have it, Gene's guy on the Teletype machines pulled off some weather reports from two ships in the Philippine Sea that showed a dangerously developing low-pressure system that could turn into a typhoon. Lieutenant Delmar Bliss, the duty officer, alerted the skipper. That's when the shit hit the fan.

I could just imagine the scene. Our commander, the FWC officer-in-charge, was a brilliant aerologist, an Annapolis graduate, with a cold and flinty personality. Weather to him was mathematics and physics, numbers and trends. It was said that when he saw the sunset over Manila Bay, instead of the incredible beauty, he saw only the percent of cloud cover, cloud height and thickness. He seldom talked to an enlisted man. Except for the section leaders, he did not know our names. And he did not suffer fools gently.

With the threatening weather reports, the skipper swung into action. He told Lt. Bliss he wanted the section leader present on the double. Lt. Bliss, a weak and indecisive man, panicked. He ran around looking for Tolliver. Gene's guys brought him down from the observation deck, drunk and staggering. Gene tried to bluff his way through. He braced in front of the commanding officer, threw his shoulders back and thundered, "Petty Officer Gene Tolliver reporting as ordered—sir," then lost his balance and fell over the duty officer's desk and on his ass.

As expected, the skipper was enraged. He relieved Gene Tolliver of his duties, and ordered an off-duty section leader to fill in. A week later, he busted Gene in rate, and two months after that, Gene rotated back to the States where he finished his two-year tour of duty.

"Jake, that was a hell of a party, wasn't it?" Don was nudging my arm—repeating the question. I jerked myself back from the memory—back to the present and the EM Club with Don. I nodded in agreement.

"But here's something you don't know—what happened after the party, after you transferred to the Armed Forces Police."

Don took a deep drag on his Old Gold, blew a smoke ring over the bar, and turned to me. "A few weeks after the party, two guys came down with the clap. It seems one of the bar girls we had there was new, just came in from Olongapo and hadn't had a medical check-up. The skipper really blew his top; he'd had enough. He ordered Lt. Bliss to conduct a full investigation. Bliss called all the section leaders together to find out who was responsible for the party—who had made the arrangements. And you know Bliss."

Yes, I did know Lt. Bliss. He was the one officer we enlisted men despised. We didn't trust him or respect him. As one old timer in the office put it, "He's all handle and no jug." Or, as another more crudely asserted, "He's not worth a shit—a real asshole."

"You know, Jake, I really sweated it out. But here's the important part. Gene Tolliver took the rap, told Bliss the blowout was his idea. He took full responsibility. I told him he didn't have to do it—at least not for me. But he said, 'Fuck it.' He was getting out of the Navy in a year to work for his dad in the construction business. He didn't care."

THE PARTY

"And, Jake, your name never came up. You're covered. But look out for Bliss. He was talking like he hates the 'dirty whores of Cavite'—his words. But he kept sniffing around, asking questions, like if any of us had slept with one, trying to find out what they were really like, what was their attraction for the men. By God, Lt. Bliss is a real weirdo."

Don stood up to go. We laid money on the bar for our drinks. As we walked out of the club, Don turned to me. "I'll leave you with this thought, Jake. Look out for Bliss. He doesn't know you're shacked up in Cavite, the only guy in our office living with a bar girl. He could make things real rough on you."

As Don and I strolled over to the mess hall, I had a bad feeling. Somehow I knew Lt. Bliss and I would tangle somewhere down the line.

CHAPTER 20

Lieutenant Delmar Bliss

The U.S. Navy, like any effective organization, has well-defined lines of authority and responsibility. This was true of Sangley's FWC. Except for the commander, each officer's main responsibility was weather forecasting. However, each officer had supplementary duties. One such duty was morale: the mental and psychological well-being of the enlisted men.

The Fleet Weather Central's morale officer was Lt. Delmar Bliss, a physically nondescript man in his early 40s, whose slouch, rumpled uniform speckled with dandruff on the shoulders, and horn-rimmed glasses were at complete odds with proper military bearing and command presence. He had the look of an absent-minded professor, walking around as if in a fog, eyes focused on some far-away object, brows furrowed as though he was struggling with some deep philosophical problem, like the meaning of life, or the question: Is there a God, and if so, is he a loving God or an angry God?

Lt. Bliss was not effective as a weather forecaster

or a morale officer. He was scheduled for day watches only, when the skipper was in and could check on his work. And when it came to activities to pump up the men's morale, such as Christmas parties, sporting events, that sort of thing, he dumped it on the section leaders to plan and run—unwilling to exert the slightest effort on our behalf. But, we were to discover there was only one thing that stirred the juices of Lt. Bliss, that obsessed him really—sex, not his own experiences, but the men's sexual encounters. And it was his fixation on sex that got me into trouble.

It all started with a directive from the base commander that put iron in the Lieutenant's back and fire in his eyes. It was the Base VD Report from sickbay—it said the Fleet Weather Central's rate of venereal disease was the highest of any division.

The U.S. Navy had been battling the scourge of venereal disease, as had most military organizations, throughout its history. Just about the first lecture a naval recruit received in boot camp was on the ravages of syphilis and gonorrhea. Slides of the most horrible cases were shown. You walked out of class thinking if you dipped your wick in the wrong place, your brain would turn to mush and your pecker would rot off. And if that didn't scare you enough, the Navy added a moral tone to its warning. The *Bluejackets' Manual*, 1940 edition cautioned:

> *When you find your mind wandering on unwholesome subjects, snap out of it and turn your mind to clean thoughts. Get interested in clean, manly subjects, such as good books, athletics, shows, etc. See the really worthwhile sights in the towns you visit. Do not hang around the dirty places that are always handy and which are always waiting to prey on you. Your position in life as a man-o'-war's man is above such things.*

Prior to World War II, there was more than a little truth to the Navy's warnings about venereal disease. First, it was downright unpleasant to have, and second, it was damn hard to get rid of. The treatment before penicillin was a year of weekly Salvarsan injections. Some regimens used mercury in conjunction with the Salvarsan. The men suffered toxic side effects from Salvarsan, one of the first chemotherapy-like drugs.

But this all changed with the advent of the miracle drug penicillin during World War II. By 1953 when I went to the P.I. the most common venereal diseases were gonorrhea (clap) and something called "nonspecific urethritis." A shot of penicillin, however, stopped them in their tracks. Penicillin worked so well that sailors joked it was better to get gonorrhea than a cold. One of the guys in my section laughed and said "you get a cold and it hangs on for a week or more. With the clap, one shot in the ass and your cock stops dripping in a day or two."

The white hat's devil-may-care attitude toward venereal disease resulted in a steady stream of new cases coming into sickbay. Sick call was first thing in the morning. The medical corpsman would separate the men reporting in, into two lines: those needing "short arm" inspections in one line and all the rest into another.

Short arm inspections were for those suspected of having a venereal disease. The symptoms of gonorrhea or urethritis (burning sensation on urination, yellow pussy discharge, and sex with a prostitute within 20 days) were so well known that the men easily found the right line to join. The corpsman would direct each man to step up and drop his trousers and shorts. He'd ask a few questions, then point to the man's penis and call out the familiar words, "skin it back and milk it down." The corpsman would take a specimen of the discharge and make a culture to confirm the diagnosis. Usually, however, there was no waiting for confirmation. The sailor got a shot of penicillin in the buttocks and left sickbay knowing he would be confined to base for 10 days to make sure he was cured.

Even though the Navy had a miracle cure for venereal disease, its fight against VD continued unabated. To the navy brass, it wasn't good enough to tell a mother back home she needn't worry if her sailor boy got a dose from an infected whore because now there was this great cure. Rather, the brass wanted to tell her the Navy would keep her boy clean and pure in the first place. Thus, there was pressure on commanders to keep the venereal disease rate down.

With the Fleet Weather Central having the highest venereal disease rate, the base commander was leaning on our skipper to clean up our act. As morale officer, it was Lt. Bliss's job to lead the charge. At our next monthly inspection, Lt. Bliss, normally listless and distracted, became a crusader, a real Billy Graham. As we stood at attention, he thundered up and down the ranks, waving the VD report, ranting and raving. "You men are supposed to be the cream of the crop here at Sangley. As a unit you've got the highest IQ. Some of you have had college, and many of you, I understand, plan to seek a college degree after you finish your navy enlistment. I would think you men would be spending your time in the base library reading good books, thinking clean thoughts about your future, about someday marrying a nice girl and having children."

Lt. Bliss slapped the stapled sheaf of papers. "And instead you're wallowing in filth, having sex with these dirty whores in Cavite." Then Lt. Bliss paused, and in a solemn, ministerial voice put forth what I'm sure he thought was the clincher. "You should be ashamed of yourselves. What would your mother think if she knew? How will you explain this to that nice girl back in the States?"

We had all heard this moralistic speech before. And coming from a man we did not respect, it held little credence. There were scantly concealed snickers within the ranks. We glanced at the skipper and noticed a crabbed look on his face. Even he, we suspected, had enough of this sanctimonious sermon.

Yet Lt. Bliss was not through. He wound up his tirade with threats. "Finally, let me remind you that not only your career in the Navy could be jeopardized, but also your chance for a decent job in civilian life. You men could be looking at a Bad Conduct Discharge."

The Lieutenant was alluding to the Navy's position that a young sailor could be allowed one mistake.

But to get venereal disease a second time was inexcusable. We were warned that this could leave a black mark on our service record. Although we had never heard of a sailor getting a BCD for a second VD infection, the threat was still there. And if you did not get an Honorable Discharge, you could lose all veterans benefits. Plus, it was well known that many an ex-serviceman had been turned down by an employer because he could not produce an honorable discharge certificate.

The monthly inspection wound down and we broke ranks with little regard for Lt. Bliss's bluster. So what if we got a second dose, we thought, there was always the Filipino doctors in Cavite. They had penicillin too, and the smart swabbie took his VD infection to them and got his shot, the Navy being none the wiser.

We white hats were keen observers of our officers, and we wondered about Lt. Bliss's vehemence regarding venereal disease. Sure it was part of his job, but there was so much anger—and all it seemed directed against the "dirty brown whores of Cavite."

Yes, Lt. Bliss was something of a puritan. Married, but without children, he did not smoke, drink, or swear—definitely singular in the U.S. Navy. And yes, his wife was a thin, nervous woman with a perpetual sour look who, we were told, was struggling to find salvation through constant study of the scriptures. Certainly, he would have little sympathy toward the "hostesses" of Cavite. But why all this passion boiling in an otherwise remote and disengaged man?

And there was something else. Lt. Bliss, we noticed, seemed to have a perverse interest in dirty stories. There was always some guy in our section relating his latest romp with one of the bar girls. Lt. Bliss, although pretending to be engrossed in his work, would listen with rapt attention.

I began to think that within the morale officer's flaccid body raged a battle between an ascetic abhorrence and a prurient curiosity about perverted sex. He brought to my mind an unforgettable character: the Reverend Mr. Davidson, the hypocritical missionary in W. Somerset Maugham's short story "Rain." And now with the full weight of the U.S. Navy behind him, Lt. Bliss could delve into the sexual lives of the men. I, it turned out, was the first to get the third degree.

One early evening, not long after Lt. Bliss's speech against VD at FWC's monthly inspection, Rosie and I were riding in a jeepney on our way to Mom's Place for a few hours of dancing, a beer or two, and maybe dinner at the Pagoda Kitchen. Since we were the only passengers, the driver stopped at the base main gate to pick up any fares going downtown. I was surprised to see Lt. Bliss wave down the driver. It was rare to see a base officer in lowbrow Cavite. Base officers and their families went to Manila for shopping or a night on the town.

Lt. Bliss stepped up into the back of the little jeepney and sat down on the facing bench seat, across from Rosie and me, so close our knees were nearly touching. There was a look of surprise on his face.

"Evening, sir," I said softly, nervous, wishing I was a million miles away.

Lt. Bliss nodded, shifted his body as if to move away from us as far as possible, then glanced at Rosie. She was dressed in the sexy outfit she wore when I first met her at Mom's: tight-fitting red blouse, black skirt, and high-heeled black shoes. There was a touch of red on her lips, a bit of eyebrow pencil and eye shadow, and a bouquet of jasmine in her hair. It was her Mom's Place look, her eye-catching, bar-girl look. It caught the morale officer's attention.

I watched as Lt. Bliss's eyes moved from Rosie's crossed muscular legs, to her short skirt hiked high enough to allow a glimpse of soft brown thigh and up to the gold heart pendant I had gotten her in Hong Kong, tucked in the cleavage of her bulging breasts.

That's where his eyes stopped and fixated.

I felt Rosie stiffen. She averted her eyes from Lt. Bliss's unwavering gaze. No one spoke. The jeepney stopped at Mom's. We excused ourselves, eased past Lt. Bliss, and got out—feeling the Lieutenant's glare as we pushed through the swinging doors.

Rosie took my arm. "That man," she whispered, "he look at me . . ." she struggled for words, "funny. I don't like."

Mom's Place was quiet, the evening trade not yet in. Two sailors swaggered in, called for beers, and fed the jukebox. Rosie and I took a few turns on the dance floor before she got into a girl-talk session with one of her old bar girlfriends. I nursed a San Miguel, thinking. Lt. Bliss won't let this incident pass. He'll come back at me somehow, I figured. Rosie and I wound up the night with pancit, fish, and rice at the Pagoda Kitchen. I did not sleep well that night.

The next morning Rosie and I slept late. It had been a warm and humid night with no breeze. We grabbed towels and hit the shower. She knew I was worried, and she had a way of freeing a man's mind of trouble. We always took the navy shower: turn on the water for a few seconds and get wet, lather, then shower off quickly, thereby conserving water. She always soaped me down. This time she lingered. It was amazing what that woman could do with her hands and a bar of soap.

We started laughing and fondling each other, and got turned on. We showered off. Rosie reached her arms around my neck, hiked her legs around my hips, and pressed her breasts against my chest. I stumbled back to our bed and laid her down. Forty minutes later we finished what we had started. Bathed in sweat, we had to shower again.

It was close to noon, and Rosie fried a pan full of eggs with biscuits, coffee, bananas and mangos. We sat, me in my skivvie shorts, Rosie in shorts and halter, slowly eating. I was thinking again. I told Rosie about Lt. Bliss.

"Is he big boss, make much trouble for you Jake," she asked, "because of me?"

"He's not the big boss, but he can make trouble. He doesn't like bar girls, doesn't want the men going with them. Don't worry about it," I said, taking Rosie's hand in mine, reassuring her. "He can't put me in the brig for going with you." I was saying this with false bravado, however, not really sure what Lt. Bliss was capable of doing.

I slipped into the civvies I had worn the night before: off-white sharkskin trousers and robin's-egg blue sport shirt, and headed back to the base to catch the evening watch at 1600 hours. In the hut I changed into my navy duds and was in the office with a half hour to spare.

Don waved me over. "Lt. Bliss wants to see you now. He didn't say why."

Oh, oh, I thought, here it comes.

I went over to Lt. Bliss at the watch officer's desk. Without comment, he walked me into the conference room and closed the door. I stood at attention while he took a chair, folded his hands on top of a manila folder on the table, and gave me a stern look.

"Becker, I'm surprised—and disappointed in you. I thought you were a good man until last night. That woman you were with, the cheap perfume, all that makeup, the short skirt showing everything, and the bosom literally falling out of her blouse—disgusting. It got me thinking." He tapped a slender finger on the table. "So I decided to do a little checking to find out just what kind of sailor you really are."

Lt. Bliss opened the manila folder and thumbed through several pages. "This morning I pulled your service record and took a look. Yes, on the surface it seemed pretty clean: a 4.0 rating, good test scores at service schools, the highest score in our office on last year's petty officer third class test, good recommendations from superiors, that sort of thing." He leaned back in his chair and gave me a satisfied look.

"But there was one thing, easy to miss," said the lieutenant smiling. "Last year you checked into sickbay with a venereal disease. That was the tip-off that there was a rotten, dirty mind lurking in that clean-cut-looking body of yours."

Damn, I thought, he's going to hold that over my head. I remembered when it happened. It was after Rosie left for Olongapo and before I moved in with Linda. I had stopped at the Pagoda Kitchen for dinner one night, then strolled upstairs to the Seven Seas Club for a drink. I stayed too long, drank too much, and ended up spending the night with a new girl at the club from Manila. She must have slipped through the required medical check-up, and I came down with gonorrhea. I spent the next ten days confined to the base to make sure I was cured.

He shifted in his chair, began strumming the table with his fingers. "So today I talked to a shipmate or two of yours, to dig a little deeper into the character of Petty Officer Third Class Jake Becker." He paused. "And what I found out sickened me."

I remained at attention, eyes straight ahead, as

Lt. Bliss eased back in his chair. He was enjoying this, I thought, the bastard.

"To begin with, you no longer attend Sunday chapel" He pointed an inquisitorial finger at me. "You've abandoned the church of your parents. Is that not true?"

Here comes the third degree, I thought. Well I won't lie. "Yes," I admitted, "I haven't been attending."

"And you know why?" he asked. Before I could answer, he replied, "Well, I'll tell you why. You don't want to hear the Word of God. You want to be comfortable in your sin with the harlot. Is that not true?"

What Lt. Bliss said was getting close to the truth. I had embraced a lifestyle foreign to everything I had been taught—in church, in Luther League, and at home. Was it because of the Navy and its carnality, the Philippine Islands and its brothels and freedom from sexual restraint, my passion for Rosie and the girls like her? And was there a bit of youthful rebellion mixed in? I hadn't stopped to think about it.

"I don't know, sir," I answered, as truthful as I could.

He eyed me closely. "I do believe it is something more grave than a mere expression of youthful indiscretion, not to be repeated. It's more than that, much more." He pushed my service record aside with a careless shrug. "In fact, I've been told you've become a shack rat, that you've gone Asiatic. In truth, you have a passion for the sinful life, drawn to it like a pig to garbage, wallowing in it day after day."

Lt. Bliss studied my face, waited for a reaction. Well I'll be damned if I give him one, I thought.

He went on. "I've found out a little more about that . . . woman of yours. Her name is Rosie, and she worked at a bar in Cavite called Mom's Place—until you registered with the police and moved in with her. Is that not true?"

Where is he getting this information, I wondered. Then it occurred to me. One of the section leaders, a Southern guy from Alabama or Mississippi hated the P.I., called the Filipinos "Flips," and the bar girls "nigger whores." And he had no time for shack rats like me, called us "nigger lovers." He'd be the only shipmate I knew that would rat me out.

"Yes, sir," I confessed, "what you say is true."

"There is more," the morale officer went on, "This Rosie of yours, I've been told, was a hot number with the sailors, couldn't get enough. If she liked the guy she would do it free."

Jesus, I thought, the lousy bastard. He likes to

hurt a guy. I was determined to keep my cool though.

"Well, sir, men talk. They say things not always true, exaggerate a little."

Lt. Bliss thought a moment, then motioned me to sit down across from him. "What is the fascination with this prostitute, this woman Rosie?" he asked, his voice subdued like a priest in a confessional. "She's been with hundreds of men. The lines around her eyes . . . she must be at least ten years older than you." He raised his hands as if in supplication. "Help me to understand."

"I can't explain," I said, truthfully, "except to say she is the most important person in my life right now."

He leaned over the table, his face close to mine. "What is so special about her?" he asked, conspiratorially. "She's cheap, tawdry." There was a leer on his face. "Is it the sex? Is it . . ." he searched for words, "strange sex, different?"

The sick bastard, I thought. He's getting his rocks off with this talk. "Sir, that's getting personal. I don't have to answer that." I caught myself. I should have prefaced that negative statement with "Sir, with all due respect," but how can you respect a man like that. I went on, "I do my work. I'm not breaking any regulations when I'm with her on liberty."

LIEUTENANT DELMAR BLISS

Lt. Bliss leaned back in his chair, his face reddened. "I have a responsibility for you men," he said, his voice taking on the stern father tone. "When I see a man making a fool of himself, violating common decency, I've got to step in and try to straighten him out. And in your case, I see a man on a downward spiral to hell." He paused, allowing the statement to sink in, then asked, "What will it take to get you to change your ways and walk the path of righteousness?"

I was angry. Who was he to tell me to change my ways? The Navy had nothing to say about my personal life as long as I obeyed the rules and regulations. I did not answer.

"Did you hear my question sailor?" he asked. "I did, sir. I have nothing more to say."

"Well," he shrugged, pushing away from the table, "if that's the way you want it—fine. But let me leave you with a bit of advice. I'm going to cut the VD rate in this office if it's the last thing I do. And I might have to make an example to get my point across." He reached over and took my service record. "You have had venereal disease once. If your name turns up on another VD report from sickbay, I'm going to throw the book at you. I'm putting a note in your record that I've warned you. If you get infected again, I will push vigorously for a bad conduct discharge." His voice was hard. "Do you understand?"

"Yes, sir," I nodded, "I understand."

"That will be all then, you're dismissed."

I scrambled to my feet, braced at attention, turned and marched out the door and back to my workstation. I took a deep breath. I've got about five months to go in the P.I., I thought, I'm going to have to watch my step.

For days I ruminated on the words Lt. Bliss had flung at me, finding them damn hard to swallow. First, came the anger. What right did he have to say I had a rotten dirty mind, a passion for the sinful life . . . wallowing like a pig in garbage, that I was on a downward spiral to hell? And what he had said about Rosie: calling her a harlot, cheap and tawdry. Who the hell was he—God Almighty?

Then came the guilt, gnawing, twisting my guts. I had been a good Lutheran: regular in church attendance growing up, president of Luther League, sang in the church choir, even taught Sunday school when I was in high school. I was reverential enough, at least on the surface, to inspire Rev. Otto Getz, my pastor at St. John Lutheran Church, to recommend me for a college scholarship so I could follow in his footsteps and become a minister. Now I wasn't going to church, and the Bible was the last thing on my mind. And my life with Rosie, how could I explain that to Mom, or anyone back home?

To add to my guilt, we were in the middle of the Lenten season, an important religious event in the Philippine Islands. Holy Week was coming up, commemorating the week of Christ's death and resurrection—all of which was important in my Lutheran upbringing. I've got to make amends, I thought.

Yet all this internal agony and the resolve to change my ways resulted in a gesture, pathetic really. In a letter to my Mom and Dad, I promised to go to church on Easter Sunday. Also, I reported that on Good Friday I observed the Filipino flagellants' efforts at penance.

Yesterday we went out in the village and watched the Filipinos during the Sacrifice. There were six of them and they were beating themselves with bamboo strips tied to a long cord. They were all bloody and if they didn't bleed enough, they had two men who were the beaters cut them on the back with razor blades. They do this every year on Good Friday to wash away their sins. The two beaters beat them with sticks and kicked them, and it really is awful the things they go through, but they do it every year up to nine and ten years. Well, I guess everyone has their own way of confessing their sins and cleansing themselves of their sins.

Three days later in a letter to my parents I reported proudly that I had attended church on Easter Sunday, said the base chapel was packed.

CHAPTER 21

A Bittersweet Time

It's May 1955, nearly two years since I steamed into Manila Bay as a young, wide-eyed sailor. In all that time I sent a stream of letters to my parents and Rev. Getz. I told about my experiences in the P.I., but kept the information circumspect. I mentioned the poverty and squalid living conditions of many Filipinos, the weather, the election of the president in 1953, and my trips to Hong Kong, Baguio, Manila, and so on. There was not a whisper about Rosie, the bar girls, venereal disease—the seamy side of my life. All that was kept secret.

Every letter though, without exception, spoke of my plans to return to the farm and my church after the Navy. But my heart and mind struggled with that eventuality. I tried to convince myself it was the right thing to do, but I could not rejoice at the prospect. Rather I felt a responsibility to do so, to live up to the expectations of my parents and Pastor Getz.

And Dad and Mom were so happy. They'd had

mixed feelings about my being a minister from the start. Although my ministry would have elevated their position in the church to near celebrity status (I would have been the first son from St. John to become a minister), it soon became clear in their letters what they really wanted was for me to be on the farm with them—on the home place.

In one letter, Mom said the farm prices were so good that Dad sold the team of workhorses and bought a new tractor. And, she said, Dad planned to rent an additional 80 acres from Old Man Johnson, who farmed next to them and was getting too old to farm the acres he had. She added that Dad said, "With Jake home and helping, we can make a go of it." In a postscript, my father scrawled, "Your mother has been sickly lately, but with you coming home in four months, it's been a tonic for her. She's her old self again."

Pastor Getz wrote: He was disappointed I wasn't going to college and study for the ministry, but he had plans for me. "You can do so much here, Jake, in the church. We need you to teach Sunday school again. The choir misses your strong bass voice; and there's the Men's Club, too."

In one of my letters, in a handwritten P.S., I mentioned I had been promoted to petty officer second class. It seems I had successfully evaded Lt. Bliss's plans and kept my nose clean.

Lt. Bliss continued his drive to cut the FWC VD rate. In this fight, however, he was losing the battle. It was an exercise in futility, like trying to swim against a Tsunami, a tidal wave. For the Philippine Islands I knew in the early 1950s was a sexual paradise for American servicemen. There were three American military bases all within a 100-mile radius from Manila: Clark Air Force Base, the huge Subic Bay Naval Station, and Sangley Point Naval Air Station. Each base had a town around it geared to please the boys with clubs, bars, massage parlors, and plenty of prostitutes.

When I arrived at Sangley in August of 1953, Cavite City, the village outside the Navy base had over 50 establishments serving American sailors, each with a coterie of bar girls. The girls served drinks and were available for sex. Five pesos ($2.50 American) was the going rate for a sailor to enjoy a sexual short-time with a bar girl. If he stayed the night, it would cost more.

And sailors coming to the P.I. from stateside duty were captivated by the Filipino bar girls, especially when compared with American prostitutes. American hookers treated sailors like all johns, with little feeling, if not contempt—men to be used. Their pimps forbade them to kiss a john, and the sex act was something to get over as quickly as possible.

Filipino bar girls, on the other hand, did not have pimps controlling their lives. They seemed free of the anger and destructive low self-esteem so common with American prostitutes; the emotional baggage carried over from a life growing up in broken homes often with sexual abuse and violence. Whether from professional pride or cultural tradition, or both, bar girls tried hard to please the sailors. Some enjoyed the sex act, kissed, had orgasms, and fell in love with sailors. With no children to complicate the relationship, young sailors sometimes fell in love with bar girls—women who treated them as special and tried in every way to please them—and did not want to leave the P.I.

The Philippine Islands at this time was in a golden age of sexual promiscuity. It was well before the scourge of acquired immune deficiency syndrome (AIDS). One never heard of genital herpes or Chlamydia infections. The Navy handed out condoms to the sailors at the gate when they went out on liberty, but not many used them. It was this attitude—not to use condoms—that got me into an emotional quandary. Rosie was pregnant and was thinking of keeping the baby.

Since we were together, Rosie had missed her period several times. When that happened she went to a Filipino physician in Cavite and got quinine, a drug obtained from the bark of the cinchona tree and used in treating malaria. Quinine, though, was toxic and it was this quality that tended to induce abortion. When Rosie took quinine it wasn't long and she miscarried.

Before, when Rosie missed her period, she went ahead and got the quinine and took it without much discussion with me, except to say she wouldn't be feeling well for a while. It was just one of those unpleasant facts that came with being a bar girl. This time things would be different.

We had gone into town one evening and seen the film "From Here to Eternity," a wonderful movie of army life in Hawaii just before the attack on Pearl Harbor by the Japanese. I was captivated by the drama and the similarities with my life in the P.I. and couldn't stop talking about it. We stopped at Mom's and after the first beer I called for a glass of fiery Tanduay rum.

We danced, our bodies pressed close, to the ballad "Harbor Lights," the lyrics about a young man leaving his girlfriend and shipping out during war time. The excitement of the film, the liquor, Rosie's body, the music, and the fact I would be leaving Rosie in less than two months got me near to tears.

When we got home, I took Rosie in my arms and kissed her deeply, and told her how much I loved her. I wanted her, passionately, desperately. I was hard, so erect my cock hurt. When I stripped, my skivvie shorts were soaked with precoital seminal fluid. We made love as if it would be the last time.

After, as we held each other, Rosie turned to me. "Jake," she whispered, brushing her fingers across my chest, "I'm pregnant."

"Oh," I said, leaning over and propping myself up on an elbow. "Have you taken the quinine?"

"No." She searched my eyes. "I have no blood for two months now."

I grew alarmed. "Why have you waited? You know the longer you wait the sicker you'll be." I was irritated. "Tomorrow we'll go and get the quinine, and you take it."

"I not take quinine." She touched my hair, smoothing it back. "I want baby—your baby."

Oh God, I thought, not this.

I sat up and took Rosie's hand. "Honey, it just won't work. I'm going back to the States. How will you live? You won't be able to work and take care of the baby. Look at Marie . . . and what she went through.

Sure she got lucky with the rich Filipino businessman. But when her looks go, he'll dump her, that's for sure—then what?"

Rosie touched my face. "Maybe you send money. Come back P.I. when you get out of the Navy."

"And what would I do here? What job could I get? Besides, I promised my parents I would work on the farm when I got out of the Navy."

"Maybe you send money for me and baby . . . come back . . . maybe some day."

Yes, I thought, I could send money. But a child needs a father. Sending money just wouldn't be good enough. Where I came from if a man got a woman pregnant, he married her. It was so common an occurrence that a favorite parlor game was to count the days between a marriage and the baby's birth, chuckling if it was less than nine months—which it often was. My parents were married in December and I was born six months later in May. No disgrace.

This code of conduct was crudely stated by a young hired man of my father's who bragged to me he was having sex with two girlfriends and liked them both. When I asked which one he would marry, he said with a laugh, "The first one I knock up."

My mind raced, thoughts in turmoil. I couldn't

marry Rosie, not here in the Philippines. The Navy would never approve. And if I waited until I was discharged, 14 months from now, came back to the P.I. and married her, and took her back to Willow Creek, that wouldn't work either.

Willow Creek was a small insular town of inbred second-generation German and Czech immigrants, some of whom considered English as a second language. The food was prepared from old Eastern European recipes with beef and potatoes the main ingredients. Their attitude about sex, in contrast to Rosie's, was narrow, cold and unyielding, like the ice and snow that covered the ground half of the year. On top of that, there were ex-servicemen in town that had served in the Philippine Islands. It wouldn't take them long to guess Rosie's background, and the word would be out in no time. No. For Rosie, a dark-skinned, uneducated (I had never seen her read or write) bar girl, daughter of poor tenant rice farmers, the hurdles were set too high for her to overcome.

Silent, I continued thinking. When I didn't respond, Rosie asked, her eyes pleading, "You say you love me. Don't you want baby?"

I held Rosie's face in my hands, kissed her lips. My heart was filled with love. "Oh, sweetheart, I love you so," I whispered. But I couldn't say no, and I couldn't say yes. Helplessly, I moaned, "What will we do?"

Along with Rosie's pregnancy, I had other worries. My transfer back to the States was coming up, and I had not received my orders. There were questions: When would I leave and how, and where would I be stationed?

My two-year tour of duty was up the middle of August, but there could be delays. About 25 men, over 40 percent of our complement, would be leaving between June and September—the height of the typhoon season, putting a severe strain on the decimated staff. In anticipation, our commander had reduced our duty sections from five to four. Yet, if push came to shove, some of us could be held back a month or more.

Now that I was a petty officer second class, there was a chance I could fly back to the States, a quick return compared to the three weeks by ship.

And where stationed? Most of the fellows rotating back for state-side duty were assigned billets on the West Coast. Three of the most important weather centrals were in San Diego, San Francisco, and Seattle. I was hoping for Seattle as I had never been there.

While I was waiting for my orders, a remarkable celestial phenomenon occurred: a total solar eclipse. As meteorologists, we knew it was coming and we were excited. The eclipse completely hid the sun at 12:20 on June 21, 1955. That day the sky was clear and the sun shown bright, and then it became as dark as night. We could see two stars. It was eerie. When it was completely dark, quite a few of the natives, who didn't know it was going to happen, were a little shook up. The eclipse lasted about seven minutes. Chickens must have gone to roost in the dark. When the sun emerged, the roosters started crowing.

As my two-year tour of duty was coming to an end, I thought about the weather we had seen in the Philippine Islands. Typhoons were the one weather phenomenon we feared the most. Although some had struck in FWC's area of responsibility, the vast southeast Pacific, none had hit Sangley Point; we had been spared their lash.

Yet there was one weather-related disaster that had hit, one we at FWC could not have forecast and that caused widespread damage, leaving 432 dead. An earthquake hit the island of Mindanao, the second major island in the Philippine chain, some 400 miles south of our island of Luzon. It got considerable press in the U.S. and my parents, concerned, wrote requesting details. In a letter, I reassured my parents that we didn't feel a thing in Northern Luzon. "One thing about these islands—if something happens on one of the islands, particularly an earthquake, the other islands don't feel anything."

Finally, my orders came in. There would be four or five of us leaving together by ship on or about August 13th. Tom Madsen, my shipmate at Lakehurst who came with me to Sangley, was one of them. They were excited, happy to be going back to the States. Everyone was asking us how it felt to be going home. I put on a happy face, but I was torn up inside. Rosie was pregnant and hadn't yet taken action to get an abortion. And I would be leaving her—that was the hard part. How could you explain to your shipmates you were in love with a bar girl, that you didn't want to leave the P.I. because of her. They would have laughed and said, "Get over it. Hell, she's just a whore, a piece of ass until you get back to God's country."

August came, and with it the rainy season. It was raining just about every day, just like it was two years before when I came to the Philippine Islands. With the weather so bad, many of the off-duty guys had card games going in the hut. At night, some came to the FWC office to catch baseball games from the States on the short wave radio or hang out at the EM Club. I was spending every free moment with Rosie, trying not to think about the last day I'd be with her.

Then it came to my last watch—a mid-watch—five days before I would board the *Barett*, a MSTS transport ship that would take me back to the States. Guys were slapping me on the back and asking my opinion on how it felt to be putting in my last watch for the good old FWC. Don Walker, my pal, was still trying to talk me into enrolling with him at the University in Mexico City on the G.I. Bill after our discharge from the Navy. He thought we could live "high on the hog" with American dollars in Mexico—get a college degree and raise a little hell with the Mexican girls. I think he added the part about Mexican girls to clinch his argument with me. Yet in my heart, that was the last thing I was thinking about.

Now that I was off the duty roster, I was a transient. Time to get my affairs in order, pack my gear. In two days I would board the *Barett* as part of an advance party, getting things ready for dependents (women and children of naval personnel) coming on board on August 12th.

It was a bittersweet time for Rosie and me. Once on the *Barett*, I might not see her again. The last two days were lovemaking and tears and hushed discussion.

A BITTERSWEET TIME

We fantasized about Rosie's pregnancy—the baby a love child. We dreamed, alternating between tears and laughter: Would the baby be a boy or girl, brown eyes or blue, tall or short (my grandfather was 6 foot 4)? Funny things: have a squinty look with eyes partly closed, like its father, have a good figure like its mother, grow up to be a good dancer like its parents . . . ?

Yet, in the end we knew, reality forced the conclusion—there would be no baby. Rosie would have to get an abortion. For what chance would the child of a bar girl have? The poverty of its life, the discrimination, the lack of opportunity for a decent education or job in a country where power, position, and family connections meant everything.

And without a father. I would not be coming back to the Philippines. I could send money, but I could not promise how much and for how long. And for Rosie, how could she raise the child and continue as a bar girl, the only work she knew and could aspire to with her lack of education and family connections.

Rosie understood. She had seen many love children born to bar girls and sailors. They ended in heartache for everyone. She agreed to have the abortion. I gave her all the money I could spare—enough for the abortion plus a couple of months' living expenses so she wouldn't have to go right back to the bars.

The last night together we went to Mom's Place, for old times sake. I thought of the first day I met her. There was a sailor and his girlfriend at Mom's, clinging to each other, in tears. They had been together for a year, and he was leaving. "How sad," Rosie had said then. "He goes back to the States in two days and she cries." Rosie told Mary, "It better not to fall in love with sailor." How ironic, I thought, for here we were, Rosie and I, in the same situation.

When we came home, before going to bed, I set the alarm clock for 0600 in the morning. I had to make muster at 0800 at the Administration Building before going aboard the *Barett*. Then we would steam the eight miles to Manila and tie up at one of the piers—I heard it would be Pier 15—to take on the naval dependents. Some time the next day we would leave for Guam on our way to the States. At least that was the plan.

We didn't sleep much that night. Rosie stayed curled in my arms, her head snuggled against my chest. My hand touched her stomach, slightly swollen now. I could feel her heart beat—or was it two beating hearts?

At first light we got up and showered. Rosie made coffee. I shook off the idea of food, I couldn't eat. We got dressed and I took one last look around, the bedroom, the kitchen, fixing in my mind the house that had been our home for almost two years.

We left the house and started walking back to the base, Rosie's hand in mine, hardly talking for fear of breaking down. It was cool, the sky overcast with rain clouds hanging heavy. At the main gate we stood for awhile as the Filipino contract workers, men and women, filed past the marine guard showing their identification cards and onto the base to begin the new day.

Then it was time. I hesitated. Would this be the last time I would see Rosie. Once through the gate, my liberty was over. There was no coming back out. Yet there was a chance. The *Barett* was to take us aboard this morning, then steam to Manila and tie up at Pier 15, one of many piers along that busy wharf, where it would take on military personnel and their dependents. We would be there until shipping out sometime the next day. I had discussed it with Rosie last night at Mom's, and we had come up with a plan. When I went through the gate, she would take the Cavite bus to Manila and wait for the *Barett* at Pier 15.

Finally, I could wait no longer. I took Rosie in my arms. There were tears in her eyes. "I love you so much," she whispered, her arms around my neck.

I brushed Rosie's hair back, took her face in my

hands and kissed her. "I love you too," I said, fighting back my own tears, trying to be a "man."

I turned and went through the gate and got on one of the dull grey navy buses that circled the base. As the bus pulled out, I looked back. Rosie was standing next to a palm tree near the gate, watching the bus leave.

I see her still, after all these years, as if looking at a photograph. Her curly black hair, a light breeze fluffing it around her shoulders, a soft blue dress, plain, the palm tree and a jeepney behind her.

Rosie, Rosie. I miss you so. Why did it have to happen? We had it all planned out—to be together again. God, if there is a God, why were you so cruel?

I made muster and we were told the *Barett* had yet to arrive, engine trouble or something. We could leave administration, but had to check back every two hours. I went back to the hut, stowed all my gear in my sea bag, and dropped it off at the Administration Building. Still no *Barett*. Now I was worried. Rosie would soon be waiting in Manila at Pier 15.

I walked over to the Fleet Weather Central to say some last goodbyes. I shook hands all around. There wasn't much to say. I had a handful of post cards with scenes of the Philippine Islands. I went into the conference room and used one of the ink pens to scratch out brief notes to family and friends.

While penning a card to Mom and Dad, I lost it. I was writing that "as much as I want to be home and back in the States, it is hard leaving the friends I have made out here." The "friends" meant Rosie. At that point I could not hold back. Tears started flowing, one dropping on the card and smearing several words. I didn't want my shipmates to see me like that. I hurried out of the office and into the head, hid myself in one of the stalls and sobbed uncontrollably. I hadn't cried like that since a little child. If my mind hadn't told me, my heart did. I would miss Rosie terribly.

The *Barett* finally arrived, two days late. We went aboard and then tied up at another pier in Manila, not Pier 15. Frantically, I looked for Rosie, praying somehow she would be at dockside. She wasn't. How could she know the *Barett* was late. She probably stayed a day or two at Pier 15, then gave up, thinking we had sailed straight from Sangley Point.

I was hurting, but I could not dwell on my feelings. I was a second class petty officer and had responsibilities. I had to go over the *Barett's* register of sailors in transit and set up a 24-hour watch list for security within the dependents' quarters. Uniformed guards had to be posted on four-hour shifts around the clock to ensure the safety and security of the wives and children. This was "officer country" where no sailor was allowed unless on official duty.

As we left Manila, I leaned over the railing and watched the familiar harbor pass by: the sunken ships, the fishing boats. Next came Sangley Point and I strained to see the little sandy beach where Rosie and I often went swimming. I watched until Sangley disappeared from sight. We steamed past Corregidor Island and out into the vast South China Sea. In Honolulu, Hawaii there is a custom that on leaving if you threw a flowered lei into the water, the direction it floats will tell you if you will ever come back. I wondered if in my life I would ever see the Philippine Islands again.

I thought about my experiences in these islands: the people, the culture, food, the land, the bar girls—Rosie. How much I had learned about life, about myself. How could I ever forget?

CHAPTER 22

Stateside and Heartache

When I wasn't checking guard posts, I was writing letters. Rosie said she would leave Cavite City when I left and go to the Greenland Nite Club in Olongapo near the Subic Bay Naval Station. I wrote, tried to explain the *Barett* delay and why we were not at Pier 15. I poured out my heart and told her how much I loved her, cared for her, missed her—things I had not told her when I was with her. I told her where I would be stationed and to write me. Although I did not know Rosie to read or write, there were bar girls that could and would help her.

When we docked in the States I took leave and traveled by train back to Minnesota. My parents met me at the station in Minneapolis. They hadn't seen me in nearly three years. There were hugs all around.

My father grabbed my arms, stepped back, and looked me over. "For all that paperwork you've been doing, you didn't get fat," he smiled. "You look fit enough to do farm work right now."

I grinned. "I got enough exercise swimming in the ocean."

Mom gave me a long look, too. "You look good, Jake. You filled out some. The navy food did right by you." She was close. I was five feet ten inches and staying around 165 pounds. I didn't tell her, but I thought it was the Filipino food: fish, rice, pansit, and fresh fruits that kept me lean, rather than the navy chow—heavy on white bread and potatoes ladled with butter.

We drove south to Willow Creek. It hadn't changed, but I had. The town didn't have the feel of "home" and neither did the farm. Had I really gone Asiatic? Or was it simply Rosie, and the terrible longing for her that made me feel indifferent to the place where I grew up.

I tried to be my old self. I put on a big smile for Pastor Getz and my friends in church. Although on leave, I went right to work on the farm with Dad and tried to get excited about my future as a farmer. It wasn't happening. Well, I thought, it's going to take some time. I'll have to keep at it.

When my leave was up, I drove to my new duty station: Sand Point Naval Air Station in Seattle, Washington. I'd had a few dollars saved, and a friend in Willow Creek sold me his 1951 Chevrolet for a good price.

I got into Seattle and checked the city map. The naval station was on Sand Point, a peninsula that jutted into Lake Washington in North Seattle. For years it had served as an air base, aviation training center, and aircraft repair depot for the U.S. Navy. After the Korean War ended, its role was reduced, and when I arrived its primary function was as a Naval Reserve training base.

I drove to the base, and the guard at the gate pointed out the Fleet Weather Central. I gave my orders to the first class yeoman handling personnel at the FWC and wandered over to introduce myself to the heavy-set section leader leaning over a plotting map.

"It rains a lot but you won't have to worry about typhoons," he grinned, shaking my hand. He poured me a cup of coffee and walked me up to the observation deck. It was a sunny day and the section leader pointed to the southeast and a stunning snow-capped mountain. "That is Mount Rainier. It's 60 miles away, and you don't often see it, rainy and cloudy as it is so often here."

The section leader showed me around the FWC, smaller than at Sangley Point, and at lunch time took me to the mess hall. I spent the rest of the afternoon getting checked out and at the end of the day watch, followed two of my new shipmates to our "digs," a two-story barracks. Our outfit was lodged on the second floor.

As I carried my sea bag in to find a bunk, I was surrounded by the usual excited and profane talk of sailors getting ready to hit the beach. "Hey asshole," said one sailor on a top bunk to his shipmate on the bottom bunk, "your fart sack looks like you shit on it"—a pause for effect—"then rolled in it." He got laughs all around. But the guy on the bottom bunk rejoined. "What you talkin' about, jerk-off?" he pointed to the top-bunk guy's scuffed shoes, "look at your shoes—dirty as hell." Then a pause. "You know a guy that won't shine his shoes, don't wipe his ass." Again laughs all around.

This kind of swabbie banter usually got my spirits up, but I couldn't shake a depressive mood. I found an unoccupied bottom bunk and tossed my sea bag on it, then went out to the car and brought in the suitcase with my civvies, which I unpacked and stowed in the metal lockers. This was my new home.

At the FWC, I was assigned to a section and soon fell into a dreary routine. I struggled to focus on work. Yet my mind and heart was still back in the P.I. with Rosie. I hadn't yet received a reply to my letters and was desperate to hear from her. The first thing I did when I reported aboard at Sand Point was to check with personnel to see if there were any letters waiting for me. There were none. Each day at mail call I prayed for something from Rosie.

Then one day the office yeoman hustled over to me at the Teletype machine, wrapped an arm over my shoulder, and handed me a letter. "It's Air Mail, Special Delivery from the Philippine Islands," he grinned. "My guess is it's the one you've been waiting for."

It was. It was from Rosie. My hands trembled. I wanted so much to read it, but not in the office. I waited until the watch was over and took it back to the barracks. When no one was around, I laid on my bunk and gently opened the little envelope with assorted multicolored stamps of the Republic of the Philippines covering the back. My eyes welled as I unfolded the single, handwritten page and silently mouthed each word.
Greenland Nite Club
Olongapo, Zambalas
Nov. 10, 1955

Dear Jake,
I received all your letters; the first one was not answered because I lost the adress you gave me. The latest one I just received it two weeks ago and you can just imagine how I feel

upon taking hold of it and read those important parts I really longed from you.

I remember when you left and you told me to see you in Pier 15. I was there just when you told me to do so but you were not there. So I went to my home province and waited for you to write me at least. However, I could not just stay there with nothing to do, so I resort to go back to work and here I am back to Greenland again. I then hope to hear from you in this adress so soon.

Well, you're too far and all what I could say is don't forget me just as how I do remember you all the time. This picture of your's can console me sometimes. I have it always with me wherever I go. Do you dream of comming back to the P.I. I hope so I glad to meet you by then. I shall pray for your return.

I must close now, & don't forget to write me as soon as possible.

Yours,
Rosie

    I reread the letter and smiled through tears at the misspellings and awkward Filipino phrasing of sentences. Although someone had written the letter for Rosie, those were her words.

For a moment I was overcome by a desperate physical longing for Rosie. My chest felt constricted. I had trouble breathing. I got up and paced the deck. There are songs written about heartache, but I always thought it was a figure of speech. Yet, I had a pain just under my breastbone.

I suffered a flight of fancy. I imagined somehow flying like a bird over the ocean to be at Rosie's side. Several years later when Bobby Darin came out with the song "Beyond the Sea" the lyrics captured exactly how I felt:

> *Somewhere, beyond the sea*
> *Somewhere waiting for me,*
> *My lover stands on golden sand . . .*

Now, some 37 years later, whenever I hear "Beyond the Sea" on one of those golden oldie stations, I feel the same old yearning.

I wrote to Rosie at the Greenland Nite Club with concern about the abortion, her health, and the work at the club. Her response broke my heart: "I went to the doctor like you told me, Jake. The doctor, he took our baby—a baby girl. The baby had brown hair like you, Jake. Our baby was gone. I cry so hard I got sick. I never had a baby before. Oh, Jake, I miss you so much."

Oh Rosie, I thought, why did I leave you? My mind reeled, broke from reality, lurched from one wild idea to another: I should never have left the P.I. I should have gone AWOL from Sangley Point, deserted the Navy, and taken Rosie to her home province. She could have had the baby there—with her parents. We could have married. I could have found a job, maybe with an American company in Manila or in the provinces. Something would have turned up.

Then I came down to earth. None of these ideas would work. Desertion from the Navy was a terrible offense. Two years in prison was not uncommon. And how would that go over with my parents, Pastor Getz, and my friends at St. John Lutheran church.

And the Navy would get me. The AFP would talk to the bar girls. There would be someone—Linda for instance—who didn't like Rosie, who would give her up, tell where her home province was. The Filipino police would be alerted to keep an eye out for me. And where would I hide? A white man with light brown hair and blue eyes. And how many jobs were there in the P.I. for weather observers?

No, I had done the rational thing. But was it the right thing? Isn't love suppose to conquer all?

More letters came. Rosie said there was much work at the club and she had been busy. If she was busy, I thought, there were other men, sailors. I felt a stab of jealousy. God, I wished I was there. Then I thought of Ted Cole, my shipmate at Sangley and his girlfriend Sally. He had asked me to move in with Sally and take care of her. Ted thought I would treat her right. Should I have sought a shipmate to move in with Rosie? Just the thought tore my guts. Yet if I truly loved her . . .

And what would Rosie do when she was too old to attract sailors for sex: when her teeth went bad, her breasts sagged, and her face wrinkled. She was nearly 30 now and looked years older. What would she do when she couldn't work in the bars. She would have to take any job to put food in her mouth. I remembered old bar girls who washed clothes and cleaned rooms for young bar girls and begged for handouts from relatives and old friends.

As our correspondence continued, Rosie's letters tore me apart, drove me into despair. She said she longed for me, to feel my arms around her, to make love to her. She had dreams about me. One night, she wrote, she was jarred awake when she heard a knock on the door, opened it, and there I was. In her dream I said the Navy had sent me back to Sangley for the rest of my 20-year hitch, after which I would get a big pension and would retire in Cavite City—and we would be together for all time. We would make babies.

It was all crazy talk. The Navy limited sailors to two-year stints at duty stations. The days of the old Asiatic Fleet when a sailor could spend his 20- or 30-year hitch in the Pacific, retire, marry a Chinese or Filipino girl, and open a bar in Shanghai or Manila were long gone.

As the months passed, more time passed between letters. As I knew, and Rosie began to realize, our life together was over. Writing about the good times we had together grew ever painful and scribbling on about our current lives brought further anguish. The heartache was too great to bear. In time the letters stopped.

Without Rosie, though, there was a hole in my heart, a need for the love and sex that she had given me. I was like a junkie in need of a drug. I had gotten hooked on Rosie, her body next to mine, her love. If it could not be Rosie, then there had to be someone else. I was frantic to find a woman to fill that need.

CHAPTER 23

Looking for Love in All the Wrong Places

Seattle was a major seaport on the Pacific Coast. Ocean-going ships poured through the Strait of Juan de Fuca, south to Puget Sound, and into Elliot Bay and Seattle's busy piers and docks. The U.S. Navy had several bases in the area: the Puget Sound Naval Shipyard at Bremerton, Whidbey Island Naval Air Base, and Sand Point. Fleet ships brought sailors into and out of these bases, and their liberty boats carried the boys into Seattle and its beer halls and bars. It was in these joints, the hangouts of sailors, that I sought love, perhaps in all the wrong places.

Two favorite hangouts of Navy sailors was the Drift Inn and the Roll Inn in downtown Seattle. At night, strolling off the street into the Drift Inn, you were hit by the sound of small-combo music, shouts and laughter, and the smell of cigarette smoke and tap beer. On entering, you had to sidle past a line of sailors bellied up to a long narrow bar. Behind the bar on the wall hung nautical gear: fish netting, lifebuoys, knotted ropes and chains. At the end of the bar was a larger room with booths and a small dance floor. At the end of the dance floor and well above the booths was a balcony on which played a three-piece band: piano, saxophone, and drums. Sailors and the girls that followed the fleet, filled the booths and waitresses scurried back and forth with trays of pitchers and glasses of beer. The dance floor was filled with swinging sailors and girls.

To meet girls at the Drift Inn, it helped to be a good dancer. The popular dance at the time was the Lindy Hop and, specifically in Seattle, the "West Coast Lindy." It was a new dance to me, but I liked the smooth, sensual swing steps and took a few lessons at a local dance studio. There were many variations to the dance, different steps and ways in which to twirl your partner, and soon I got good at it. Now with a car and some skill on the dance floor, the Drift Inn became a familiar haunt.

The girls, or more accurately the women, who frequented the Drift Inn were not saints, desperately protecting their virginity. For most, that barrier had been breached years before and was but a distant memory. Many of the women were divorced, or married to sailors on six-month cruises, or were working gals out for a good time. For the sailors the Drift Inn was a great pick-up joint. The ambience of the place reeked of illicit sex. In fact, at closing time, the piano player, a lusty middle-aged woman, sang a signature ballad that ended with the suggestive lyrics: "It's one o'clock motel time." Time for a sailor to take his newfound ladylove to the nearest motel for the night.

With wheels and some skill on the dance floor, I was spending most free nights at the Drift Inn and having a good time. The women liked to dance and it was an easy way to get to know them. One woman in particular, Fran, loved to do the slow Lindy, and she was very good. When we danced she anticipated my every move, and together we drew admiring glances. Soon we were a twosome, sharing the same booth and exchanging our life histories.

In her early 30s, Fran was a big woman, about 5 foot 7 inches and carried about 145 pounds on a solid frame. She had light brown hair, good skin, and dressed in fashion. She was a clerk in the women's department of a large, downtown department store and had an apartment on Queen Ann Hill. She didn't wear a wedding ring, and I assumed she was single.

Fran was easy to be with, and soon I asked her out for dinner and a movie. Later, at her apartment, she invited me in for a drink. I ended up spending the night. In the morning, as I pulled on my clothes, I noticed a wedding ring on the bureau of her bedroom. I asked her about it.

"Well, I'm married," she said casually, a slight smile on her face, "but I don't like to wear the ring when I'm out on the town. My husband is a sailor and won't be back for four months. A person gets lonely."

Over coffee and toast, Fran filled me in. Her husband was a first class quartermaster on a cruiser out on a six-month cruise to the Orient: Japan, Guam, and the Philippines. He had one year left on a 20-year hitch before he could retire. They'd been married for two years. This was her second marriage, she said, the first one to an "abusive son-of-a-bitch," then added, "pardon my French," with a look that suggested she was too refined to use that swear word casually.

I didn't like the idea of sleeping with a married woman, but it grew easy to rationalize away with thoughts such as: Well, if she wasn't sleeping with me, it would be someone else, what harm would it do, her husband won't know and she doesn't care . . .

As time went on it became apparent that Fran wasn't looking for some hot romance. She liked to go out, dance, have some drinks and a laugh or two. I was as good as any guy to provide that. And sex wasn't a big thing for her. She was deathly afraid of getting pregnant. Abortion was illegal and prevention was the only alternative. She used a diaphragm and insisted I use a condom too. On our first night she handed me a Trojan and said "You can't take chances. These damn diaphragms aren't foolproof."

Besides going to the Drift Inn, we liked the Roll Inn tavern up on 10th or 11th Avenue. It was like the Drift Inn, but the music was from a juke box. The big hits there were Frank Sinatra's "Learnin' the Blues," and "Jealous Lover."

Then one morning a few months later in Fran's apartment, as she was dressing to go to work, she turned to me and casually announced, "Jake, we can't see each other any more. Dan's ship is due in two weeks, and I don't want him to know about us."

I knew this was coming, eventually, Fran's husband coming back, but Fran's lack of feeling as she said it surprised me. I was at the kitchen table nursing a cup of coffee when it came. I pushed my coffee aside. "You mean this is it, no more dancing, no contact of any kind?"

"Nothing against you," she said, smoothing on lipstick, "but I get a navy allotment check regularly, and when Dan retires we can live real nice on his navy pension. You understand, don't you?"

"Sure," I said. "I don't blame you. A woman's got to look out for herself."

There wasn't much said after that. I offered to drop her off at work. When we pulled up at the store entrance, Fran reached over and gave me a hug. "It's been fun," she said. "Take care of yourself."

"Sure," I said. "I hope it'll be clear skies and smooth sailing for you."

Fran got out of the car, and at the door, turned, waved, and blew me a kiss. That was it. I was glad she ended it. Other than dancing, we had nothing going for us. For Fran, it seemed, making love was an obligation to repay me for taking her out.

So here I was, cast adrift again. And just as lonely as I was on the first day I came to Sand Point. I was having trouble making the adjustment from Filipino bar girls to American women. I was looking for Rosie in a sea of white faces. I couldn't free myself of her memory.

And, on top of that, I was troubled with guilt. I felt the first stirrings while still in the P.I. in May of 1955, when Pastor Getz of St. John Lutheran Church sent me a questionnaire requesting the dates of communion I had taken during the past year. I had not gone to communion once. Then, back in Willow Creek on leave, I resumed my usual every Sunday attendance. Friends of mine were getting married to local girls, nice girls. Now in Seattle, I was looking for a woman of easy virtue, someone to sleep with.

It got me thinking. Maybe I should clean up my act, date a "good girl," one I could marry. Ironically, the chance came at the Drift Inn.

The piano player and vocalist, Clara, had an 18-year-old daughter that on occasion, usually a Friday or Saturday night, would come downtown with her mother. While Clara did her thing at the Drift Inn, her daughter, Louise, would take in a movie and maybe have a soda or banana split afterward. That done, Louise would come to the Drift Inn, climb the backstairs to the balcony, and take a chair by her Mom. She'd listen to the music and take furtive glances at the revelry on the dance floor below. Sometimes she would bring a school book to busy herself until closing time when she would go home with Clara.

If I'd seen Louise walking down the street, I would not have paid any attention, just another teenage girl. But when I first saw her walk into the Drift Inn, wearing white anklets and penny loafers and a dress that could be a uniform in a Catholic girls' school, I was struck by the contrast. What was she doing here?

My interest piqued, I asked one of the waitresses. "Yeah; that's Clara's daughter, nice kid though, just out of high school. She can't hang around the bar, not old enough to drink, has to stay in the balcony."

"Think she'd go out with a sailor?" I asked, the possibility floating around in my head.

"Who knows, but you'd have to get past Clara. She's like a mother bear when it comes to Louise."

I looked forward to seeing Louise. When she came to the Drift Inn, I'd look up at the balcony and hope to catch her glance. Sometimes on breaks, she would go out and get coffee and a sandwich for Clara. She seemed shy, never talked to the bartenders and hardly glanced at the sailors. I wanted to know her, but first I had to know Clara.

On breaks, Clara had a habit of working the booths. She would stop here and there, cracking a joke, laughing. She saw it as part of her job. When she came by my booth, I always said something, commented on the music, requested a song, anything. Then one night at closing, a night when Louise was not there, I went up to Clara as she was getting ready to leave. She was standing next to the piano, slipping on her coat. The other musicians, two guys on sax and drums, were laughing and heading down the back steps to the bar for a nightcap.

After some lame questions about music, I got right into it. "I'm stationed out at Sand Point. I come here a lot. I see your daughter . . . I was wondering . . ."

Clara stopped, put her purse down, and cut me off in mid-sentence, "You were wondering what?"

"Your daughter Louise. I was wondering if I could ask her for a date?" This wasn't going to be easy, I could tell.

There was strained silence, then, "Listen, I don't want my daughter going out with sailors. She's just out of high school. Plans to go into nurses' training in the fall, make something of herself."

"Well, I'm not a career guy. I'm getting out of the Navy in September. I'm going to work with my parents on the farm. I'm not after what you think."

"Yeah, I know what you guys say. I wasn't born yesterday." Clara leaned against the piano, gave me the once over. "I see you here a lot, see you dancing. Pretty chummy with the same woman—and she's no kid."

"That was just dancing," I lied. "She's married and her husband just got back from a cruise."

Clara thought awhile, adjusted her coat and gave

me a long look. "What's your name?"

"Jake. Jake Becker."

"Listen, Jake, I'm tired. It's been a long day. I've got to get home." She turned and over her shoulder said, "Let me think about it."

Well, I thought, at least she asked for my name. It wasn't a complete brush off.

In the days that followed, I continued my quest to soften up Clara. To date Louise became close to an obsession. Somehow, I thought, this might turn my life around, get me on the track of Christian righteousness. I frequented the Drift Inn, hoping to charm Clara into thinking I was a decent human being.

Sometimes, on slow nights, I got a booth to myself. When the band was on break, I would wave Clara over to sit with me. I polished my persona: a Sunday school teacher, sang in the church choir, eventually would take over my parent's farm. She shared her life story, said she had married a sailor and was now divorced.

"The bastard left me after 15 years," she said frowning, "and me with a five-year-old child, Louise, and no job. Yeah, dumped me for a floozy he met in Hawaii while on a navy cruise." I offered her a cigarette and watched as she drew deeply on the Chesterfield.

She continued, "And now this chippy's got his pension and I'm out in the cold. It's a damn good thing I could play a piano and sing a little. It puts food on the table."

In time we got on. I listened to her problems and she listened to mine. Soon it was Clara and Jake. Then one night Louise stopped by our booth with coffee for her Mom. I motioned for her to sit. While she slid in next to Clara, I ordered a soda for her. While Louise sipped the nonalcoholic drink with downcast eyes, I asked her about her plans for nurses' training. Clara sat quiet and watched our talk. I supposed she was gauging the chemistry between us.

"I've always wanted to be a nurse," said Louise, her soft brown hair tumbling around her shoulders. "I want to help people." She looked into my eyes, "I think I would be good."

We talked a few minutes, she asked how I liked the Navy. When the break was over, Louise went back to the balcony with Clara. There was something about this girl I liked. Perhaps it was the purity, the simplicity that was so refreshing. Just the fact she wanted to be a nurse suggested she had a warm heart, would be a good wife and mother. That she was a plain Jane as far as looks were concerned should not stop me from going further with this relationship. Sex wasn't everything.

I asked Clara for their home telephone number. I got it and a stern warning. "You treat my little girl right, you hear?"

"I'll be good, Clara," I promised.

I called Louise and made a date to take her to a Saturday night movie when she came downtown with her mother. That night I met Louise at the Drift Inn. I let her pick out the movie. We ended up seeing a teenage flick, starring someone like Mickey Rooney or Tab Hunter. After the movie, we went to a high school hangout for hamburgers and cokes. She said she had a great time. I took her back to the Drift Inn and drove back to the base. The night was over. I never held her hand.

We went out several more times, more bobby-soxer films, ice cream and soda. I was careful not to get fresh, do anything to frighten her. She was delighted. She loved the movies, giggled at the jokes, and teared up when the boy and girl got into a fight. I was bored silly. Yes, I thought, she is a nice girl—but good God!

Then maybe it was me. What had happened to me in the Philippine Islands! Had I become an animal, a saliva-dripping beast that needed wild passionate sex to satisfy its carnal needs.

It all ended one Sunday afternoon. Louise wanted to go roller skating; it was her passion she said. I told her I had never skated before. "It's easy," she said, her eyes bright. "All my friends go. It's at the community center. They play music and we skate dance."

When we went to the community center, Louise saw two couples from her high school graduating class and waved them over. She introduced me as a friend of her mother. I was in civilian clothes so they did not know I was a sailor. Louise had white shoe skates. I rented clamp skates and tightened them on my shoes with a skate key. The music was playing and Louise dragged me out to skate with her friends. I stumbled, then wobbled like a drunk, hardly keeping on my feet. I was a regular clown, everybody stopped to watch. I got laughs all around. I pulled off my skates and said I'd watch. Total humiliation.

Later, we went to Clara's apartment. There was a great movie on television, Louise said. It was another young romance picture. We watched the movie and held hands. When the film got mushy, I reached over to put my arm around Louise. I thought I might try to steal a kiss. As my arm slipped around Louise's shoulders, she stiffened, fear coursed her face. She jumped up and ran to the kitchen. "I'll pop popcorn, okay?" We ate popcorn, hands at our sides, and watched the movie to the end. I thanked Louise and left for the base. I never saw her again. I hope she found a "good" guy.

I gave up on romance. Rather than hang out at the Drift Inn, a shipmate and I took in events at Seattle's municipal auditorium. We saw professional wrestling matches, Seattle's famous hydroplane boat races on Lake Washington, and, on one occasion, witnessed two giants of the big band era, Gene Krupa and Buddy Rich, in a battle of the drums.

When the weather was nice, my pal and I took a scenic drive from Seattle to Vancouver, British Columbia. One incident stays in my mind. We stopped in a tavern. It was clean with red and white tablecloths. There were a number of men, drinking and talking, but no women. I asked the bartender about it, and he said there were places in Vancouver just for men—and it was legal. It was a hell of a law as far as we were concerned. We left immediately.

In May of 1956, I got promoted to first class aerographer's mate and to section leader as well. And on top of that, I was made barracks supervisor over 40 white hats. I was accountable for more than myself now. With four months to go before my discharge, I found that I was pretty good as a supervisor. I treated the men as I would have wanted to be treated—the "golden rule." I had no discipline problems. Only one man caused me concern, and that was for what he was doing to himself, not his work.

 Dave was a thin man with black hair, a dark complexion, and a Roman nose that reflected his native American heritage. He did his work well enough, but he was a bundle of nerves. His self-medication of choice was vodka and gin, and four packs of Pall Malls a day. Watching him plot a weather map was painful. With a cigarette constantly smoldering between the fingers of his left hand, Dave would lean over his map in deep concentration, pressing down hard with his pencil to keep his writing hand steady, his weather symbols a tracing of quivering, dark heavy lines. Every minute or so, Dave would lean back in his chair and drag deeply on his cigarette two or three times, then back to work. Dave never seemed to carry matches or a lighter, he didn't have to—he lit a fresh cigarette from the butt-end of the last.

 I talked to Dave once or twice about cutting back on the cigs and booze, but he shook it off with a friendly smile and shrug of his shoulders. So be it, I thought.

 With the section running smooth and the weather mild with few surprises, work was easy. The hours dragged, especially the mid-watches, midnight to 0800 hours. To pass the time, I read books from the base library. One project was to read the complete volume of Sherlock Holmes short stories. I read most of them. Another diversion was music. The radio dial in the office was set for a constant rendition of the current top-40 songs. There was always someone mouthing the lyrics or whistling softly the current hot number. My taste centered around the sentimental ballads by songsters like Frank Sinatra, Tony Bennett, and Jo Stafford, and the vocal groups: the Ames Brothers and the Four Aces. The first time we heard Elvis Presley sing "Hound Dog," one guy said, "what the hell kind of music is that?" reflecting our general thinking. Rock n' roll was foreign to us, not at all romantic.

CHAPTER 24

Back to the Farm

A few weeks before my discharge, our skipper, Commander Paul T. Johnson, called me into his office. He had my service record in his hand. "You've done good work here, and you have a clean record. We would like you to reenlist, make the Navy a career." I thanked him, then told him of my promise to my parents to go back to the farm to help out. He nodded in understanding, shook my hand, and offered me "good luck."

A day or two later, I sat down with our office personnel man, a first class yeoman, to complete my discharge papers. He took one more shot at getting me to reenlist. He leaned over, his voice low, "You reenlist, we can give you three years in Japan, the Fleet Weather Central in Yokosuka." He leaned back and smiled. That was choice duty. I had put in for Japan at Lakehurst, but all the billets were gone before my chance came up. Other than the P.I., that was the best inducement to get me to ship over. "Thanks," I said, "but my mind is made up."

On September 7, 1956, I took my mustering-out pay of $300, a Good Conduct Medal, and walked out of the Fleet Weather Central office a free man. Two of my shipmates got their discharges the same day. Their homes were on the East Coast. Since I was the only one with a car, I asked them to join me, and we would share driving on a round-the-clock jaunt to Minneapolis. From there, they could take a bus or train east.

There would be one stop on the way, however: Walla Walla, the old mining town near the Blue Mountains of southeastern Washington State. In our hot hands was a perfume-laced Christmas card from the "Girls" of a well-known bordello there, inviting us to stop for a good time. For years our office had received a Christmas card from this house of ill repute, and always it was posted in a hallowed position on the office bulletin board for all to see and sniff. To stop and partake of their services was an honored tradition of the sailors of Sand Point whenever going east. To fail to stop would besmirch the memory of all those gallant gobs that had gone before.

It was well after midnight when we pulled off U.S. Highway 12 and into the darkened streets of Walla Walla. From the address we had and from descriptions by old salt shipmates, we had no trouble finding the bawdy house. On our knock, a small light above the door went on. A heavy-set woman in her fifties opened the door. "Can I help you boys?" she asked.

One of my pals slipped the Christmas card in her hand and said, "We're sailors from Sand Point Naval Air Station in Seattle. We'd like to use your services."

"Ah, yes," she smiled. "Good boys, all. It's a little late, but come in. I'll tell the girls you're here."

The madam led us into a living room that reminded me of pictures of Victorian whorehouses, all red and pink satin and velvet. We took seats in comfortable stuffed chairs and waited. Soon the madam came in trailed by five scantly clad women who sat, hands folded demurely, on a long couch across from us. "Take your pick, boys," said the madam brightly. "They're all good girls, guaranteed to suit your fancy."

We each made our selection and followed the girls up a flight of stairs to rooms on the second floor. My lady-of-the-evening walked me into a room with just the basics: bed, bureau, two chairs, a wash basin and towels. "What'll it be sailor?" she asked, as if she was a waitress taking a coffee order, "straight or around the world?"

"Straight," I answered, about as enthusiastic as she was.

Within 30 minutes I was back downstairs where my pals were waiting. We hit the road and, except for meals and toilet stops, kept rolling until we got to Minneapolis. I let them off and headed for home.

It was early evening when I pulled into Willow Creek. I drove down main street and past St. John Lutheran Church. My future loomed before my eyes. On Sunday I'd go to church with Mom and Dad. Everyone would shake my hand and welcome me home. Pastor Getz would greet me with his arm around my shoulders. He knew I wasn't going to college to study for the ministry; I'd written him several times about that. He was disappointed, but he had plans for me: teaching Sunday school, singing in the choir, and becoming a leader in the Men's Club.

I thought about these things, and I did not feel good. How could I teach 11 and 12-year-old kids about the Bible? Or sing hymns about the glory of Jesus Christ? Could I do that with my past and live with myself? If I could—then there is a name for a man like that—hypocrite.

I headed south on the gravel road to the farm. I had written my parents I'd be home this day or the next. As I neared the farm, I pulled off the road next to the driveway and turned off the key. It was getting dark, and there was no traffic. I rolled down the window. It was quiet, hardly a sound. A soft breeze blew over my face, carrying with it the rich earthy smells of the fields. I looked over to the barn. A light was burning and through an open door, I could see my father hunched over milking the cows—as he had done every morning and night for most of his life. In the house, the kitchen light was on. Mom was washing dishes after the evening meal—the unbroken routine.

I lingered, deep in thought. This was the farm—the home place—that Dad had promised Grandpa Fritz would stay in the family. I started the Chevy and drove slowly down the driveway to what would be my home for the rest of my life. Somehow, there was no joy in my heart.

Epilogue

2009

Jake's memoir ends there, but I can tell you the rest of the story.

When Jake and I got out of the Navy, we kept in touch, writing letters back and forth. He said he tried to make it on the farm, helped his father milk cows, and did all the usual farm chores—even helped his mother gather eggs and vegetables from the garden. But, he said it wasn't long until he was bored silly.

And it didn't go well for him at the Lutheran church either. His minister wanted him to start teaching Sunday school and sing in the choir right away. He begged off, saying he needed time to adjust to civilian life. He did join the church Men's Club, but all they talked about was broken toilets and mold in the basement. He said his mind went numb. I chuckled at that; mine would have too.

Jake started spending evenings at the American Legion Club in Willow Creek, drinking with the World War II and Korean veterans—and drinking more than he should. His folks were upset and his minister got on his case. There were words.

Jake pulled out, went to Iowa City and enrolled at the University of Iowa on the G.I. Bill. At the time, I was going to the University of Florida at Gainesville; I liked the warm weather. We never did make it to the university in Mexico City.

I didn't hear from Jake for about six months, then got a telephone call. He was so excited. He said he planned to go back to the Philippine Islands and be with Rosie. He'd started writing her and she couldn't wait. Along with taking a full course load at the university, he was working nights as a bartender at a saloon near the campus. He was sending Rosie money so she could quit her job as a bar girl at the Greenland Nite Club in Olongapo and move to Cavite City and live with her brother Carlos, now married and working as a jeepney mechanic.

I asked Jake about employment opportunities in the P.I. He said he had it all figured out. He'd go to Manila and find work with an American company there. By the end of the year, he would have completed some university courses and thought that would count for something.

Jake was crazy in love, that was for sure. I didn't

say much, just that I was happy for him. But I had a bad feeling; I just could not see it working out.

Then in June of 1957, I got a call from a bartender in the saloon where Jake worked. He got my number from Jake's employment application as the person to call in case of an emergency.

Jake, he said, was going to pieces. Jake had gotten a letter saying his girlfriend in the Philippine Islands had been killed in a jeepney accident. Jake was living alone in an apartment off campus, drinking heavily, and had quit coming to work.

I had an old junker at the time and drove through the night to Iowa City. The bartender friend and I went to Jake's apartment. He was passed out on the sofa, empty bottles of rum scattered about.

With the help of the university's health service, we got Jake into a veterans hospital. After a month or two in the hospital's psychiatric unit on medication, Jake was discharged.

Jake was never the same, but he straightened out enough to finish his bachelor's degree and get an advanced degree in economics.

In 1961, at the height of the Cold War with Russia, I got a letter from Jake. He was working for a U.S. agency concerned with national security. Although he didn't name it, it was clear to me that it was the Central Intelligence Agency—the C.I.A.

As the years went by, Jake and I stayed in contact. I had finished a degree in meteorology, got a job with the U.S. Weather Service, and got married. I'd get a card or letter from Jake, usually around Christmas, and always from some foreign city—in the beginning, a capitol of an African country—later a city in Europe. He never said much—nothing about his work—usually talked about the weather and the local culture. Once in a while he'd mention a woman's name, but never the same one twice.

In the early 1990s, both Jake and I retired. My wife and I were living in Lexington, Kentucky. Our three kids were now married and on their own.

Jake was living in Northern Minnesota, near the Canadian border on the edge of the Boundary Waters Canoe Area. He lived alone in a log cabin near a lake, the nearest neighbor, a Korean War veteran like himself, was about a half mile away. Jake said he liked the peace and quiet.

My wife died of cancer of the pancreas in 2000. I was alone. I traveled and visited the kids and grandchildren, but I soon tired of that—they were probably sick of me as well.

2009

In February 2001, I called Jake and suggested we get together somewhere where it was warm. He agreed. I got on the Internet and found a resort in Scottsdale, Arizona. It wasn't fancy, but it had suites with two beds, a living room and kitchen. We checked in for three weeks and every winter thereafter until Jake died.

The resort had a large swimming pool surrounded by palm trees, with tables and chairs and a bar at one end. In the evening, Jake and I would sit and drink rum cocktails and feel the breeze as it rippled the palm leaves. It almost made us feel like we were back in the Philippine Islands.

In the morning we'd have breakfast made to order by Mexican cooks. Jake would always have a plate of bacon or ham and eggs. He didn't seem to worry about cholesterol or high blood pressure. I don't think he cared.

In the summer, I'd spend a month or two with Jake at his cabin. Sometimes we'd go fishing, catching just enough walleye pike to fix for dinner. Other times Jake would take me on walks on deer trails or along the lake shore.

Jake's cabin was sparsely furnished: a leather-bound easy chair with reading lamp, a fireplace, sofa, and kitchenette with table and chairs. Shelving along the walls was filled with books: histories, biographies, memoirs, mostly, and two volumes of *The Complete Short Stories of W. Somerset Maugham*. Jake thought Maugham was the best storyteller in the English language.

In the evening, Jake liked to sit on the deck. We'd sit, whiskey in hand, and look out over the lake. Toward dark, we'd hear the cry of the loon and at night the howling of the timber wolves. Jake admired the wolf: the way they formed in packs, like a family, the way they would fight for one another, and die, if necessary, for their pups. He didn't think humans measured up.

Jake was a patriot, he loved his country. He didn't talk much about his service with the CIA, but from the few things he said, he wasn't some analyst pushing papers at Langley. I got the feeling he was involved in covert activities, real cloak-and-dagger stuff. Sometimes I think he wished he had died somewhere in the field on assignment, on a mission for his homeland.

In 2004, Jake developed heart trouble. His doctor prescribed medications and told him to go easy on alcohol and salt.

The last time I saw Jake was at his cabin the summer of 2007. He didn't look well; seemed all in. I noticed his ankles were swollen, and he got breathless walking the few yards to the lake shore. And he was drinking more than usual. I grew concerned and told him so. He just looked at me and shrugged his shoulders.

I remember the last night. We were drinking on the deck, all mellow and nostalgic, and started reminiscing about the Philippine Islands. I asked Jake if he ever thought about Rosie. "Every day, Don," he said, "every day."

In February 2008, just before Jake and I planned to be in Arizona, I got a call from the old Korean War veteran who lived near Jake. He said he hadn't heard from Jake for a while, so the day before, he had walked over to his place. There was no reply to his knock, so he pushed open the unlocked door. Jake was sitting in his easy chair, frozen rigid. On a stand near his arm was a half empty bottle of rum and a glass. Jake's dead hand clutched a photograph of a young sailor and an Asian woman. The vet said on the back of the photo was scrawled: Jake and Rosie, registration photo, Cavite City, 1954.

As Executor, I had to make funeral arrangements. Jake wanted to be cremated and his money used to pay off his debts and to carry out his wishes. The rest was mine.

When I went through Jake's personal effects, I

discovered that when Rosie died in the jeepney accident, her brother Carlos had sent Jake all Rosie's intimate items, things she had kept guarded and protected: a jewelry box containing a gold, heart-shaped pendant and chain, registration papers signed by Jake and Rosie, photographs and a bundle of love letters Jake had sent her tied in a red ribbon. Jake had kept them in an old sea chest.

Also, I found out Jake had sent money to Rosie's brother for her burial in the Cavite City cemetery and for flowers and candles to be put on her grave every year on All Saints Day. Every Christmas Jake had sent Carlos, his children, and grandchildren money for gifts. In letters and cards to Jake, they referred to him as Uncle Jake. I guess Jake had a family after all.

Jake wanted his ashes sent to Carlos to be interred in Rosie's grave. It was March now, sunny and warm in the Philippine Islands. I had never been back, and I had plenty of time on my hands, so I decided to fly out and deliver Jake's ashes to Carlos in person.

Rosie's brother, a small gray-haired man not much younger than me, met me at the airport in Manila with a big smile and a fervent handshake. We took a jeepney back to Cavite City and Carlos's home where I was introduced to his wife and their grown sons and grandchildren.

It was a celebration and, because of Jake, I was treated like part of the family. There were platters of Filipino food, beer and rum, and Jake and Rosie's registration photo sat in the center of the table with burning candles on each side. I remembered Jake saying how Carlos liked American cigarettes, so I brought several cartons of Marlboros and passed packs around. I hadn't smoked for years, but I broke open a pack and lit up with the rest of the guys, smoking and drinking San Miguel and Tanduay rum.

I stayed with Carlos and his wife as a guest. The next day Carlos took me on a tour of Cavite City. I didn't recognize it; it had changed with so many American fast food joints. Sangley Point Naval Air Station had closed in 1971, with the Philippine government taking over the property.

We drove out to the cemetery. Carlos and I dug a little hole on top of Rosie's grave. I poured in Jake's ashes. Rosie's name and the dates of her birth and death were on her marker. I gave Carlos money to have an inscription added to the marker reading "Jake and Rosie—together for eternity."

Back home in Kentucky, I took Jake's personal items: the jewelry box with pendant and chain, Jake and Rosie's registration papers and photo, Jake's love letters to Rosie, and Jake's memoir and locked them away in a bedroom safe to be opened upon my death. In my will, I left it all to my oldest son who plans to write a family history. I figure he'll learn something about his old man and his shipmate Jake—about our lives and times when we were young.

My wife is buried in a national cemetery for veterans. I will be buried next to her, amidst row upon row of white gravestones on a carpet of green. There's a grove of pine trees, too, and it's so quiet you can hear the whisper of the wind through their branches. Jake would like the place.

The End

ABOUT THE AUTHOR

Don Walker (a pseudonym) was a sailor in the U.S. Navy from 1952–56 and served at the naval bases depicted in this book. *Manila Bay* is based on his unpublished memoir of those days, written after his retirement from government service in the 1990s.

CPSIA information can be obtained at www.ICGtesting.com
Printed in the USA
BVOW011825211211

278945BV00001B/5/P